YOU CAN'T GET LOST IN CAPE TOWN

Women Writing Africa
A Project of The Feminist Press at The City University of New York
Funded by The Ford Foundation

Women Writing Africa is a project of cultural reconstruction that aims to restore African women's voices to the public sphere. Through the collection of written and oral narratives to be published in six regional anthologies, the project will document the history of self-conscious literary expression by African women throughout the continent. In bringing together women's voices, Women Writing Africa will illuminate for a broad public the neglected history and culture of African women, who have shaped and been shaped by their families, societies, and nations.

The Women Writing Africa Series, which supports the publication of individual books, is part of the Women Writing Africa project.

The Women Writing Africa Series

ACROSS BOUNDARIES
The Journey of a South African Woman Leader
A Memoir by Mamphela Ramphele

AND THEY DIDN'T DIE
A Novel by Lauretta Ngcobo

CHANGES
A Love Story
A Novel by Ama Ata Aidoo

HAREM YEARS
The Memoirs of an Egyptian Feminist, 1879–1924
by Huda Shaarawi
Translated and introduced by Margot Badran

NO SWEETNESS HERE
And Other Stories
by Ama Ata Aidoo

TEACHING AFRICAN LITERATURES IN A GLOBAL LITERARY ECONOMY
Women's Studies Quarterly 25, nos. 3 & 4 (fall/winter 1998)
Edited by Tuzyline Jita Allan

ZULU WOMAN
The Life Story of Christina Sibiya
by Rebecca Hourwich Reyher

YOU CAN'T GET LOST IN CAPE TOWN

Zoë Wicomb

Historical Introduction by Marcia Wright
Literary Afterword by Carol Sicherman

The Women Writing Africa Series

THE FEMINIST PRESS AT THE CITY UNIVERSITY OF NEW YORK

Published by The Feminist Press at The City University of New York
The Graduate Center
365 Fifth Avenue
New York, NY 10016
feministpress.org

First Feminist Press edition, 2000

Library of Congress Cataloging-in-Publication Data

Wicomb, Zoë
    You can't get lost in Cape Town / Zoë Wicomb ; historical introduction by
Marcia Wright ; literary afterword by Carol Sicherman.— 1st Feminist Press ed.
    p. cm. — (The women writing Africa series)
    Includes bibliographical references.
    ISBN: 1-55861-224-0 (cloth: alk. paper). —ISBN: 1-55861-225-4 (pbk.:
alk. paper)
    1. Coloured people (South Africa)—Fiction. 2. Young women—South
Africa—Fiction. 3 Cape Town (South Africa)—Fiction. I. Title. II. Series

    PR9369.3.W53 Y6 2000
    823—dc21   99-053119

This publication is made possible, in part, by a grant from The Ford Foundation in
support of the Feminist Press's Women Writing Africa project. The Feminist Press is
grateful to Florence Howe, Joanne Markell, Caroline Urvater, and Genevieve
Vaughan for their generosity in supporting this publication.

Printed on acid-free paper by RR Donnelley & Sons

Manufactured in the United States of America

05 04 03 02 01 00   5 4 3 2 1

CONTENTS

HISTORICAL INTRODUCTION

Although *You Can't Get Lost in Cape Town*, Zoë Wicomb's portrait of a young coloured[1] woman's coming to age in apartheid-ruled South Africa, spans the mid-1950s to the mid-1980s, this episodic novel is not a period piece. Indeed, to grasp the complex consciousness of those known in the twentieth century as the Cape Coloured people, one must reach back not just fifty years, but to a time far anterior to apartheid. What is more, this portrayal of one young woman's life and expanding awareness is highly relevant to the present, when the struggle in South Africa is defined not by race-led laws but rather by class aspirations and economic disadvantages that carry forward a history of vulnerability.

Wicomb's protagonist, Frieda Shenton, and her immediate family resolutely defy easy categorization, even when the characters themselves indulge in stereotyping. The Shentons are exceptional among coloured people in Little Namaqualand, an impoverished, semiarid area beyond the rich wheat farms and vineyards north of Cape Town. With respect to their neighbors, the Shentons are well educated and, invested in social improvement, proud of their growing command of the English language and of their patrilineal name-giver, a Scot. Frieda's father, a primary school teacher, is recognized as a local notable, above the "commonality," while Frieda's mother has something more equivocal in her identity: Griqua parentage.[2] Mrs. Shenton has embraced the ideal of the "lady" and continually warns her daughter against compromising behavior. The young and then mature Frieda must cope with and transcend essentially conservative anxieties that feed the stereotypes purveyed by her

viii   *Introduction*

mother, which reveal a perspective prevalent among the coloured petty bourgeoisie. In telling Frieda's story, Wicomb explores class, race, gender, and culture across a wide register.

The social arena in Little Namaqualand into which Frieda is born encompasses a confusing array of identities. These identities fall short of being ethnicities, that is, coherent groups claiming a common ancestry. Rather, individuals carry or are assigned identities that may be fragments of their ancestry but bespeak stereotypical behaviors or features. A preliminary understanding of the roots of these various identities will enrich appreciation for Wicomb's work, which restores coloured experience and history as it contextualizes, revises, and humanizes it. Wicomb does this on a personal scale, bringing forth characters who—albeit in sometimes oblique ways— comment on, align themselves with, or represent various indigenous and settler groups, ranging from the indigenous Namaqua to the coloured Griqua to the white Boers and British. *You Can't Get Lost in Cape Town* depicts not only the strong cultural hold of these identities but also their limits and shifting nature, as well as the painful history of colonization, displacement, and apartheid that accompanies them.

The Namaqua of Namaqualand were among the groups of Khoikhoi, the indigenous African pastoralists encountered by the Dutch in their initial settlements at the Cape in the mid-seventeenth century. By the middle of the nineteenth century, the Namaqua group of Khoi had yielded to the incoming Basters (literally meaning *hybrid*), mixed-race groups of frontierspeople.[3] The absorbed

Namaqua surface in Wicomb's work through Skitterboud, the servant who figures in "A Fair Exchange."

Of all these mixed-race frontierspeople, by far the most prominent were the Griqua, a group substantially involved in the nineteenth-century northward extension of Cape colonial culture. In the early 1800s, patriarchally led settlements of Basters moved north of the Orange River, beyond the limits of the Cape Colony, where they exercised greater political autonomy while seeking to maintain their economic and cultural ties to the Cape Colony. The name *Griqua* was adopted at one of the key settlements, Klaarwater, renamed Griquatown "because, 'on consulting among themselves they found a majority were descended from a person of the name of Griqua', that is, from the eponymous ancestor of the Khoikhoi clan, the /Karihur ('Chariguriqua')."[4] The Griqua leadership and following continued to be materially oriented toward the Cape Colony, Christian and literate in aspiration, but hardly united among themselves. By the twentieth century, the Griqua had long passed their prime as frontierspeople. Some were dislodged from commercial sheep farming in the Orange Free State by white farmers. Others, in what became annexed as the northern Cape, were ultimately forced to emigrate east, extruded by the forces of capitalism and colonial authority that accompanied the exploitation of the diamond fields. A remnant of Griqua later journeyed to Little Namaqualand, where they added to a sparse, heterogeneous population occupying a space of very little economic potential.

Another identity that figures in the milieu of Little Namaqualand is that of the Boers, later called Afrikaners, who had been settling in this marginal environment from the eighteenth century onward. *Boer* was a term current before *Afrikaner*, but subsequently often used by the British to suggest a poor white element and a generally backward culture. Under apartheid, which specifically climaxed an Afrikaner Nationalist campaign to elevate their *volk*, Boers were regarded by the disenfranchised as a privileged group. Even as poor whites, they belonged to the political master class. For Mrs. Shenton, however, the word is still loaded with class distinctions; Boers lacked the refined quality of the more "civilized" British.

These identities and their accompanying stereotypes consolidated—particularly during the apartheid regime—in a brittle cultural and economic hierarchy, positioning Africans as the lowest group, with Indian and coloured groups then following, and privileging white European settlers. This hierarchy plays out, in overt ways, within given groups. Frieda's coloured classmate Henry Hendrikse, for example, who has dark features and who knows the Xhosa language, is disparagingly referred to in the beginning of the work as "almost pure kaffir" (116). Later in the work, after black resistance has surfaced, Henry's roots are not to be easily dismissed. Frieda's acquaintance with Africans is slight, but she is presented as fascinated by the difference of indigenous people, who are distant and alien even as they occupy the same space. Henry Hendrikse remains an intentionally unclarified character, although evidently a "registered Coloured."

In fact, for over a century, Western-acculturated Xhosa people had been settled in the northwestern Cape, brought in purposefully by the colonial authorities to serve as a buffer community against the raiding "Bushmen."[5] Other Xhosa immigrated in association with the London Missionary Society, and even more as workers on the railway and in the copper mines that had boomed and then failed in Little Namaqualand in the mid- to late nineteenth century.

It is worth recalling that from 1853 on, in the Cape Colony, civil rights were theoretically shared equally by men, regardless of race, if they were materially qualified. White legislators acted to stem the increase in the black electorate. One means was to build a dualism, with the Transkei as a native territory politically excluded from the rest of the Cape Colony. Even where the "colour-blind" constitution prevailed, the threshold of qualifications was raised, especially in the 1890s. In 1936, new enrollment of Africans ceased. The process of disenfranchisement would be completed under apartheid.

UNDER APARTHEID

You Can't Get Lost in Cape Town illuminates the interplay of these identities not only in Little Namaqualand but in Frieda's expanding world. The novel, set and written during apartheid, also dramatizes how politically charged and changing these identities can be. Wicomb considers the ambiguous role of many coloureds, oppressed by whites and yet susceptible to the promise of state-granted privileges that guaranteed them protection from competition for employment from the even more oppressed Africans coming from desperate conditions in the Transkei and Ciskei of the Eastern Cape.

The barrage of apartheid legislation passed after the National Party came to power in 1948 aimed to achieve total segregation. One of the very first laws was the Prohibition of Mixed Marriages Act (1949). In 1950, in remorseless succession, came the Group Areas Act, authorizing racially exclusive areas of residence and removals to effect them; the Population Registration Act, categorizing all South Africans into four primary "racial categories": "White," "Coloured," "Indian," and "Bantu"; and the Immorality Act, prohibiting sex between the races. Clearly the ideologists aspired to control the most intimate relationships, leaving no sanctuary in private life. Anyone associating beyond the prescribed racial boundaries became criminalized.

In one of the most aggressive, explicitly political steps taken in the first years, the apartheid regime introduced a bill to exclude coloured voters from parliamentary constituencies in the Cape Province. The colour-blind franchise had legitimated an exaggerated sense of the "civilized," as opposed to the uncouth or culturally "other." Such a system of franchise had discriminated against unpropertied Boers, as well as ordinary coloured or African subjects. The determination to purge the non-white electorate, first by excluding the Africans and then disenfranchising coloured voters, had been an explicit program of certain Afrikaner Nationalists from the time of the unification of South Africa in 1910. Although the Cape franchise was constitutionally "entrenched," requiring a two-thirds majority of the parliament to alter, that majority in the all-white parliament was achieved in 1935 for the purpose of disqualifying Africans on the basis of their race and ethnicity.

The proposed coloured exclusion precipitated a constitutional crisis; only in 1956 were parliamentary objections about the exclusion and judicial appeals defeated.[6] Most politics had been urban based: the franchise issue would not have aroused the largely apolitical community Wicomb evokes in Little Namaqualand. Unlike Africans and Indians, before 1950 coloured people were not required to carry identity passes and, consequently, did not share in the attendant tradition of resistance.[7] In the 1950s, however, the coloured population came under a similar administrative overrule, that of the Coloured Affairs Department, a parallel to the Bantu Affairs Department. The draconian combination of the Population Registration and Group Areas Acts circumscribed their freedom to own property within their province.

The Group Areas Act as implemented in the 1960s and 1970s displaced urban-dwelling people from historically mixed residential areas, to be confined in putatively homogeneous townships. During the thirty-four years from 1950 through 1984 in the Cape Province, only 840 white families were moved, compared with 65,657 coloured families.[8] In *You Can't Get Lost in Cape Town* several episodes reflect the herding of people into coloured townships in Little Namaqualand. The references are somewhat veiled, but removals inflect the portrait of Auntie Truida in "Jan Klinkies" and the defeat that weighed on Mr. Shenton when he had to move, "to be boxed in" in a coloured village (29). In the book, this forced retreat is converted into a hope for the future when the small proceeds from the sale of the Shenton's former home are invested in Frieda's two years of education at an Anglican secondary school, enabling her to matriculate and move on to the University of the Western Cape (UWC).

In fact, the UWC would become a hotbed of Black Consciousness, a movement of young activists who had grown up under apartheid, led by such people as Steve Biko. Established under provisions of the Extension of University Education Act of 1959, the UWC was apartheid-defined as for coloureds only. Frieda is wry about the limited consciousness she possessed at the time of the boycott of memorial services for the April 1966 assassination of Prime Minister Verwoerd, who was, among other things, chief architect of the racially defined education system. Frieda suggests that the huddle of young men behind the school boycott was not deeply politicized.

In 1973 students suddenly exploded, moving away from the muted protest described in *You Can't Get Lost in Cape Town*. Black Consciousness developed the polarity of white versus black as the epitome of the struggle, and aligned Indian, coloured, and black South Africans in common struggle. UWC students bonded with their peers in other nonwhite universities, declaring on June 5, 1973, in their first major manifesto:

> We reject completely the idea of separate ethnic universities because it is contrary to the historic concept of a university—that of universality— but are forced by the laws of the land to study at the [coloured] University of the W. Cape. . . .[9]

They pointed out the inequities in pay between white and coloured teaching staff and the overwhelming preponderance of white lecturers (seventy-nine) over black lecturers (twelve). They concluded that the institution was run by Afrikaners for Afrikaners, which is to say that it provided employment for Afrikaners who were Nationalist clients committed to the regime. In the first flush of radicalization, the UWC students rejected Afrikaans, although it was their mother tongue, in favor of English. Later thinking brought them to repossess Afrikaans as a language of liberation.[10]

Frieda's love affair with the English language and literature is her passport to the wider world, specifically

Britain. Living in Britain from 1972 to 1984, she is removed from the main cut and thrust of the confrontations of students and of an increasingly aroused populace with the enforcers of apartheid.

The egalitarian stance of the UWC manifesto might have rooted the students in a tradition of South African political dissent that advanced equality and unity, as manifested, for example, by the Non-European Unity Movement (NEUM), which since 1943 had followed a Marxist line independent of the South African Communist Party. A movement attractive to schoolteachers, it had recruited a few Indians, Africans, and whites, as well as coloureds. A revived Unity Movement, however, failed to capture the mood of the times. The students drew on Black Consciousness. The movement contained elements of spontaneity, impatience with structural analysis, intolerance of compromising elders, and great heroism. Black became a metaphor for nonwhite, a very suitable one for a struggle against the white racist regime.

When in 1983 a new Tricameral Parliament provided for a separate chamber where coloureds would legislate on their "own affairs," several parties offered candidates. The strongest was the Labour Party, essentially the voice of the most skilled and organized coloured labor unions. Coloured voters stayed away from the polls in these elections, which extended franchise to coloured and Indian voters but excluded Africans. Many coloured voters were made aware by the active campaign of the United Democratic Front (UDF) of the falsity of democracy when racial segregation remained intact.[11]

Frieda returns from Britain after a twelve-year absence still politically naïve, as are most of her friends (with the exception of her friend Moira) and certainly her family,

who are still defined by their localities and histories in South
Africa. She encounters once again the depth of coloured
acquiescence.

Wicomb published this book originally in 1987, three
years before the end of apartheid, while state violence and
insurrection were at a height. Close readers of *You Can't
Get Lost in Cape Town* at that time would have been cau-
tioned and perhaps less surprised than many political
observers when, in the months before the 1994 general
elections, the coloured voters moved from "undecided"
to support of the National Party, which courted them as
part of an enlarged constituency of Afrikaans-speakers.
They delivered the Western Cape provincial government
to the old Afrikaner ruling party, while in most other
provinces the African National Congress swept the
elections. Peter Marais, one of the victorious candidates, wrote of his personal sense of identity:

> My language, Afrikaans, provides the first indica-
> tion of where I am located because many things flow
> from language. My religious affiliation is another fea-
> ture of my identity. . . . As a *bruin man* (brown man)
> of Griqua and Afrikaner descent, I do not wish to have
> another "bruin man" telling who I am; or that I am noth-
> ing. On the contrary, I am something. I am a Griqua
> with Afrikaner blood.[12]

It is apparent from such a testimony that Griqua in the
new South Africa was becoming an ethnicity around which
to mobilize. The eventual political alliance of Griqua cultural chauvinists, however, is not a foregone conclusion.
In the last chapter of the novel, Wicomb dramatizes this
shift in perspective; the Griqua suddenly enjoy a more

positive valence. Wicomb questions the politics of ethnicity as much as the rigid racism of apartheid.

RESPECTABILITY AND COLOR

At the heart of the ambiguity for coloured peoples are
the implications of their mixed ancestry and two sorts
of prejudice: prejudice against them because of color and
prejudice against such women in particular as (pre-
sumptively) available for sexual liaisons. These markers
are inflected differently across time and circumstance.

Mixing in the seventeenth century occasionally
involved visible and highly placed persons. Detailed
examinations are now being made of the life of the
late-seventeenth century Khoikhoi woman Eva, the
protégé of and interpreter for the first Dutch governor,
wife of a company official, and, finally, a mother in
reduced circumstances. Her Khoi name, Krotoa, is adopted by those who promote her as the foremother of the new
South Africa.[13] In the seventeenth and eighteenth centuries, some other marriages between white men and Khoi
or coloured women were solemnized in church. A few
descendants of these marriages became citizens, burghers,
with full civil rights.[14] For example, among the leadership
in colonial coloured resistance was the Reverend James
Read, Jr., the son of a London Missionary Society missionary and a Khoi-descended woman.[15]

That the Dutch East India Company imported and owned
slave retainers whom it housed collectively in Cape
Town, however, created a very different situation. Cape
Town has been called "the tavern of the two seas," the port
where vessels bound for or returning from the Far East called
for provisions and respite. The slave lodge became a
place to find partners in casual sex and children were born

with anonymous fathers, some of them European sailors.
Toward the end of the eighteenth century, German soldiers brought in as mercenaries by the Dutch East India
Company added to the mixture by making country marriages. By the time the British took over the Cape
Colony in 1808, "free people of colour" were of many
shades. There were a number of slaves of mixed parentage, and increasing ambiguity as to whether the "tame
Hottentots"—Khoi within colonial society or grouped
around mission stations—were melting into the same category. With the abolition of slavery and other degrees of
formal servitude, the process of acculturation accelerat-
ed. In the Cape Colony, the civil rights of free people were
equal. Contracts between masters and servants, however, put the servant in a weak position. And most coloureds
were servants. On farms, with arrangements dating from
the days of slavery, the domestic privacy of laborers'
families was minimal. The Cape Marriage Order of 1839
provided for the regularization of marriage and induced
a flow of couples to the churches.[16]

An example of deep prejudice within colonial society has been given by Pamela Scully through the case of
Anna Simpson, the wife of a laborer who in April 1850
brought rape charges before the circuit court. The defen-
dant confessed and was sentenced to death, only to
have the sentence commuted because of white citizens'
protests that Anna Simpson was coloured: "The woman
and her husband are Bastard coloured persons, and that
instead of her being a respectable woman, her character
for chastity was very indifferent."[17] On the score of
respectability, in the eyes of white moralizers, women of
color were lacking unless proven otherwise.

The impoverishment of the majority of those considered

to be coloured resulted from their lack of capital and ability to secure and retain land, their indebtedness, and the failure of wages to rise in real terms. It has been reckoned that pay for coloured workers did not improve relative to the cost of living between the 1840s and the interwar period.[18] There may have been some real increases in the 1940s and 1950s, but they were stalled and reversed as the full effects of apartheid took hold. Coloured wages declined steeply relative to white wages. Declining real wages affected women as well as men in the formal economy; women had to work ever harder, by whatever means, to meet their household needs. The attitude of the canteen worker Tamieta at the University of the Western Cape in "A Clearing in the Bush" reflects many women's aversion to the risk of lost employment, as well as compromises of respectability.

The Population Registration Act was one of the most painful measures for coloureds. Each person had to carry an identity card declaring her or his race category. Entitlement to educational facilities, to residential areas, to employment, to association all followed. When the Population Registration rubrics were dictated, "Coloured" subcategories distinguished "Cape Coloured," "Cape Malay" (Muslims), "Griqua," and "other Coloured."[19] These reflected potential fault lines to exploit in a policy of divide and rule. But the overarching categories "Coloured," "European"(or "White"), "Bantu" (African), and "Asian" (or "Indian") served as racial cyphers for juridical purposes. Members of the same families received different racial classifications. Assignments could be altered each year, unilaterally by officials or following appeal. In 1970, for example, the Ministry of Interior unilaterally reclassified seven persons from "Coloured" to "Bantu," and acted favorably on petitions in twenty-two cases to be changed from "White" to Coloured," twenty-three from "Coloured" to "White," and fourteen from "Bantu" to "Coloured." Race Classification Boards reclassified one "White" to "Coloured," four "Coloured " to "White," and twenty-nine from "Bantu" to "Coloured." The report does not specify where in South Africa these persons resided.[20] From Wicomb's writing, readers will appreciate that consciousness of race and cultural status was sharply registered within the ranks of coloureds. Mrs. Shenton's ironic reference to the chauffeur's possible legal status as a "registered Coloured" bespeaks her uncertainty over the identity of the apparently white driver (4).

A case that drew great attention to the excruciating consequences of population registration was that of Sandra Laing. Laing was the daughter of poor but "respectable" whites, whose features did not conform to the Caucasian model. She was dismissed from her white school and reclassified "Coloured" by officials. On protest and following a court case, she was reclassified "White," but never again settled into her privileged entitlements. She finally married an African.[21]

These notes will have underscored the irony of Wicomb's title. *You Can't Get Lost in Cape Town* comes from a confident statement by Frieda's longstanding white boyfriend as she is about to go off to have an abortion in the white part of the city. Frieda Shenton, for her part, does not have a sense of direction, even though she ends up in the clinic and is able to deny that she is coloured in order to have the procedure. What is wonderful about this character is her unwillingness to follow in the tracks of others, her observance of the humanity of her own extended family and members of Namaqualand society regardless of her mother's indoctrination and projection of them as dangerous, throwbacks to poor, uncultured antecedents. The important reconciliation that appears at the book's end reminds us most tellingly of a general point of the work—that rehearsed, constraining histories can be transcended, at least momentarily.

Marcia Wright
New York
December 1999

NOTES

1. *Coloured*, a term referring to mixed-race individuals in South Africa, is discussed with more texture later in this introduction. In the context material for this edition of *You Can't Get Lost in Cape Town*, *coloured* appears, for the most part, without quotation marks and an initial capital. *Cape Coloured* has been capitalized as a historical marker; similarly, when the term denotes the specific apartheid classification named in the Population Registration Act of 1950, it appears with an initial capital and in quotations. In an essay on shame and identity, Zoë Wicomb briefly comments on the changing use of the term *coloured*, especially with respect to apartheid and liberation politics. She writes, "Such adoption of different names [i.e., black, "Coloured," Coloured, etc.] at various historical junctures shows perhaps the difficulty that the term *coloured* has in taking on a fixed meaning, and as such exemplifies postmodernity in its shifting allegiances, its duplicitous play between the written capitalization and speech that denies or at least does not reveal the act of renaming" ("Shame and Identity: The Case of the Coloured in South Africa," in *Writing South Africa: Literature, Apartheid, and Democracy, 1970–1995*, ed. Derek Attridge and Rosemary Jolly [New York: Cambridge University Press, 1998], 93–94).

2. Griqua, an ethnicity among coloured South Africans, is a designation and political identity treated later in this introduction.

3. J. S. Marais, *The Cape Coloured People, 1652–1937* (1939; reprint, Johannesburg: Witwatersrand University Press, 1968), chap. 3. The other classic study is W. M. Macmillan, *The Cape Colour Question: A Historical Survey* (1927; reprint, London: Hurst, 1968).

4. Martin Legassick, "The Northern Frontier to c. 1840: The Rise and Decline of the Griqua People," in *The Shaping of South African Society, 1652–1840*, ed. Richard Elphick and Hermann Giliomee, 2d ed. (Middletown: Wesleyan University Press, 1989), 382. Such distillations of one trace element from a number of sources (in this case, the naming of a common ancestral link) is, of course, part of ethnicity-building, as a vigorous literature on the invention of tradition makes clear.

5. Marais, *Cape Coloured*, 85. Poppie Nongena is a poignant example of an acculturated, Afrikaans-speaking woman of the Western Cape; see Elsa Joubert, *Poppie Nongena* (New York: W. W. Norton, 1985).

6. Thomas G. Karis and Gail M. Gerhart, introduction to *Challenge and Violence, 1953–1990*, vol. 3, *From Protest to Challenge: A Documentary History of African Politics in South Africa, 1882–1964*, ed. Thomas G. Karis and Gwendolyn M. Carter (Stanford: Hoover Press, 1977), 10–11.

7. A Western Cape woman who married a "Bantustan" citizen from the Eastern Cape lost her rights of residence. This situation is powerfully reflected in Joubert's *Poppie Nongena*. The account of Poppie's experiences working in fish processing factories on the west coast of the Cape Province, not far from the interior of Little Namaqualand, opens the opportunity for reflection on underclass women's lives as compared with the aspirant, precarious middle class explored by Wicomb.

8. Elaine Unterhalter, *Forced Removal: The Division, Segregation and Control of the People of South Africa* (London: International Defence and Aid Fund, 1987), 146.

9. Thomas G. Karis and Gail M. Gerhart, eds., *Nadir and Resurgence, 1964–1979*, vol. 5, *From Protest to Challenge: A Documentary History of African Politics in South Africa, 1882–1990*, ed. Thomas G. Karis and Gail M. Gerhart (Bloomington: University of Indiana Press, 1997), 525.

10. Ibid., 103.

11. Bill Nasson, "Political Ideologies in the Western Cape," in *All, Here, and Now: Black Politics in South Africa in the 1980s*, ed. Tom Lodge, Bill Nasson, Steven Mufson, Khenla Shubane, and Nokwanda Sithole (New York: Ford Foundation, 1991).

12. Peter Marais, "Too Long in the Twilight," in *Now That We Are Free: Coloured Communities in a Democratic South Africa*, ed. Wilmot James, Daria Caliguire, and Kerry Cullinan (Boulder: Lynne Rienner, 1996), 60.

13. See, for example, Julia Wells, "Eva's Men: Gender and Power in the Establishment of the Cape of Good Hope, 1652–74," *Journal of African History* 30(1998): 417–37, and Yvette Abrahams, "Was Eva Raped? An Exercise in Speculative History," and Christina Landman, "The Religious Krotoa (c. 1642–1674)," *Kronos: Journal of Cape History* 23: 3–21, 22–35.

14. Richard Elphick and Robert Shell, "Intergroup Relations: Khoikhoi, Settlers, Slaves and Free Blacks, 1652–1795," chap. 4 in *The Shaping of South African Society, 1652–1840*, ed. Richard Elphick and Hermann Giliomee, 2d ed. (Middletown, Conn.: Wesleyan University Press, 1989).

15. Timothy Keegan, *Colonial South Africa and the Origins of the Racial Order* (Charlottesville: University of Virginia, 1996), 238. See also Robert Ross, "Missions, Respectability and Civil Rights: The Cape Colony, 1828–1854," *Journal of Southern African Studies* 25 (September 1999): 333–45.

16. Pamela Scully, *Liberating the Family? Gender and British Slave Emancipation in the Rural Western Cape, South Africa, 1823–1853* (Portsmouth: Heinemann, 1997), 116, 127–28.

17. As quoted in Scully, *Liberating*, 155–56.

18. Marais, *Cape Coloured*, 266.

19. *Apartheid: The Facts* (London: International Defense and Aid Fund, 1983), 16. The original default category "Coloured" also included "Indian," "Chinese," and "other Asiatic."

20. Muriel Horrell, et al., comp., *A Survey of Race Relations in South Africa 1971*, vol. 25 (Johannesburg: Institute of Race Relations, 1972), 60.

21. W. A. de Klerk, *The Puritans in Africa: A Story of Afrikanerdom* (London: Rex Collings, 1975), 268–70. De Klerk, a maverick Cape Afrikaner writer, criticizes the apartheid regime and makes a major point of the case of Sandra Laing as one evidence of the absurdity of the system. A docudrama, *The Search for Sandra Laing* (video: 50 minutes, color, ATV production in affiliation with the African National Congress, 1978; distributed by IDERA, Canada), provides a searing reenactment of the story.

YOU CAN'T GET LOST IN CAPE TOWN

Origins trouble the voyager much, those roots
that have sipped the waters of another continent . . .

it is solitude that mutilates,
the night bulb that reveals ash on my sleeve.

ARTHUR NORTJE

Don't travel beyond
Acton at noon in the intimate summer light
of England

ARTHUR NORTJE

In writing the history of unfashionable families one is apt
to fall into a tone of emphasis which is very far from being
the tone of good society, where principles and beliefs are
not only of an extremely moderate kind, but are always
presupposed, no subjects being eligible but such as can be
touched with a light and graceful irony.

GEORGE ELIOT, The Mill on the Floss

BOWL LIKE HOLE

At first Mr Weedon came like any white man in a motor car, enquiring about sheep or goats or servants.

A vehicle swerving meteor-bright across the veld signalled a break in the school day as rows of children scuttled out to hide behind the corner, their fingers plugged into their nostrils with wonder and admiration. They examined the tracks of the car or craned their necks in turn to catch a glimpse of the visitor even though all white men looked exactly the same. Others exploited the break to find circuitous routes to the bank of squat ghanna bushes where they emptied their bowels and bladders. On such occasions they did not examine each other's genitals. They peered through the scant foliage to admire the shiny vehicle from a safe distance. They brushed against the bushes, competing to see, so that the shrivelled little leaf-balls twisted and showered into dust. From this vantage point they would sit, pants down, for the entire visit while the visitor conducted his business from the magnificence of his car.

At an early age I discovered the advantage of curling up motionless in moments of confusion, a position which in further education I found to be foetal. On these topsy-turvy days I crept at great risk of being spotted to the kitchen which jutted out at a near ninety degrees of mud-brick wall from the school building. Under the narrow rectangular table I lay very still. The flutter inside subsided the instant I drew my knees up and became part of the arrangement of objects, shared in the solidity of the table and the cast-iron buckets full of water lined up on it. I could depend on Mamma being too absorbed by the event to notice me. Or if she did, she would not shout while the car squinted at the kitchen door.

So under the kitchen table I invariably found myself when vehicles arrived. And at first Mr Weedon arrived like any other white man enquiring about sheep or goats or servants.

As the time between sunrises and sunsets began to arrange itself into weeks and months and seasons, Mr Weedon's arrivals became regular. Something to do with the tax year, at the end of March, Mamma explained. The children still ran out to whisper and admire from a distance, and I with a new knowledge of geography still crept under the kitchen table, but with the buckets of water was now swept along on the earth's elliptical journey around the sun.

Mr Weedon spoke not one word of Afrikaans. For people who were born in England the g's and r's of the language were impossible, barbaric.

'A gentleman, a true Englishman,' Mamma said as she handed Father his best hat. For the Mercedes could be seen miles away, a shining disc spun in a cloud of dust. A week or so after the autumn equinox he arrived. He did not blow a horn like the uncouth Boers from the dorp. There was no horn in the back seat. Neither did he roll down a window to rest a forearm on the door. Perhaps the chrome was too hot even in autumn and he did not wish to scorch the blond hairs on his arm. With the help of the person who occupied the driver's seat, Mr Weedon's door was opened, and despite a light skirmish between the two men, he landed squarely on both feet. The cloud of dust produced by the car and the minor struggle subsided. So Mr Weedon puffed deeply on a thick cigar, producing a cloud of smoke. Mr Weedon loved clouds. Which may explain why his eyes roved about as he spoke, often to rest ponderously on a fleecy cloud above.

'A true gentleman,' Mamma whispered to herself from the kitchen window as he shook hands with Father, 'these Boers could learn a few things from him.'

'Well and how are you, how's the wife?' The English r's slid along without the vibration of tongue against palate. Mamma's asthma mentioned, he explained how his wife suffered with hers. And Cape Town so damp in winter she was forced to spend a hideous season in the Bahamas. Father tutted sympathetically. He would hate to spend several days away from home, let alone months.

'Yes,' said Mr Weedon, braiding his lapel with delicate fingers. How frail we all are . . . an uncertain world . . . even health cannot be bought . . . we must all march past as Death the Leveller makes his claim, and he looked up at a floating cloud in support of his theory of transience.

Father too held his chin slightly to the left, his goitre lifted as he scanned the sky. Possibly to avoid the cigar smoke, for he supported the school of thought that doubted whether God intended man to smoke; why else had he not provided him with a chimney?

Mr Weedon dropped his cigar and rubbed his palms together, which indicated that he was ready for the discussion held annually in the schoolroom. Father smiled, 'Certainly,' and tapped the black ledger already tucked

under his arm. He rushed to open the door and another
cloud of dust ensued as the man who opened doors tried to
oust him. Everyone mercifully kept their balance and the
man retreated sourly to lean against his Mercedes.

'Good Heavens,' whispered Mamma, 'he's picking his
nose.' Was she talking to me? Even in the topsy-turviness
of the day I dared not say anything, ask who or where. Only
the previous day I had been viciously dragged by the hair
from under the table with threats of thrashings if ever I was
found there again. It was not worth the risk. Fortunately
she went on. 'I wouldn't be surprised if he were Coloured,
from Cape Town I suppose, a play-white . . . one can
never tell with Capetonians. Or perhaps a registered
Coloured. Mr Weedon being a civilised man might not
mind a brown person driving his car.'

So she knew that I was there, must have known all
along, for I had been careful not to move. I turned my head
towards the window and through the iron crossbars of the
table saw in her two great buttocks the opposing worlds she
occupied. The humiliation of the previous day still smarted;
she was not to be trusted and I pursed my lips in disgust
when she sat down, occupying her two worlds so fully.

'Oom Klaas Dirkse has been off work again. You must
take him an egg and a mug of milk, and no playing on the
way.'

A brief silence, then she carried on, 'And I've warned
you not to speak Afrikaans to the children. They ought to
understand English and it won't hurt them to try. Your
father and I managed and we all have to put up with things
we don't understand. Anyway, those Dirkse children have
lice; you're not to play with them.'

As if the Dirkse children would want to play with me.
Kaatjie Dirkse may lower her head and draw up her thin

shoulders, but her plaited horns would stand erect and quiver their contempt.

Oh how Mamma spoiled things. The space under the table grew into the vast open veld so that I pressed against the wall and bored my chin into clasped knees. Outside the shiny Capetonian leaned against his car; only Kaatjie Dirkse would have dared to slink past him with a single sullen glare. The murmur from the schoolroom rose and fell and I was glad, very glad, that Kaatjie's horns crawled with lice.

'Stay there, you're not to hang over the lower door and gawp,' Mamma hissed unnecessarily. She heard the shuffling towards the school door and, finding her hands empty, reached for the parts of our new milk separator. These she started to assemble, tentatively clicking the parts into place, then confidently, as if her fingertips drew strength from the magic machine. Its scarecrow arms flung resolutely apart, the assembled contraption waited for the milk that it would drive through the aluminium maze and so frighten into separation. I watched her pour the calf's milk into the bowl and turn the handle viciously to drown the sound of the men's shuffling conversation outside. Out of the left arm the startled thin bluish milk spurted, and seconds later yellow cream trickled confidently from the right.

'That's Flossie's milk. She's not had any today,' I accused.

'We'll milk again tonight. There'll be more tonight,' and her eyes begged as if she were addressing the cow herself, as if her life depended on the change of routine.

Father did not report back to the kitchen. He was shown to the front seat of the car in order to accompany Mr Weedon to the gypsum mine on the edge of the settlement. Mr Weedon's cigar smoke wrapped itself in blue bands around Father's neck. He coughed and marvelled at the modesty of the man who preferred to sit alone in the back seat of his own car.

Children tumbled out from behind the schoolroom or the ghanna bushes to stare at the departing vehicle. Little ones recited the CA 3654 of the number plate and carried the transported look throughout the day. The older boys freed their nostrils and with hands plunged in their pockets suggested by a new swaggering gait that it was not so wonderful a spectacle after all. How could it be if their schoolmaster was carried away in the Mercedes? But it was, because Father was the only person for miles who knew enough English, who could interpret. And Mr Weedon had a deep fear of appearing foolish. What if he told a joke and the men continued to look at him blankly, or if they with enamelled faces said something irreverent or just something not very nice? How they would laugh later at his blank or smiling face. For Mr Weedon understood more than he admitted, and was not above the occasional pretence.

With Father by his side Mr Weedon said the foreign Good Afternoon to the miners, followed by a compliment on how well they looked, their naked torsos glistening with sweat, rivalling only the glory of the pink desert rose that they heaved out of the earth. Distanced by the translation, the winged words fluttered; he was moved to a poetic comparison. A maddening rhythm as the picks swung with a bulge of biceps in unison, up, cutting the air, the blades striking the sunbeams in one long stroke of lightning; then down the dark torsos fell, and a crash of thunder as the blades struck the earth, baring her bosom of rosy gypsum. Mr Weedon, so overcome, was forced to look away, at a cloud that raced across the sky with such apparent panting that in all decency he had to avert his eyes once again.

And so midst all that making of poetry, two prosaic

mounds rose on either side of the deepening pit. One of these would ultimately blend in with the landscape; fine dust cones would spin off it in the afternoons just as they spun off the hills that had always been there. There was no telling, unless one kicked ruthlessly and fixed an expert eye on the tell-tale tiredness of the stone, that this hill was born last year and that had always been. The other mound of gypsum was heaved by the same glistening torsos on to lorries that arrived at the end of the week. These hobbled over gravel roads to the siding at Moedverloor from where the transformed plaster of paris was carried away.

Mr Weedon turned a lump of jagged gypsum in the sun so that its crystal peaks shimmered like a thousand stars in the dead stone.

'For my daughter,' he said, 'a sample of nature's bounty. She collects rocks, just loves the simple things in life. It's nature, the simple things,' he said to Father, who could not decide whether to translate or not, 'the simple things that bring the greatest joy. Oh Sylvia would love our Brakwater, such stark beauty, and his gaze shifted . . . 'the men are doing a marvellous job' . . . as his eyes settled on a rippled chest thrown back.

'These man-made mountains and the bowls they once fitted into, beautiful and very useful for catching the rain, don't you think?'

So he had no idea that it never rained more than the surface of the earth could hold, enough to keep the dust at rest for a day or so. Father decided not to translate.

'Tell them that I'm very happy with things,' and he turned, clicking his fingers at the man who opened doors. An intricate system of signals thus triggered itself off. The boot of the car flew open, a cardboard box appeared, and after a particularly united blow at the rock the men laid down their picks and waited in semaphoric obedience. Mr Weedon smiled. Then they stepped forward holding out their hands to receive the green and white packet of Cavalla cigarettes that the smiling man dealt out. Descants of 'Dankie Meneer' and he flushed with pleasure for he had asked many times before not to be called Baas as the Boers insisted on being called. This time not one of the men made a mistake or even stuttered over the words. A day to be remembered, as he reviewed the sinewed arms outstretched, synchronised with simple words of thanks and the happy contingent of the kind angle of sun so that a bead of sweat could not gather at his brow and at a critical moment bounce on to the green and white Cavalla packet, or, and here he clenched his teeth, trail along the powdered arm of a miner who would look away in disgust.

'I don't smoke thank you, sir,' Father seemed very tall as his rigid arm held out the box. Mr Weedon's musings on harmony splintered to the dissonance of Father's words, so that he stared vacantly at the box of one hundred Cavallas held at him between thumb and index finger. Where in God's name was the man who opened doors?

Was the wind changing direction? Moisture seeped on to his brow and little mercurial drops rolled together until a shining bead gathered dead centre then slid perpendicularly to the tip of his nose where it waited. Mr Weedon brushed the back of his hand across the lower half of his face, rubbed the left jaw in an improvised itch and said, 'Well we must be off.' The box of cigarettes had somehow landed in his free arm.

The men waited, leaning on their picks, and with the purr of the engine shouted a musical Goodbye Sir in Afrikaans, words which Mr Weedon fortunately knew the meaning of. The wheels swung, a cigar moved across the back window and a cloud of dust swallowed all. The men screwed their eyes and tried to follow the vehicle. When it finally disappeared over the ridge they took up their picks once more.

'Here he co-omes,' the children crooned, as they do about all vehicles flashing in the distance. I ran to meet Father who would be dropped just above the school. From behind a bush I watched the Mercedes move on. A cloud of dust shaped itself into a festive trail following the car. A dozen brackhounds, spaced at intervals along the road and barking theatrically, ran in the manner of a relay race alongside the vehicle until the next dog took over.

I trotted to keep up with Father's long stride, my hand locked in his. His eyes like the miners' were red-rimmed in his powdered face. He handed me a lump of gypsum which I turned about in the sun until its crystal peaks shimmered like a thousand stars in the dead stone.

'That was quick,' Mamma said. Obscure words of praise that would invite him to give a full account.

'Funny,' Father replied, 'Mr Weedon said that the mine was like a bowl in the earth. Bowl like hole, not bowl like howl. Do you think that's right?'

She frowned. She had been so sure. She said, 'Of course, he's English, he ought to know.'

Then, unexpectedly, interrupting Father as he gave details of the visit, she turned on me. 'And don't you think you'll get away with it, sitting under the table like a tame Griqua.'

But revenge did not hold her attention. A wry smile fluttered about her lips. She muttered. 'Fowl, howl, scowl and not bowl.' She would check the pronunciation of every word she had taken for granted.

I knew that unlike the rest of us it would take her no time at all to say bowl like hole, smoothly, without stuttering.

JAN KLINKIES

Perhaps Father's cousin, Jan Klinkies, was not so strange. He had after all prised off a length of wire from the roll to serve as a belt. Unless such a belt is still attached to the roll which then is dragged heavily along, it is unfair to typecast a man merely because he bunches his trousers generously with a length of wire. Or because he is neither a coffee nor a Rooibos tea-drinker or because he is keen on empty cans.

These things, however, constituted the sum total of what was said about him. There was no malicious gossip. No one said how thin his legs had grown, that his teeth once were white and regular, that he should do this or that. Jan Klinkies, I knew even before this visit, did not do things. He had once done things and references to his words or actions were always references to the past. For his past did not grow pot-bellied with time. Old stories about Jan Klinkies did not shrink to single images in order to make way for fresh ones. And fresh stories did not wrap around the old like coloured cellophane, covering here and there in a fold through which the old is dimmer, the cellophane doubly coloured. An event some two years before had sealed off the past and all that concerned Jan Klinkies now was in the present.

So he bunches his trousers, refuses to take coffee or tea
with his relatives, is mad for empty tin cans.

Which presumably exempted him from such things as
wrinkles, birthdays, the worry about a nest egg or the
condition of his soul. He certainly did not go to church but
spent Sundays in the comfort of his crusty corduroys, and
no one complained. Not that he was neglected. Brothers,
sisters, aunts and cousins regularly put their heads together
on sad and windy afternoons. They tutted and shook their
heads vigorously, saying, Blood is thicker than water.

So twice a year Father visited Jan Klinkies who remained
stubbornly unconscious of the fundamental truth upon
which these visits were based. He may have noticed that
the visitors came in a particular order but it is doubtful
whether he correlated the viscosity of blood with the
frequency of these visits, for he snarled at all alike.

His eyes slid along the line of Father's raised arm and
proffered hand. If he associated the posture with the
shaking of hands, he dismissed the idea immediately. What
he looked like, whether his face was toasted or cracked by
the sun, his hair tangled or combed, can be of no interest
without a knowledge of his appearance two years before. He
wore a broad-rimmed hat pulled down over his ears and
there were two broad strips of elastoplast on his left hand
which confirmed Auntie Minnie as the previous visitor.

Jan Klinkies stood on the stoep and stared as we
approached. Then, as Father extended a hand, he rushed
down the steps and stubbed the toe of a veldskoen into the
earth as if it were a meteorological device, for he then flung
his face skyward and recited what could only be the SABC
report of the wind for that day. Which suggested that he
listened to the weather broadcast each morning even though
the dust lay inches thick on the radio in the kitchen.

But if his wife could be relied on, Jan Klinkies was not above duplicity. She would not have been surprised if it were the only weather report he had ever heard, many years ago, and which he repeated in the knowledge that the family rota was so large that no one would remember from one visit to another. Besides, he spoke so indistinctly, a rattle in the throat as he reeled off the information, that one barely caught the gist. There was no time to check the details even if he repeated the report in the course of the day. Then the voice came so unexpectedly that you cocked an ear as the words whistled through his barely parted lips. He was either after an onomatopoeic rendering of the wind or it was a deliberate attempt to disguise the words. Whatever his reason, he was certainly successful at both.

Auntie Truida was admired by visiting children who sucked into brittle transparencies the boiled sweets that she stealthily passed to them from the tin on the sideboard. But not everyone had a high opinion of Truida, the wife. It was true that she was not given to lies. Some remembered her valour during the business of the loss of the land. How she submitted to the will of God and saw it as the blessing in disguise which is God's favourite method. How patiently she explained and interpreted the pages and pages of documents about the western strip of land and the Group Areas Act and found a dictionary to look up the word 'expropriation,' for she was thorough in whatever she did. To all of which Jan Klinkies developed the irritating habit of saying no. But Truida made plans: they would better themselves, leave the mangey little farm and with the compensation money buy a house on the Cape Flats. And staring at her scaly grey hands she swore that she would burn the scrubbed oak table and have green marbled formica. There would be an indoor lavatory and the child would learn English and Jan would earn a decent wage, perhaps learn a trade, attend evening classes . . . and here she stumbled as her eye alighted on a more serious than ever decline of his jaw. Still, she carried on, she'd be a shop assistant, make friends with town women in high heels, for she had seen the jaw drop before, and recover, and everyone thought, Very sensible, and told her so for praise must be given where praise is due.

Still this did not persuade the entire family to a high opinion of her. Truida, in spite of her light skin, came from a dark-complexioned family and there was certainly something nylonish about her hair. Not that anyone actually knew of the primus stove in the back room and the metal comb and the thick sweet smell of brilliantine welded to shafts of hair. The fashion of the french knot that Truida so foolishly adopted confirmed suspicions. There was no doubt that the little hairs in the nape of the neck were rolled up tightly like fronds unfurled by the cautious hot comb. Truida had in other words made a good marriage and Jan had regrettably married beneath him. The family ignored her father's spiteful comments about Jan's lower lip that sometimes drooped until a trickle of saliva brought him back, sometimes at as special and lively an occasion as a Christmas gathering.

So opinion was divided. Father and others were not so sure whether even in the unfortunate circumstances . . . the trousers, the empty cans, the refusal to drink coffee, the desecration of her home . . . it was not immoral of her to leave a lawful husband. A double scandal seemed unnecessary, showed a heathenish disregard of the family. So that they were not prepared to believe everything Truida said.

Jan Klinkies wandered off after the weather recital,

tugging at the waist. Why was it that the trousers, khaki and far too wide, sagged at the waist in spite of the improvised wire belt? He clearly did not experiment, did not arrange equidistant little folds in the band before securing them with the wire. Or sew loops through which to thread the wire. Instead he haphazardly bunched the fabric together, drew the wire around his middle and twisted the ends. So that the wire ends shunted and bumped together as he walked and naturally people complained about this eternal tugging at the waist. Like people who sniff and sniff to prevent mucus from dribbling out of the nostrils, when from a jacket or trouser pocket or even a handbag, much to the surprise of those present, they produce a perfectly adequate handerchief upon which to drain the lot. Jan Klinkies was not altogether insensitive to the problem. He had discovered a flaw in the stitching around the waistband and so sensibly hooked a pinkie into the improvised pocket. But this did not alter matters much. He wandered off discreetly tugging at the waist with a crooked little finger hooked in the waistband in the way that everyone found so potentially indecent.

Father stumbled about with hammer and pliers repairing the fence, tapping at this and that in the awkward moments when Jan Klinkies popped up unexpectedly from behind a bush or a wall. I had an idea that we were not altogether welcome. Entry for me had been a humiliating business, an undignified scrambling over the fence laced with barbed wire. The gate was barricaded with a hillock of tarnished cans, and as further security the house refuse was heaped in front of it. Our host had stood on the stoep watching from beneath his broad-rimmed hat, as if the nature of our reception depended upon the method of mastering the obstacles. His trousers stayed up beautifully, not a suspicion of sagging as he stood with arms folded. Then he came to watch as Father dug a hole for the refuse with a spade that I passed over the fence. Father shovelled the mountain of cans away from the gate. A wondrous variety of cans: besides the tall cylindrical container of canned pilchards, there was the elliptical Fray Bentos can in two sizes, soft-cornered rectangles of sardine cans, squat condensed-milk cans and others of which you could only guess the spent contents, for all the cans were scrupulously stripped of their labels.

There was no telling whether Jan Klinkies welcomed or resented this shovelling aside, whether he minded the discarded cans mounded in an obelisk on that particular spot. His face remained set. No tell-tale smile of approval played on his lips; he did not clench his teeth in anger. But I suspected that careful aesthetic considerations had been at play. The cans so callously shoved aside might have been placed one by one, interrupted by the stepping back to appraise from a distance and perhaps replace or reposition. There is the business of balance, for instance; the wrong shape could bring the lot toppling down and you'd have to tap sliding cans carefully back into place. And a starting pattern can gradually lose its regularity until a completely new one is formed. It is perhaps only the beginning, the first small mound that you step back from, that is totally pleasing. With such a great number and variety of cans the permutations of summit and slope must be endless. Perhaps it was precisely that consideration that made Jan Klinkies appear a detached observer.

The entrance was briskly cleared. There was plenty to do. The potatoes had not been earthed up, the cabbage seedlings elbowed each other ruthlessly for breathing space, the goat lay listless in need of some or other drug. And all the while Jan Klinkies shuffled about, heaping empty cans at the base of the tree where he carefully examined them for rust or dents or other blemishes. He also prowled about and spied on us from behind scant bushes through which his eyes shone like a jackal's.

Aha, hum, said Father, clearing his throat and forgetting himself when our host came upon us suddenly, 'Ahum, a cup of Boeretroos would be just the thing now. A strong cup of coffee.' Jan Klinkies turned very red and rattled, 'Whatcomfortsaboerispoisontome.' Four times and I had just stopped counting when it came again, tattered with use so that only the contraction Boerpoison came out.

I was sent to make tea. I knew that he had given up Rooibos tea with its illustration of an ox wagon scaling the Drakensberg. The figures alongside the wagon were in Voortrekker dress, so Rooibos too offended him, in spite of his once-favourite sister Sissie's pleading for its lack of tannin, its goodness for the urinary system. So I made Five Roses with the inoffensive label of a rosette of five on the silver wrapping suggesting nothing other than its name. The men drank their tea outside in the sun. I had mine in the kitchen which I scanned for irregularities, for clues. But the pots and pans like any others were heavy and black on the Jewel stove, and from a beam large enamel mugs hung at an angle at which mugs of that size would. Two or three modest cobwebs clung to the beam. There was nothing of interest. Besides, the dust rose from the earth floor choking curiosity.

Through the window I watched them sitting in the sun on their haunches. Father beamed at the unexpected pleasure of taking tea together, observing the ritual of men breaking off from work. They slurped their tea noisily and in concert. The pauses were liberally interspersed with the one-sided conversation conducted by Father.

'The potatoes don't look too bad this year. When did they go in?' Jan Klinkies held the tea in his mouth and stared at Father, who felt obliged to continue.

'Last month, first week of last month, no later. I'd bet on it.' They slurped their tea comfortably in concert. Until Jan Klinkies was caught with the mug just poised at his lips.

'Is there enough to last through the winter? I'd have thought the little patch by the chicken run could be used as well, chickens have used it for so long, it should be good soil, give a good yield.' A long silent savouring of tea. Then Father prefaced his remarks with gentle nodding.

'You could be right, those fowls need the space. And ja, there are plenty potatoes for one and even for a family dinner now and again.'

For a moment Jan Klinkies took command of his slack jaw, but the resulting discomfort which might induce one to shift the pressure through talking made him drop the jaw again within seconds. He walked off with the mug of tea held carefully in front of him.

'The floor is dusty,' said Father, returning his mug to the kitchen. 'We must smear it.' By which he meant that I should, since I am a girl.

One could be fastidious about handling a cow-pat with bare hands, but the mixture of cow dung and a dollop of clay pounded to a smooth paste with a splash of water loses many of the unpleasant properties of freshly released dung, even though the texture resembles it more closely. And applied to the floor it is transformed by its function and so becomes sweet smelling. It is therefore in anticipation that the mixture in the bucket squelches luxuriously between playful fingers; that you apply it first thickly for idle sculpting before smoothing it down to a thin layer of sealant. Then the roughness of fibre presses up against the palm and is left like a sprinkling on the surface. The door left ajar, the freshly smeared room, just dried, suggests such lush green meadows as the cows have never seen.

The kitchen floor was done. There was a fair amount left in the bucket. It seemed a pity to waste it, to pour the mixture away in rivulets down a slope or splash it over a ghanna bush, foully disfiguring wherever it chanced to land. I thought of doing the diningroom floor. The diningroom was never used. It had lost its original function of seating deaf great-aunts at family gatherings. I tiptoed across the kitchen, smoothing the stunted footprints on the wet dung behind me. I battled with the three bolts that warned against entry.

The room was small. A square table with tucked-in extensions stood in the corner. Four chairs, tucked in, touched each other's knees sedately at four right angles, forming a lesser square under the table. Two more chairs of the same family fitted the corners facing me as I surveyed the room from the doorway. Two persons sitting on these chairs would face each other squarely, knees held close together in decorum with the room. To my left, fitting the fourth corner, was the sideboard with a glass-fronted display area which once was packed with objects worthy of a privileged position. Three of these were left, abandoned on their backs or sides as the others were hurriedly taken away. A band of gold on white porcelain, a painted something on blue opaque glass, a flash of silver; I could not be sure in the darkened room. Perhaps they were not whole objects; perhaps they were mere fragments of things shattered in a reckless removal.

I did not hear anyone cross the kitchen floor. There was simply a shadow beside me in the doorway and then he sprinted over to the sideboard and stretched his arms and planted his feet wide apart in a modified crucifixion pose.

Jan Klinkies, my cousin once removed, did not seem himself at all. Between his long legs, just beneath the inverted V of his crotch pressed against the cupboard space below the display cabinet, was a piece of paper stuck on to the wood. In the shape of a star and of a dull goldish colour. I left the room with the bucket still swinging in my right hand. The star was familiar. But the floor, as I turned to check his position, the floor was covered with patterned linoleum as of course a dining-room floor would be. Hardly in need of cow dung. Silly of me, and I remembered that it was not really a star at all, but almost a star, the label of the Gold Cross condensed-milk can.

Father was waiting. We were ready to go. The afternoon wind was rising. Not that anything was suddenly carried off; things merely shuffled in readiness. The tree barely moved, but the branches stooping heavily under the hundreds of cans tied to them with wire rattled and sent off beams of blinding light at angles doubtlessly corresponding to a well-known law.

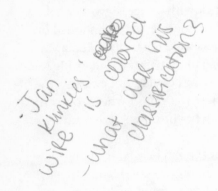

WHEN THE TRAIN COMES

I am not the kind of girl whom boys look at. I have known this for a long time, but I still lower my head in public and peep through my lashes. Their eyes leap over me, a mere obstacle in a line of vision. I should be pleased; boys can use their eyes shamelessly to undress a girl. That is what Sarie says. Sarie's hand automatically flutters to her throat to button up her orlon cardigan when boys talk to her. I have tried that, have fumbled with buttons and suffered their perplexed looks or reddened at the question, 'Are you cold?'

I know that it is the act of guiding the buttons through their resistant holes that guides the eyes to Sarie's breasts.

Today I think that I would welcome any eyes that care to confirm my new ready-made polyester dress. Choosing has not brought an end to doubt. The white, grey and black stripes run vertically, and from the generous hem I have cut a strip to replace the treacherous horizontal belt. I am not wearing a cardigan, even though it is unusually cool for January, a mere eighty degrees. I have looked once or twice at the clump of boys standing with a huge radio out of which the music winds mercurial through the rise and fall of distant voices. There is no music in our house. Father says it is distracting. We stand uneasily on the platform. The train is late or perhaps we are early. Pa stands with his back to the boys who have greeted him deferentially. His broad shoulders block my view but I can hear their voices flashing like the village lights on Republic Day. The boys do not look at me and I know why. I am fat. My breasts are fat and, in spite of my uplift bra, flat as a vetkoek.

There is a lump in my throat which I cannot account for. I do of course cry from time to time about being fat, but this lump will not be dislodged by tears. I am pleased that Pa does not say much. I watch him take a string out of his pocket and wind it nervously around his index finger. Round and round from the base until the finger is encased in a perfect bandage. The last is a loop that fits the tip of his finger tightly; the ends are tied in an almost invisible knot. He hopes to hold my attention with this game. Will this be followed by cat's cradle with my hands foolishly stretched out, waiting to receive? I smart at his attempts to shield me from the boys; they are quite unnecessary.

Pa knows nothing of young people. On the morning of my fourteenth birthday he quoted from Genesis III . . . in pain you shall bring forth children. I had been menstruating for some time and so knew what he wanted to say. He said, 'You must fetch a bucket of water in the evenings and wash the rags at night . . . have them ready for the next month . . . always be prepared . . . it does not always come on time. Your mother was never regular . . . the ways of the Lord . . .' and he shuffled off with the bicycle tyre he was pretending to repair.

'But they sell things now in chemists' shops, towels you can throw away,' I called after him.

'Yes,' he looked dubiously at the distant blue hills, 'perhaps you could have some for emergencies. Always be prepared,'

and lowering his eyes once again blurted, 'And don't play
with boys now that you're a young lady, it's dangerous.'

I have never played with boys. There were none to play
with when we lived on the farm. I do not know why. The
memory, of a little boy boring a big toe into the sand,
surfaces. He is staring enviously at the little house I have
carved into the sandbank. There are shelves on which my
pots gleam and my one-legged Peggy sleeps on her bank of
clay. In my house I am free to do anything, even invite the
boy to play. I am proud of the sardine can in which two clay
loaves bake in the sun. For my new china teapot I have
built a stone shrine where its posy of pink roses remains
forever fresh. I am still smiling at the boy as he deftly pulls a
curious hose from the leg of his khaki shorts and, with one
eye shut, aims an arc of yellow pee into the teapot. I do not
remember the teapot ever having a lid.

There is a lump in my throat I cannot account for. I
sometimes cry about being fat, of course, especially after
dinner when the zip of my skirt sinks its teeth into my flesh.
Then it is reasonable to cry. But I have after all stood on
this platform countless times on the last day of the school
holidays. Sarie and I, with Pa and Mr Botha waving and
shouting into the clouds of steam, Work Hard or Be Good.
Here, under the black and white arms of the station sign,
where succulents spent and shrivelled in autumn grow once
again plump in winter before they burst into shocking
spring flower. So that Pa would say, 'The quarters slip by so
quickly, soon the sun will be on Cancer and you'll be home
again.' Or, 'When the summer train brings you back with
your First Class Junior Certificate, the aloe will just be in
flower.' And so the four school quarters clicked by under
the Kliprand station sign where the jewelled eyes of the
iceplant wink in the sun all year round.

The very first lump in my throat he melted with a fervent whisper, 'You must, Friedatjie, you must. There is no high school for us here and you don't want to be a servant. How would you like to peg out the madam's washing and hear the train you once refused to go on rumble by?' Then he slipped a bag of raisins into my hand. A terrifying image of a madam's menstrual rags that I have to wash swirls liquid red through my mind. I am grateful to be going hundreds of miles away from home; there is so much to be grateful for. One day I will drive a white car.

Pa takes a stick of biltong out of his pocket and the brine in my eyes retreats. I have no control over the glands under my tongue as they anticipate the salt. His pocketknife lifts off the seasoned and puckered surface and leaves a slab of marbled meat, dry and mirror smooth so that I long to rest my lips on it. Instead my teeth sink into the biltong and I am consoled. I eat everything he offers.

We have always started our day with mealie porridge. That is what miners eat twice a day, and they lift chunks of gypsum clean out of the earth. Father's eyes flash a red light over the breakfast table: 'Don't leave anything on your plate. You must grow up to be big and strong. We are not paupers with nothing to eat. Your mother was thin and sickly, didn't eat enough. You don't want cheekbones that jut out like a Hottentot's. Fill them out until they're shiny and plump as pumpkins.' The habit of obedience is fed daily with second helpings of mealie porridge. He does not know that I have long since come to despise my size. I would like to be a pumpkin stored on the flat roof and draw in whole beams of autumn's sunlight so that, bleached and hardened, I could call upon the secret of my glowing orange flesh.

A wolf whistle from one of the boys. I turn to look and I know it will upset Pa. Two girls in identical flared skirts arrive with their own radio blaring Boeremusiek. They nod at us and stand close by, perhaps seeking protection from the boys. I hope that Pa will not speak to me loudly in English. I will avoid calling him Father for they will surely snigger under cover of the whining concertina. They must know that for us this is no ordinary day. But we all remain silent and I am inexplicably ashamed. What do people say about us? Until recently I believed that I was envied; that is, not counting my appearance.

The boys beckon and the girls turn up their radio. One of them calls loudly, 'Turn off that Boere-shit and come and listen to decent American music.' I wince. The girls do as they are told, their act of resistance deflated. Pa casts an anxious glance at the white policeman pacing the actual platform, the paved white section. I take out a paper handkerchief and wipe the dust from my polished shoes, a futile act since this unpaved strip for which I have no word other than the inaccurate platform, is all dust. But it gives me the chance to peer at the group of young people through my lowered lashes.

The boys vie for their attention. They have taken the radio and pass it round so that the red skirts flare and swoop, the torsos in T-shirts arch and taper into long arms reaching to recover their radio. Their ankles swivel on the slender stems of high heels. Their feet are covered in dust. One of the arms adjusts a chiffon headscarf that threatens to slip off, and a pimply boy crows at his advantage. He whips the scarf from her head and the tinkling laughter switches into a whine.

'Give it back . . . You have no right . . . It's mine and I want it back . . . Please, oh please.'

Her arm is raised protectively over her head, the hand flattened on her hair.

'No point in holding your head now,' he teases. 'I've got it, going to try it on myself.'

Her voice spun thin on threads of tears, abject as she begs. So that her friend consoles, 'It doesn't matter, you've got plenty of those. Show them you don't care.' A reproachful look but the friend continues, 'Really, it doesn't matter, your hair looks nice enough. I've told you before. Let him do what he wants with it, stuff it up his arse.'

But the girl screams, 'Leave me alone,' and beats away the hand reaching out to console. Another taller boy takes the scarf and twirls it in the air. 'You want your doekie? What do you want it for hey, come on tell us, what do you want it for? What do you want to cover up?'

His tone silences the others and his face tightens as he swings the scarf slowly, deliberately. She claws at his arm with rage while her face is buried in the other crooked arm. A little gust of wind settles the matter, whips it out of his hand and leaves it spreadeagled against the eucalyptus tree where its red pattern licks the bark like flames.

I cannot hear their words. But far from being penitent, the tall boy silences the bareheaded girl with angry shaking of the head and wagging of the finger. He runs his hand through an exuberant bush of fuzzy hair and my hand involuntarily flies to my own. I check my preparations: the wet hair wrapped over large rollers to separate the strands, dried then swirled around my head, secured overnight with a nylon stocking, dressed with vaseline to keep the strands smooth and straight and then pulled back tightly to stem any remaining tendency to curl. Father likes it pulled back. He says it is a mark of honesty to have the forehead and ears exposed. He must be thinking of Mother, whose hair was straight and trouble-free. I would not allow some unkempt youth to comment on my hair.

The tall boy with wild hair turns to look at us. I think that they are talking about me. I feel my body swelling out of the dress rent into vertical strips that fall to my feet. The wind will surely lift off my hair like a wig and flatten it, a sheet of glossy dead bird, on the eucalyptus tree.

The bareheaded girl seems to have recovered; she holds her head reasonably high.

I break the silence. 'Why should that boy look at us so insolently?' Pa looks surprised and hurt. 'Don't be silly. You couldn't possibly tell from this distance.' But his mouth puckers and he starts an irritating tuneless whistle.

On the white platform the policeman is still pacing. He is there because of the Blacks who congregate at the station twice a week to see the Springbok train on its way to Cape Town. I wonder whether he knows our news. Perhaps their servants, bending over washtubs, ease their shoulders to give the gossip from Wesblok to madams limp with heat and boredom. But I dismiss the idea and turn to the boys who certainly know that I am going to St Mary's today. All week the grown-ups have leaned over the fence and sighed, Ja, ja, in admiration, and winked at Pa: a clever chap, old Shenton, keeps up with the Boers all right. And to me, 'You show them, Frieda, what we can do.' I nodded shyly. Now I look at my hands, at the irrepressible cuticles, the stubby splayed fingernails that will never taper. This is all I have to show, betraying generations of servants.

I am tired and I move back a few steps to sit on the suitcases. But Father leaps to their defence. 'Not on the cases, Frieda. They'll never take your weight.' I hate the shiny suitcases. As if we had not gone to enough expense, he insisted on new imitation leather bags and claimed that people judge by appearances. I miss my old scuffed bag and slowly, as if the notion has to travel through folds of fat, I realise that I miss Sarie and the lump in my throat hardens.

Sarie and I have travelled all these journeys together. Grief gave way to excitement as soon as we boarded the train. Huddled together on the cracked green seat, we argued about who would sleep on the top bunk. And in winter when the nights grew cold we folded into a single S on the lower bunk. As we tossed through the night in our magic coupé, our fathers faded and we were free. Now Sarie stands in the starched white uniform of a student nurse, the Junior Certificate framed in her father's room. She will not come to wave me goodbye.

Sarie and I swore our friendship on the very first day at school. We twiddled our stiff plaits in boredom; the *First Sunnyside Reader* had been read to us at home. And Jos. Within a week Jos had mastered the reader and joined us. The three of us hand in hand, a formidable string of laughing girls tugging this way and that, sneering at the Sunnyside adventures of Rover, Jane and John. I had no idea that I was fat. Jos looped my braids over her beautiful hands and said that I was pretty, that my braids were a string of sausages.

Jos was bold and clever. Like a whirlwind she spirited away the tedium of exhausted games and invented new rules. We waited for her to take command. Then she slipped her hand under a doekie of dyed flourbags and scratched her head. Her ear peeped out, a faded yellow-brown yearning for the sun. Under a star-crammed sky Jos had boldly stood for hours, peering through a crack in the shutter to watch their fifth baby being born. Only once had she looked away in agony and then the Three Kings in the eastern sky swiftly swopped places in the manner of musical chairs. She told us all, and with an oath invented by Jos we swore that we would never have babies. Jos knew everything that grown-ups thought should be kept from us. Father said, 'A cheeky child, too big for her boots, she'll land in a madam's kitchen all right.' But there was no need to separate us. Jos left school when she turned nine and her family moved to the village where her father had found a job at the garage. He had injured his back at the mine. Jos said they were going to have a car; that she would win one of those competitions, easy they were, you only had to make up a slogan.

Then there was our move. Pa wrote letters for the whole community, bit his nails when he thought I was not looking and wandered the veld for hours. When the official letter came the cooped-up words tumbled out helter-skelter in his longest monologue.

'In rows in the village, that's where we'll have to go, all boxed in with no room to stretch the legs. All my life I've lived in the open with only God to keep an eye on me, what do I want with the eyes of neighbours nudging and jostling in cramped streets? How will the wind get into those back yards to sweep away the smell of too many people? Where will I grow things? A watermelon, a pumpkin need room to spread, and a turkey wants a swept yard, the markings of a grass broom on which to boast the pattern of his wingmarks. What shall we do, Frieda? What will become of us?' And then, calmly, 'Well, there's nothing to be done. We'll go to Wesblok, we'll put up our curtains and play with the electric lights and find a corner for the cat, but it won't be our home. I'm not clever old Shenton for nothing, not a wasted drop of Scots blood in me. Within five years we'll have enough to buy a little place. Just a little raw brick house and somewhere to tether a goat and keep a few chickens. Who needs a water lavatory in the veld?'

The voice brightened into fantasy. 'If it were near a river we could have a pond for ducks or geese. In the Swarteberg my pa always had geese. Couldn't get to sleep for months here in Namaqualand without the squawking of geese. And ostriches. There's nothing like ostrich biltong studded with coriander seeds.' Then he slowed down. 'Ag man, we won't be allowed land by the river but nevermind hey. We'll show them, Frieda, we will. You'll go to high school next year and board with Aunt Nettie. We've saved enough for that. Brains are for making money and when you come home with your Senior Certificate, you won't come back to a pack of Hottentots crouching in straight lines on the edge of the village. Oh no, my girl, you won't.' And he whipped out a stick of beef biltong and with the knife shaved off wafer-thin slices that curled with pleasure in our palms.

We packed our things humming. I did not really understand what he was fussing about. The Coloured location did not seem so terrible. Electric lights meant no more oil lamps to clean and there was water from a tap at the end of each street. And there would be boys. But the children ran after me calling, 'Fatty fatty vetkoek.' Young children too. Sarie took me firmly by the arm and said that it wasn't true, that they were jealous of my long hair. I believed her and swung my stiff pigtails haughtily. Until I grew breasts and found that the children were right.

Now Sarie will be by the side of the sick and infirm, leaning over high hospital beds, soothing and reassuring. Sarie in a dazzling white uniform, her little waist clinched by the broad blue belt.

If Sarie were here I could be sure of climbing the two steel steps on to the train.

The tall boy is now pacing the platform in unmistakable imitation of the policeman. His face is the stern mask of someone who does not take his duties lightly. His friends are squatting on their haunches, talking earnestly. One of them illustrates a point with the aid of a stick with which he writes or draws in the sand. The girls have retreated and lean against the eucalyptus tree, bright as stars against the grey of the trunk. Twelve feet apart the two radios stand face to face, quarrelling quietly. Only the female voices rise now and again in bitter laughter above the machines.

Father says that he must find the station master to enquire why the train has not come. 'Come with me,' he commands. I find the courage to pretend that it is a question but I flush with the effort.

'No, I'm tired, I'll wait here.' And he goes. It is true that I am tired. I do not on the whole have much energy and I am always out of breath. I have often consoled myself with an early death, certainly before I become an old maid. Alone with my suitcases I face the futility of that notion. I am free to abandon it since I am an old maid now, today, days after my fifteenth birthday. I do not in any case think that my spirit, weightless and energetic like smoke from green wood, will soar to heaven.

I think of Pa's defeated shoulders as he turned to go and I wonder whether I ought to run after him. But the thought of running exhausts me. I recoil again at the energy with which he had burst into the garden only weeks ago, holding aloft *Die Burger* with both hands, shouting, 'Frieda, Frieda, we'll do it. It's all ours, the whole world's ours.'

It was a short report on how a Coloured deacon had won his case against the Anglican Church so that the prestigious St Mary's School was now open to non-whites. The article ended sourly, calling it an empty and subversive gesture, and warning the deacon's daughters that it would be no bed of roses.

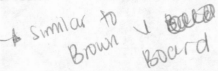

Similar to Brown ✓ Board

'You'll have the best, the very best education.' His voice is hoarse with excitement.

'It will cost hundreds of rand per year.'

'Nonsense, you finish this year at Malmesbury and then there'll be only the two years of Matric left to pay for. Really, it's a blessing that you have only two years left.'

'Where will you find the money?' I say soberly.

'The nest egg of course, stupid child. You can't go to a white school if you're so stupid. Shenton has enough money to give his only daughter the best education in the world.'

I hesitate before asking, 'But what about the farm?' He has not come to like the Wesblok. The present he wraps in a protective gauze of dreams; his eyes have grown misty with focusing far ahead on the unrealised farm.

A muscle twitches in his face before he beams, 'A man could live anywhere, burrow a hole like a rabbit in order to make use of an opportunity like this.' He seizes the opportunity for a lecture. 'Ignorance, laziness and tobacco have been the downfall of our people. It is our duty to God to better ourselves, to use our brains, our talents, not to place our lamps under bushels. No, we'll do it. We must be prepared to make sacrifices to meet such a generous offer.'

His eyes race along the perimeter of the garden wall then he rushes indoors, muttering about idling like flies in the sun, and sets about writing to St Mary's in Cape Town.

I read novels and kept in the shade all summer. The crunch of biscuits between my teeth was the rumble of distant thunder. Pimples raged on my chin, which led me to Madame Rose's Preparation by mail order. That at least has fulfilled its promise.

I was surprised when Sarie wept with joy or envy, so that the tears spurted from my own eyes on to the pages of

Ritchie's First Steps in Latin. (Father said that they pray in Latin and that I ought to know what I am praying for.) At night a hole crept into my stomach, gnawing like a hungry mouse, and I fed it with Latin declensions and Eetsumor biscuits. Sarie said that I might meet white boys and for the moment, fortified by conjugations of *Amo*, I saw the eyes of Anglican boys, remote princes leaning from their carriages, penetrate the pumpkin-yellow of my flesh.

Today I see a solid stone wall where I stand in watery autumn light waiting for a bell to ring. The Cape south-easter tosses high the blond pigtails and silvery laughter of girls walking by. They do not see me. Will I spend the dinner breaks hiding in lavatories?

I wish I could make this day more joyful for Pa but I do not know how. It is no good running after him now. It is too late.

The tall boy has imperceptibly extended his marching ground. Does he want to get closer to the policeman or is he taking advantage of Father's absence? I watch his feet, up, down, and the crunch of his soles on the sand explodes in my ears. Closer, and a thrilling thought shoots through the length of my body. He may be looking at me longingly, probing; but I cannot bring my eyes to travel up, along his unpressed trousers. The black boots of the policeman catch my eye. He will not be imitated. His heavy legs are tree trunks rooted in the asphalt. His hand rests on the bulge of his holster. I can no longer resist the crunch of the boy's soles as they return. I look up. He clicks his heels and halts. His eyes are narrowed with unmistakable contempt. He greets me in precise mocking English. A soundless shriek for Pa escapes my lips and I note the policeman resuming his march before I reply. The boy's voice is angry and I wonder what aspect of my dress offends him.

'You are waiting for the Cape Town train?' he asks unnecessarily. I nod.

'You start at the white school tomorrow?' A hole yawns in my stomach and I long for a biscuit. I will not reply.

'There are people who bury dynamite between the rails and watch whole carriages of white people shoot into the air. Like opening the door of a birdcage. Phsssh!' His long thin arms describe the spray of birdflight. 'Perhaps that is why your train has not come.'

I know he is lying. I would like to hurl myself at him, stab at his eyes with my blunt nails, kick at his ankles until they snap. But I clasp my hands together piously and hold, hold the tears that threaten.

'Your prayer is answered, look, here's Fa-atherrr,' and on the held note he clicks his heels and turns smartly to march off towards his friends.

Father is smiling. 'She's on her way, should be here any second now.' I take his arm and my hand slips into his jacket pocket where I trace with my finger the withered potato he wears for relief of rheumatism.

'No more biltong, girlie,' he laughs. The hole in my stomach grows dangerously.

The white platform is now bustling with people. Porters pile suitcases on to their trolleys while men fish in their pockets for sixpence tips. A Black girl staggers on to the white platform with a suitcase in each hand. Her madam ambles amiably alongside her to keep up with the faltering gait. She chatters without visible encouragement and, stooping, takes one of the bags from the girl who clearly cannot manage. The girl is big-boned with strong shapely arms and calves. What can the suitcase contain to make her stagger so? Her starched apron sags below the waist and the crisp servant's cap is askew. When they stop at the far end of the platform she slips a hand under the edge of the white cap to scratch. Briefly she tugs at the tip of her yellow-brown earlobe. My chest tightens. I turn to look the other way.

Our ears prick at a rumbling in the distance which sends as scout a thin squeal along the rails. A glass dome of terror settles over my head so that the chatter about me recedes and I gulp for air. But I do not faint. The train lumbers to a halt and sighs deeply. My body, all but consumed by its hole of hunger, swings around lightly, even as Father moves forward with a suitcase to mount the step. And as I walk away towards the paling I meet the triumphant eyes of the tall boy standing by the whitewashed gate. Above the noise of a car screeching to a halt, the words roll off my tongue disdainfully:

Why you look and kyk gelyk,
Am I miskien of gold gemake?

A CLEARING IN THE BUSH

Tamieta, leaning against the east-facing wall, rolls her shoulders and like a cat rubs against the bricks to relieve the itching of her back. Which must mean something ominous, such a sudden and terrible itch, and as she muses on its meaning, on its persistence, the rebellious flesh seems to align itself with the arrangement of bricks now imprinted on her back. She longs for the hot press of the sun that will brand the pattern of narrow new bricks into her flesh, iron the itch out of existence. She will never get used to this Cape Town weather so cold and wet in winter. It's about time summer showed its face; there hasn't been any sunshine for days. As for the itch, who thinks of conditions of the flesh that have just disappeared? When it should be freshest in the memory, that is the time when we do not think of an itch at all.

'Ag, a person mustn't complain,' she mutters to herself. 'This is the first morning of spring and even if it's not going to last, there's enough warmth to be soaked up against this wall.'

If only she knew what the omen was, for it's no good disregarding these things; they'll catch up with you all the same. Now, if it had been yesterday – and did she not yesterday look up at a hesitant sun and toy with the idea of taking her coffee outside, to lean against this nice wall? – yes, if it had been yesterday then she would have been able to exclaim as Charlie's Springbok radio bleeped the news, 'This is so. An itch of the back early in the morning means there's going to be an assassination.'

And as she drains her coffee grounds into the rough grass she remembers. Beatrice's wool. She promised to get to Bellville South after work to get a couple of ounces from her lay-by at Wilton Wools. Perhaps it's not an omen but a reminder: the itch leading to the bricks leading to the pattern in Beatrice's nimble hands. Knit four, purl one, chanting earnestly as she clicks her bricks into place. And the wool cleverly chosen by Beatrice to build a jersey in the colours of bricks and mortar. Ooh that child of hers is now clever. She can do just about anything with her hands and also her head, of course, because if your hands can do good so must the head. That is what the Apostle says and quite right too since it's all part of the same person.

As Tamieta braces herself for the day of labour in the canteen, her eyes fall on the bricks of this nice new wall and to her surprise must admit that it is not the colour of bricks at all. Really these are a greyish-black, with iridescent blue lights admittedly, but certainly not brick-red or brick-brown. Well, at least it isn't just our people who get it wrong; as far as she can think, people just haven't noticed, or people in spite of the evidence just go on talking nonsense. But she castigates herself for having been duped by a false association. She ought to have seen the futility of a reminder so early in the day when there is no need to remember. And now at this very moment the itch returns with new virulence. Tamieta has never known her flesh threaten to break free of its containing skin; such an itch must have a marrow-deep meaning.

Raising her head in order to scratch more effectively, she sees the first student settling into a seat on the top floor of the library. She has never been in there, even though it is the block closest to the cafeteria. Here, along these paths linking the four buildings that the government has given specially for our people, this is where Beatrice will walk one day, flying in and out of glass doors in her baby-louis heels and a briefcase bulging under her arm. But her skirts will be a decent length, not creeping above the knees like a few of the girls have started wearing them.

She climbs the steps to the cafeteria kitchen just as Charlie's sing-song voice calls, 'Tamieta, the mutton is chopped.' He has a voice to match his swagger and her ears twitch for a note of mockery, for it is amazing how that boy persists in thinking of her as a plaasjapie. That's why he slips in handfuls of English words as if she can't understand. Let him go on thinking it's so special to come from District Six.

Tamieta's energetic leap up the steps makes me wriggle in my seat. Large and slothful I sit pressed in my carrell on the top floor of the library making no progress whatsoever with the essay on *Tess of the D'Urbervilles* which should have been handed in yesterday. Failure to do it will lose me the right to take the end-of-year examination yet I have been unable even to start the thing. At the very moment yesterday as I strained for an excuse, trembling at the thought of a visit to Retief's office somewhere along a carpeted corridor, a pet abdominal tapeworm hissed persuasively into the ear of its Greek host, whose trembling hand grew still for a second to aim a fatal shot at the Prime Minister. Today I arrived early and hid here on the top

floor amongst large botanical tomes since a tapeworm
cannot protect me for ever. Along the margin of this blank
sheet of foolscap I have drawn triangles and parallelograms,
clean geometrical lines. I have no talent for likenesses and
it is Retief's I wish to capture in this margin, someone to
whom I can address the wormy tangle of questions that
wriggle out of reach each time I pick up my pen. The Parker
pen, a solemn gift from Father, lies before me, capped,
uncooperative. I read through Retief's notes once more. A
pity in some respects that I did not get to see his room.
James, who once was in the same position, except that his
mother's illness offered a legitimate excuse, says that close
up Retief's skin is not white at all, rather a liverish-yellow
with fine red veins, and that his speaking voice is hardly
recognisable to a student who only hears him lecture in the
large theatre. And what, I wonder, would I have
interrupted in that room? In that functional cubicle of new
uncluttered design the rugby-playing Retief will barely be
able to stretch his legs while he copies out in longhand the
lecture notes of the correspondence university to which we
are affiliated. Pressed against the door I would have said,
through a plate glass of awe and fear, something, something
credible, so that he would draw up his long legs in attentive
sympathy and say in a strange voice, 'But there is absolutely
nothing to worry about, of course I understand my dear
Miss . . . er . . .'

I could say anything to him and it is a relief to know that
it does not matter in the slightest how I deliver my lie, for
he does not know me, doesn't know any of us, and will not
recognise me the next day.

I uncap my pen and read through Retief's dictated
lecture. His pigeon head bobs up and down in empathy
with the bowed heads of students before him as he pecks at

his words in clipped English. The novel, he says, is about Fate. Alarmingly simple, but not quite how it strikes me, although I cannot offer an alternative. The truth is that I do not always understand the complicated language, though of course I got the gist of the story, the interesting bits where things happen. But even then, I cannot be sure of what actually happens in The Chase.

Wessex spreads like a well-used map before me, worn and dim along the fold-lines, the lush Frome Valley and the hills so picture-green where Persephone skips sprinkling daisies and buttercups from her clutched apron, caring not two hoots about the ones that fall face down destined to die. The scuffed green strip is The Chase where God knows what happened. Seduced, my notes say. Can you be seduced by someone you hate? Can trees gnarled with age whisper ancient ecstasies and waves of darkness upon dark lap until the flesh melts? I do, of course, not know of these matters, but shudder for Tess.

Beyond these pale buildings gleaming ghostly in the young spring light there is a fringe of respectably tall Port Jackson and bluegum trees that marks the clearing of university buildings from the surrounding bush. These raggle-taggle sentinels stand to tin-soldierly attention and behind them the bush stretches for miles across the Cape Flats. Bushes, I imagine, that send out wayward limbs to weave into the tangled undergrowth, for I have never left the concrete paths of this campus. Even summer couples may step out arm in arm to flaunt their love under the fluffy yellow flower of the Port Jackson, but never, surely, do they venture beyond. Somewhere beyond the administration block where today the flag flies half mast, they say there is a station where the train stops four times daily on the way to and from the Cape Flats. Skollie boys sit all day long on the deserted platform, for there is no ticket office, and dangle their legs above the rails while they puff at their dagga pils. But even from this height there is no visible path winding through the bush. The handful of students who use the train must daily beat like pioneers a path through the undergrowth.

Along the top of my page enclosing the essay title, 'Fate in Tess,' I have now drawn an infantile line of train carriages. I cannot start writing. I have always been able to distinguish good from bad but the story confuses me and the lecture notes offer no help.

Murder is a sin which should outrage all decent and civilised people.

The library is beginning to fill up and a boy I vaguely recognise as a Science student passes twice, darting resentful looks at me. No doubt I am in the seat that he has come to think of as his very own. Perhaps I should leave. Perhaps he can't work for being in a strange seat. ~No, don't leave~

Through the window I watch James in his canary-yellow jersey, his jacket tucked under his arm, trotting to the Arts block for the English lecture. I shall get the notes from him. James is a good friend; he is not like other boys. It is the distant sound of the nine o'clock siren that makes my courage fountain and the opening sentence spill on to the page in fluent English: 'Before we can assess the role of fate in the novel we must consider the question of whether Tess is guilty or not, whether she has erred in losing her virginity, deceiving her husband and killing her lover.'

Exhausted by my bold effort I can go no further. Outside, the pathways are deserted. English 1 students are by now seated in their row, shoulders hunched over Retief's dictation. The surly boy walks past me once again with a large volume under his arm. The hatred in his lingering look is unmistakable. I pack up my things hurriedly and before I reach the door the boy leaps up from his exposed seat at a central table and lurches indecently into the carrell so that I blush for the warm imprint of my buttocks which has not yet risen from the thin upholstery. It should be more comfortable on the first floor where I usually work amongst familiar faces, but by the time I reach the bottom of the stairs a reckless thirst propels me out, right out of the library towards the cafeteria where Tamieta's coffee pots croon on the hot plate. *racial segregation still exists in the high school*

She mutters, 'It's not ready,' and clatters the lids of her pots and turns on a fierce jet of water so that Charlie jumps out of the spray and shouts, 'Jeez-like Auntie man, that's mos not necessary man.'

He tilts his face for the gracious acceptance of an apology but Tamieta's head remains bent over the sink. He cannot bear the silence and by way of introduction hums an ironic tune.

'That ou in there,' pointing at the door that leads into the lecturers dining room, 'that ou said just now that Verwoerd was the architect of this place,' Charlie offers.

'It's because you listen to other people's conversations that you forget the orders hey. You'll never get on in this canteen business if you don't keep your head. Never mind the artitex; clever people's talk got nothing to do with you,' Tamieta retorts.

Charlie laughs scornfully. He discards the professional advice because he will not believe that a speaker could fail to be flattered by an eavesdropper. So that recognising the root of the error he will not mind being brought curry instead of bredie. Besides, he, Charlie, had only got an order wrong once, several weeks ago.

'I know you don't need architects in the platteland. Not

if you build your houses out of sticks and mud, but here in Cape Town there are special big-shot people who make drawings and plan out the buildings.' He speaks slowly, with pedagogical patience. 'So that's what I mean; the Prime Minister got even more important things to do and a lecturer should know better. That ou must be from the Theology School over there', driving a thumb in the wrong direction. 'Those moffies know buggerall there.'

Tamieta's fingers are greedy beaks pecking into the pastry bowl and she fixes her eyes on the miracle of merging resistant fat and flour. She will not be provoked by this blasphemous Slams who has just confirmed her doubts about the etymology of his 'Jeez-like.' They know nothing of God and yes it is her Christian duty to defend her God, but this Charlie is beyond the pale. The Old Man will have to look after himself today. She adds the liquid slowly, absorbed by the wonder of turning her ingredients into an entirely new substance. But it will not last. Her melktert to rival all tarts, perfectly round and risen, will melt in so many mouths, and that will be the end of it.

' . . . just reading the Bible all day long makes them stupid, those preacher chaps from the platteland . . .' Charlie's voice weaves through her thoughts. This boy will not stop until she speaks out against his irreverence and Tamieta sighs, weary with the demands of God. Even the bonuses have strings attached. What, for instance, is the point of having a Sabbath when you have to work like a slave all Saturday in order to prepare for the day of rest? When she first started in service with Ounooi van Graan, my word how she had to work. All the vegetables peeled the night before, the mutton half roasted in the pot and the sousboontjies all but cooked. And now in her own home in Bosheuwel, working all Saturday afternoon to make Sunday the day of rest. Oh what would she give to spread out the chores and do the ironing on Sundays. Instead she has to keep a watchful eye on Beatrice whose hands itch for her knitting needles. She feels for the child as they sit after the service and the special Sunday dinner wondering what to do so that she would yawn and shut her eyes and pray for strength to hold out against the child's desire to make something durable. For knitting on a Sunday pierces God directly in the eyes. It is her sacred duty to keep that child out of the roasting fires of hell for, not being her own, she is doubly responsible.

It was on her first visit back to Kliprand that she found cousin Sofie merry with drink and the two-year-old toddler wandering about with bushy hair in which the lice frolicked shamelessly. Then she pinned the struggling child between her knees and fought each louse in turn. She plaited her hair in tight rows that challenged the most valiant louse, and with her scalp soaked in Blue-butter the little Beatrice beamed a beauty that is born out of cleanliness. And Tamieta knew that she, not unlike the Virgin Mary, had been chosen as the child's rightful mother. She who adored little ones would have a child without the clumsiness of pregnancy, the burden of birth and the tobacco-breathed attentions of men with damp fumbling hands. Sofie agreed, weeping for her own weakness, and found parents for the other two, so that the validity of choosing a child at one's convenience was endorsed by the disposal of those she could no longer care for.

Eight good years together testify to the wisdom of the arrangement. Beatrice loves the yearly visits to Kliprand where Ousie Sofie awaits them with armfuls of presents, not always the sort of thing a girl would want in Town, but so jolly is Sofie telling her fabulous stories with much noise and actions that they all scream with mirth. A honey mouth that cousin of hers has, full of wise talk which only gets a person into trouble. Just as well she has kept to the country; Cape Town would not agree with her.

Beatrice has brought nothing but good luck. After serving the terrible English family in Cape Town – they paid well but never talked to her, nor for that matter did they talk to each other except in hushed tones as if someone in the family had just died – came Tamieta's lucky break at the UCT canteen where she could hold her head up high and do a respectable job of cooking for people whose brains needed nourishing. She was the one who kept the kitchen spotless, who cooked without waste and whose clockwork was infallible; it was only right that she should be chosen to run the canteen at the new Coloured university. The first kitchen boy was quiet, eager to please, but this Charlie is a thorn in her flesh. Full of himself and no respect for his elders. Why should he want to go on about the pondokkies of country folk? She casts a resentful look at the girl just sitting there, waiting for her coffee with her nose in her blinking book. She too is from the country. Tamieta knows of her father who drives a motor car in the very next village, for who in Little Namaqualand does not know of Shenton? The girl speaks English but that need not prevent her from saying something educated and putting this Charlie in his place. She, Tamieta, will turn on him and say as she rolls the pastry, pliant under her rolling pin, strike him with a real English saying which will make that know-all face frown. She has not worked for English people without learning a thing or two. She has learned to value their weapon of silence, and she has memorised Madam's icy words to the man with the briefcase, 'Fools rush in where angels fear to tread.' Oh to see Charlie's puzzled look before he pretends to know exactly what it means. Her fingers stiffen as the boy rises with his board of chopped onions, but what if he were just to laugh at her if she said it now? If only she could leave him alone, but Tamieta calls out just as he is about to drop the onions into the pan. Curtly, 'It needs to be finer than that.' Charlie's onion tears stream down his face.

'See how you make me cry, Tamieta? This is the tears of all my young years, and I'll have none left for your wedding. They say you getting married, Tamieta, when is the happy day?'

He runs his hand over the mirror surface of his greased hair, asserting his superiority. This Charlie with his smooth hair and nose like a tent will find every opportunity to humiliate her. She ought to ask him to wash his hands. No one wants Brylcreem-flavoured bredie. But her legs ache and her back starts up again, the itching pores like so many seething hot springs, so that she really can't give a damn. The stove will tend to the germs. This is no ordinary itch.

Tamieta turns to Charlie. 'We must get a move on. All tomorrow's work has to be done this morning as well 'cause this afternoon is the memorial and the cafeteria will be closed.'

'Ooh-hoo,' the boy crows loudly, 'I'm going up Hanover Street to get the material for our Carnival uniforms. We start practising next week and this year the Silver Blades is going to walk off with all the prizes.'

'Sies,' Tamieta remonstrates, 'I don't know how you Slamse can put yourself on show like that for the white people to laugh at on New Year's Day.'

'Oh, you country people know nothing man, Tamieta man. The best part is when we come out at midnight in our costumes. Have you ever been in the city for the midnight?'

Tamieta seals her face and maintains a scornful silence.

'No,' he continues, 'you won't have seen the lights all down Adderley Street, man, twinkling like home-made stars, man, like all the planets just jiving in the streets. Then all the bells start ringing and that's when we run out from the shadows with the black polish.'

His hips grind as he dances towards her, waving his spread palms. She cannot ignore him and when she retreats with her wooden spoon, Charlie grabs his knees with mirth and crows breathlessly, 'That's when we get all the whities and rub the black polish all over their faces.'

'I must be a baboon to listen to all this nonsense. Where will a white person allow a troop of coons to even touch their faces? I may have been born in a pondok but I wasn't born yesterday, you know.'

''Strue Tamieta, 'strue,' he begs her to believe him. 'It's been going on for years now, it's a tradition you know,' and taking up his chopping knife he adds soberly, 'I suppose the whities who come there know it's going to happen and come specially for the black polish, but perhaps there is, yes there must be, one or two who get the fright of their lives when we jump out from the shadows.'

Tamieta sets the cups out on the counter. She really can't be listening to this boy's nonsense and if he doesn't know that he's supposed to spend the afternoon at the ceremony, well then, that's his problem.

'Here,' she calls to the Shenton girl, 'here, the coffee's ready.'

Midst these unlikely sounds of clattering cups and the regular fall of the knife, the bass of the bean soup and the sizzling onion smells, the essay is going tolerably well. There are human voices in the background, the amicable hum of

Tamieta and Charlie, harmonising with the kitchen sounds that will materialise into bean soup favoured by the students and bredie for the staff.

I have followed the opening thrust with two more paragraphs that wantonly move towards exonerating Tess. Retief's notes are no good to me. He will not be pleased. Things are going well until an ill-timed ten o'clock siren sounds, signalling a visit to the lavatory. Since the collapse of the beehive I have not found a satisfactory way of doing my hair although the curve of my flick-ups is crisp as ever. Fortunately one can always rely on Amami hairspray. I wet my fingers at the tap to tug at the crinkly hairshaft of an otherwise perfectly straight fringe. Cape Town with its damp and misty mornings is no good for the hair. Thank God there is no full-length mirror to taunt me although I have a feeling that the waistband of my skirt has slackened. After a final glance at the now stabilised fringe and a rewarding thumb between my blouse and waistband, I am ready to face coffee-break.

The boys who play klawerjas at the back of the room are already installed and they let out the customary wolf whistle as I re-enter the cafeteria. Fortunately my table is right at the front so that I do not have to endure the tribute for long. It is of course encouraging to know that a few moments before the mirror does pay dividends, that the absorption with a card game can be pierced by a pleasing female tread. My pulse quickens. Though I sit with my back to them I don't know what to do. There is no question of carrying on with the essay. These males have a sixth sense. Whilst being held by the game they somehow know when a girl moves and will not fail to pucker the lips and allow the hot draught of air to escape even as you bend to retrieve a sheet of paper from the floor. There must be some girls who never get whistled at but I don't think I know of any. We are all familiar with the scale of appreciation, from the festive tantara for the beauties to the single whiplash of a whistle for the barely attractive. Then there is the business of who is whistling at you, and since you cannot possibly look, since you drop your eyes demurely or stare coldly ahead, and while you shiver deliciously to the vibrations of the whistle there can be a nagging discomfort, an inexplicable lump that settles like a cork in the trachea. Should it be some awful country boy with faltering English and a feathered hat . . . but such a contingency is covered by the supportive group whistle. You will never know the original admirer so it is best not to look, not to speak.

I am pleased to see James and tidy away my folder to make room for him. But he collects a cup of coffee, drops his bag at my table and with a dismissive hallo goes straight to the back where he joins the boys. Unusual for him but it really does not matter. I stretch my legs and with my heels draw in James's bag to support my calves. Perhaps I should take my folder out again and try to work, but there is no point; the others will be here soon. Instead I decide on another cup of coffee. It is not an extravagance; I shall not have one this afternoon. With my ten-cent piece I tap on the stainless-steel counter until I realise that the sound is not drowned by the rowdy klawerjas players. No one has whistled. Have I in spite of my narrowing waistline become one of those who does not merit a second look?

When Moira enters she stands for a moment framed in the doorway, blinking, for the sun has come out again. It is one of those just-spring days when the sun plays crazy kiss-catch games and the day revolves through all the seasons of the year. So Moira blinks in this darkness after the glare outside. The silence of her entry is unnerving.

Moira has never moved in this room without a fanfare of whistles and an urgent drumming on the tables. She hesitates as if that exhalation of hot air is the only source of kinetic energy that will produce motion in her exquisite legs. Moira is indisputably beautiful. The smooth skin. The delicately sculpted form. The sleek brown hair.

But now her eyes are troubled, her hovering form uncertain, so that I wave at her and lo, the legs swing into mobility, the left foot falls securely on the floor and she propels herself expertly towards me. 'Coffee or tea,' I whisper loudly and point at the table where my folder lies. Like an automaton she changes direction and manoeuvres into a chair.

'What's going on in here? Where's James?' she asks.

James always sits with us. We have learned to make allowances for the filtered version of friendship that boys offer; nevertheless his behaviour today is certainly treacherous. Why has he gone without explanation to join the dark tower of boys peering down on to the table at the back? It is clearly not the klawerjas game that holds their attention. Someone screened from our vision is talking quietly, then bangs a fist on the table. The voices grow more urgent. We watch James withdraw from the inner circle and perch on the back of a chair shaking his head, but he does not look across at us.

By now the cafeteria is full. There is a long queue for coffee. The boys drift instinctively to the back to join the dark bank of murmuring males while the girls settle with their coffees at separate tables. Moira is agitated. What can they be talking about? We listen carefully but the sounds remain unintelligible. The group is no longer cohesive. It is too large, so that sub-groups mutter in cacophony, someone laughs derisively and above the noise the sound of Mr

Johnson's gravel voice, herding the stragglers back into the fold. He is the older student who in his youth had something to do with politics and now wears the bereaved look of someone who cannot accept the death of the movement.

'I think,' says Moira, 'we should go and join them. If they've got something important to discuss then it's bound to affect us so we ought to go and find out.'

'Oh no,' I remonstrate anxiously. I can only think of crossing the room in slow motion, elephantine, as my lumbering thighs rub together. A deadly silence except for the nylon scratching of left pantyhose against right, then right against left, before the ambiguous sound from the lungs of that bulwark rings plangent in my ears. I do not recognise this register; can a whistle be distorted by slow-motion? I fail to summon the old familiar sound, its pitch or timbre. Some day, I think wildly, there will be a machine to translate a whistle, print it out boldly as a single, unequivocal adjective: complimentary . . . or . . . derisive? A small compact machine to carry conveniently in the pocket which will absorb the sound as confidently as I have done. The meaning must lie there in the pitch, audible, measurable; otherwise, surely, we would never have considered it as anything other than a sound, an expression of time. How did we ever know with such certainty that it spelled admiration?

Moira is determined to go until I say, 'They will whistle as we approach.'

She slumps back in her chair and tugs listlessly at her skirt that has risen above the knee. In the seated position these shrinking hemlines assert a dubious freedom. We console ourselves that we might have risked it in last year's skirts and curl our toes newly released from the restrictive points of last year's shoes.

When James strides over he stands for a moment with one foot on the chair while he lights a cigarette and languidly savours the smoke before it curls out of his nostrils.

'Hey,' he teases as his eyes fall on my folder. 'Have you done that essay yet? Retief asked after you this morning.'

I have no desire to banter with him. Has it occurred to James that Retief has no idea who any of us are? James turns the chair around and sits astride it, spreading his legs freely. He does not read the resentment in our unyielding postures.

The day slips into mid-winter. The sky darkens and a brisk rain beats against the glass. The wind tugs at the building, at this new brick and glass box placed in a clearing in the bush, and seems to lift it clean off the ground.

'My word,' says James and treats us to a lecture on the properties of glass as building material. It is clear that he will nurse the apple of knowledge in his lap, polish its red curve abstractedly until we drool with anticipation. Only then will he offer us little lady-like bites, anxious for the seemly mastication of the fruit and discreet about his power to withdraw it altogether.

'Come on, what's all this about?' Moira asks, pointing to the table at the back.

'We're organising the action for this afternoon's memorial service. We must be sure that nobody goes. If we . . .'

'But no one would want to go,' I interrupt.

'The point is that there are too many cowards who don't want to but who are intimidated into going. Fear of reprisals is no small thing when there is a degree at stake, but if no one, and I mean not a soul, goes, then there'll be nothing to fear. Obviously we can't call a public meeting so it's up to every one of us to get round and speak to as many people as possible. Everyone must be reassured that no one will go. You two are going to Psychology next, aren't you? So make sure that you get there early and get the word around. I'll miss it and go to Afrikaans-Nederlands I instead. There'll be someone in every lecture room this morning and a couple of chaps are staying in here. Mr Johnson and others are going round the library. The idea is that every student must be spoken to before one o'clock.'

We nod. I had hoped to miss all my classes today in order to finish the essay. I shall have to think of something since Retief will certainly not accept it after today, especially not after the boycott of the service.

'Do you feel any sense of horror or shock or even distaste at the assassination?' I ask.

Moira taps her beautiful fingers on the table. James gets up. 'I'd better get along and speak to Sally's table over there,' he says.

'Well, do you?' I persist. 'Can you imagine being a member of his family or anyone close to him?'

'No,' she says. 'Do you think there's something wrong with us? Morally deficient?'

'Dunno. My father would call it inhuman, unchristian. It seems to me as if common humanity is harped on precisely so that we don't have to consider the crucial question of whether we can imagine being a particular human being. Or deal with the implications of the answer. All I can tell of the human condition is that we can always surprise ourselves with thoughts and feelings we never thought we had.'

Moira laughs. 'You're always ready with a mouthful of words. I'm surprised that you have any trouble with knocking off an essay.'

As we go off towards the Arts block we watch the gardeners in their brown overalls putting out hundreds of chairs in the square to accommodate all the students and staff. The chairs are squashed between the flowerboxes where the spring-green of foliage just peeps over the concrete. I try to think what they are but cannot imagine flowers tumbling over that concrete rim now lashed by the shadow of the wind-tossed flag.

Later I lean against the brick wall at the back of the cafeteria, my knees drawn up and the folder resting on the plane of my thighs. The soil is somewhat damp but I do not mind since a luke-warm sun has travelled round to this wall. Besides, there is nowhere else to go; the library as well as the cafeteria is shut and I wouldn't like to sit in the deserted Arts block.

A heavy silence hangs over the campus. The bush is still as if the birds are paying their respects to the dead Verwoerd. This freshly rinsed light won't last; such a stillness can only precede the enervating sweep of the south-easterly wind. I watch an ant wriggle her thorax along a blade of grass before I turn to my watch to find that the minute arm has raced ahead. The ceremony will start in fifteen minutes. It will probably last an hour and before that my essay must be finished and delivered. I read Retief's notes and start afresh. This will have to be my final copy since there is no time to develop ideas, let alone rephrase clumsy language. My attempt to understand the morality of the novel has to be abandoned. Retief will get what he wants, a reworking of his notes, and I will earn a mark qualifying for the examination.

It is not easy to work in this eerie silence. The stillness of the trees, the dark bush ahead inspire an unknown fear, a terror as if my own eyes, dark and bold as a squirrel's, stare at me from the bush. I am alone. The lecturers settling into their mourning seats under the flag some three hundred yards away offer no reassurance. If only a bird would scream or an animal rush across the red carpet of Rooikrans pods along the fringe of the bush, this agitation would settle. When the tall Australian bluegums shiver in the first stir of air, I retrieve my restless fingers raking through the grass to attend to Tess, luscious-lipped Tess, branded guilty and betrayed once more on this page. Time's pincers tighten round my fingers as I press on. This essay, however short and imperfect, must be done before three o'clock.

I start at the sound of gravel crunched underfoot. Surely there is no one left. Students in the hostel would keep to their rooms; others have rushed off for the 1.30 bus, too anxious to hitch the customary lift to the residential areas. I get up cautiously, tiptoe to the edge of the wall and peer round to see a few young men in their Sunday suits filing from the Theology College towards the square. They walk in silence, their chins lifted in a militaristic display of courage. I have no doubt that they have been asked to support the boycott. But they will think their defiance heroic and stifle the unease by marching soldier-like to mourn the Prime Minister.

Their measured tread marks the short minutes that go on sounding long after they have disappeared. I scribble wildly these words that trip each other up so that the page is defaced by inches of crossed-out writing and full stops swelled by a refractory pen that shrinks before a new sentence. Just as I finish, the gilt braid of fleece overhead slips under cover of a brooding raincloud. There is no time to make a fair copy. It is nearly three o'clock and I do not have the courage to wait for a bus or a lift at the main entrance where tall, fleshy cacti with grotesque limbs mock the human form. With difficulty I slip the essay without an explanatory note under Retief's close-fitting door then brace myself for the bush, for I must find the path that leads to the little station and wait for the Cape Flats train.

Tamieta shifts in her seat and lifts her wrist to check again the ticking of her watch. If this thing should let her down, should wilfully speed up the day so that she is left running about like a headless chicken amongst her pots . . . But she allows her wrist to drop in her lap; the unthinkable cannot be developed any further. And yet she has just fallen breathless in her chair, the first in the last row, only to find no one here. Not a soul. All the chairs in front of her are empty, except for the first two rows where the Boers sit in silence. Only two of the lecturers are women who, in their black wide-rimmed hats, are curious shapes in the distance. Tamieta had no idea that the ceremony was for white people only. Oh, what should she do, and the shame of it flames in her chest. Wait until she is told to leave? Or pick up the bag of working clothes she has just tucked under her chair and stagger off? But a few heads had turned as she sat down; she has already been seen, and besides how can she trust these legs now that her knees are calcified with shame and fear? She longs for a catastrophe, an act of justice, something divine and unimaginable, for she cannot conceive of a flood or a zigzag of lightning that will have her tumbling in scuffed shoes with her smoking handbag somersaulting over or entwined with the people at the front. There is no decent image of a credible demise to be summoned in the company of these mourners, so she fishes instead in her handbag for the handkerchief soaked in reviving scent. Californian Poppy, the bottle says, a sample that Beatrice had written away for and which arrived in the post with the picture on the label hardly discernible as a flower, just a red splodge, and as she inhales the soothing fragrance her mind clears into a sharp memory of the supervisor. Mr Grats said distinctly as he checked the last consignment of plates, 'Tomorrow is the ceremony, so close up straight after lunch. It won't last more than an hour so you still have an afternoon off.'

Unambiguous words. Mr Grats is a man who always speaks plainly. Besides, they would not have put the chairs out if Coloureds were not allowed, and her new-found security is confirmed by the arrival of the first students. She recognises the young men from the seminary, the future Dutch Reformed or rather Mission Church ministers, and her chest swells with relief which she interprets as pride in her people. They slip noiselessly into the third row but there are only eleven and they have no effect on the great expanse between her and the front.

Tamieta looks at her watch. It is five minutes past two. She would not expect students to be late for such an important ceremony; why should they want to keep Coloured time on an occasion like this and put her to shame? Where is everybody? And she sniffs, sniffs at the comforter impregnated with Californian Poppy.

The rector strides across from the Administration block in his grand cloak. He bellows like a bull preparing to storm the empty chairs.

'Ladies and gentlemen, let those of us who abhor violence, those of us who have a vision beyond darkness and savagery, weep today for the tragic death of our Prime Minister . . .'

He is speaking to her . . . Ladies and gentlemen . . . that includes her, Tamieta, and what can be wrong with that? Why should she not be called a lady? She who has always conducted herself according to God's word? Whose lips have never parted for a drop of liquor or the whorish cigarette? And who has worked dutifully all her life? Yes, it is only right that she should be called a lady. And fancy it coming from the rector. Unless he hasn't seen her, or doesn't see her as part of the gathering. Does the group of strangers backed by the dark-suited Theology students form a bulwark, an edifice before which she must lower her eyes? How could she, Tamieta Snewe, with her slow heavy thighs scale such heights?

' . . . these empty chairs are a sign of the barbarism, the immense task that lies ahead of the educator . . .'

Should she move closer to the front? As his anger gives way to grief, she can no longer hear what he says. In Tamieta's ears the red locusts rattle among the mealies on the farm and the dry-throated wind croaks a heart-broken tale of treachery through the cracks of the door. She must wait, simply wait for these people to finish. Never, not even on a Sunday afternoon, has she known time to drag its feet so sluggishly. If she could pull out of her plastic bag a starched cap and apron and whip round smilingly after the last amen with a tray of coffee, perhaps then she could sit through the service in comfort. And the hot shame creeps up from her chest to the crown of her head. The straw hat pinned to the mattress of hair released from its braids for the occasion (for she certainly does not wear a doekie to church like a country woman) smoulders with shame for such a starched cap long since left behind.

So many years since the young Mieta carried water from the well, the zinc bucket balanced on her head, her slender neck taut and not a drop, never a drop of water spilled. Then she rolled her doekie into a wreath to fit the bottom of the bucket and protect her head from its cutting edge. So they swaggered back, the girls in the evening light when the sun melted orange in an indigo sky, laughing, jostling each other, heads held high and never a hand needed to steady the buckets.

If only there were other women working on the campus she would have known, someone would have told her. As for that godless boy, Charlie, he knew all right, even betrayed himself with all that nonsense about the carnival while she sniffed for his treachery in quite the wrong direction. Of course he knew all along that she would be the only person there. And at this moment as he stands in Hanover Street with the pink and green satins flowing through his fingers, he sniggers at the thought of her, a country woman, sitting alone amongst white people, foolishly singing hymns. And he'll run triumphant fingers through his silky hair – but that is precisely when the Jewish draper will say, 'Hey you, I don't want Brylcreem on my materials, hey. I think you'd better go now.' And that will teach Charlie; that will show him that hair isn't everything in the world.

The words of the hymn do not leave her mouth. A thin sound escapes her parted lips but the words remain printed in a book, written in uneven letters on her school slate. Will the wind turn and toss her trembling hum southward into the ear of the dominee who will look up sternly and thunder, 'Sing up aia, sing up'?

Oh, how her throat grows wind-dry as the strips of biltong beef hung out on the farm in the evening breeze. The longing for a large mug of coffee tugs at her palate. Coffee with a generous spoonful of condensed milk, thick and sweet to give her strength. How much longer will she have to sit here and wait for time to pass? This time designated by strangers to mourn a man with a large head?

For that was what the newspaper showed, a man with the large head of a bulldog, and Tamieta, allowing herself the unknown luxury of irreverence, passes a damp tongue over her parched lips.

She will watch the plants in the concrete flowerbox by her side. She does not know what they are called but she will watch these leaves grow, expand before her very eyes. By keeping an eye trained on one leaf – and she selects a healthy shoot resting on the rim – she will witness the miracle of growth. She has had enough of things creeping up on her, catching her unawares, offering unthinkable surprises. No, she will travel closely with the passage of time and see a bud thicken under her vigilant eye.

It is time to rise for prayer, and as she reminds herself to keep her lowered eyes fixed on the chosen leaf the plastic bag under her chair falls over and the overall, her old blue turban and the comfy slippers roll out for all the world to see. But all the eyes are shut so that she picks up her things calmly and places them back in the bag. Just in time for the last respectful silence. The heads hang in grief. Tamieta's neck aches. Tonight Beatrice will free the knotted tendons with her nimble fingers. She does not have the strength to go into town for the wool, but Beatrice will understand. Tamieta is the first to slip out of her seat, no point in lingering when the rain is about to fall, and with her handbag swinging daintily in the crook of her right arm and the parcel of clothes tucked under her left, she marches chin up into the bush, to the deserted station where the skollie-boys dangle their feet from the platform all day long.

You can't get lost in Cape Town

In my right hand resting on the base of my handbag I clutch a brown leather purse. My knuckles ride to and fro, rubbing against the lining . . . surely cardboard . . . and I am surprised that the material has not revealed itself to me before. I have worn this bag for months. I would have said with a dismissive wave of the hand, 'Felt, that is what the base of this bag is lined with.'

Then, Michael had said, 'It looks cheap, unsightly,' and lowering his voice to my look of surprise, 'Can't you tell?' But he was speaking of the exterior, the way it looks.

The purse fits neatly into the palm of my hand. A man's purse. The handbag gapes. With my elbow I press it against my hip but that will not avert suspicion. The bus is moving fast, too fast, surely exceeding the speed limit, so that I bob on my seat and my grip on the purse tightens as the springs suck at my womb, slurping it down through the plush of the red upholstery. I press my buttocks into the seat to ease the discomfort.

I should count out the fare for the conductor. Perhaps not; he is still at the front of the bus. We are now travelling through Rondebosch so that he will be fully occupied with white passengers at the front. Women with blue-rinsed heads tilted will go on telling their stories while fishing leisurely for their coins and just lengthen a vowel to tide over the moment of paying their fares.

'Don't be so anxious,' Michael said. 'It will be all right.' I withdrew the hand he tried to pat.

I have always been anxious and things are not all right; things may never be all right again. I must not cry. My eyes travel to and fro along the grooves of the floor. I do not look at the faces that surround me but I believe that they are lifted speculatively at me. Is someone constructing a history for this hand resting foolishly in a gaping handbag? Do these faces expect me to whip out an amputated stump dripping with blood? Do they wince at the thought of a hand, cold and waxen, left on the pavement where it was severed? I draw my hand out of the bag and shake my fingers ostentatiously. No point in inviting conjecture, in attracting attention. The bus brakes loudly to conceal the sound of breath drawn in sharply at the exhibited hand.

Two women pant like dogs as they swing themselves on to the bus. The conductor has already pressed the bell and they propel their bodies expertly along the swaying aisle. They fall into seats opposite me – one fat, the other thin – and simultaneously pull off the starched servants' caps which they scrunch into their laps. They light cigarettes and I bite my lip. Would I have to vomit into this bag with its cardboard lining? I wish I had brought a plastic bag; this bag is empty save for the purse. I breathe deeply to stem the nausea that rises to meet the curling bands of smoke and fix on the bulging bags they grip between their feet. They make no attempt to get their fares ready; they surely misjudge the intentions of the conductor. He knows that they will get off at Mowbray to catch the Golden Arrow buses to the townships. He will not allow them to avoid paying; not he who presses the button with such promptness.

I watch him at the front of the bus. His right thumb strums an impatient jingle on the silver levers, the leather bag is cradled in the hand into which the coins tumble. He chants a barely audible accompaniment to the clatter of coins, a recitation of the newly decimalised currency. Like times tables at school and I see the fingers grow soft, bending boyish as they strum an ink-stained abacus; the boy learning to count, leaning earnestly with propped elbows over a desk. And I find the image unaccountably sad and tears are about to well up when I hear an impatient empty clatter of thumb-play on the coin dispenser as he demands, 'All fares please' from a sleepy white youth. My hand flies into my handbag once again and I take out the purse. A man's leather purse.

Michael too is boyish. His hair falls in a straight blond fringe into his eyes. When he considers a reply he wipes it away impatiently, as if the hair impedes thought. I cannot imagine this purse ever having belonged to him. It is small, U-shaped and devoid of ornament, therefore a man's purse. It has an extending tongue that could be tucked into the mouth or be threaded through the narrow band across the base of the U. I take out the smallest note stuffed into this plump purse, a five-rand note. Why had I not thought about the busfare? The conductor will be angry if my note should exhaust his supply of coins although the leather bag would have a concealed pouch for notes. But this thought does not comfort me. I feel angry with Michael. He has probably never travelled by bus. How would he know of the fear of missing the unfamiliar stop, the fear of keeping an impatient conductor waiting, the fear of saying fluently, 'Seventeen cents please,' when you are not sure of the fare and produce a five-rand note? But this is my journey and I must not expect Michael to take responsibility for everything. Or rather, I cannot expect Michael to take responsibility for more than half the things. Michael is scrupulous about this division; I am not always sure of how to arrive at half. I was never good at arithmetic, especially this instant mental arithmetic that is sprung on me.

How foolish I must look sitting here clutching my five-rand note. I slip it back into the purse and turn to the solidity of the smoking women. They have still made no attempt to find their fares. The bus is going fast and I am surprised that we have not yet reached Mowbray. Perhaps I am mistaken, perhaps we have already passed Mowbray and the women are going to Sea Point to serve a nightshift at the Pavilion.

Marge, Aunt Trudie's eldest daughter, works as a waitress at the Pavilion but she is rarely mentioned in our family. 'A disgrace,' they say. 'She should know better than to go with white men.'

'Poor whites,' Aunt Trudie hisses. 'She can't even find a nice rich man to go steady with. Such a pretty girl too. I won't have her back in this house. There's no place in this house for a girl who's been used by white trash.'

Her eyes flash as she spits out a cherished vision of a blond young man sitting on her new vinyl sofa to whom she serves gingerbeer and koeksisters, because it is not against the law to have a respectable drink in a Coloured home. 'Mrs Holman,' he would say, 'Mrs Holman, this is the best gingerbeer I've had for years.'

The family do not know of Michael even though he is a steady young man who would sit out such a Sunday afternoon with infinite grace. I wince at the thought of Father creaking in a suit and the unconcealed pleasure in Michael's successful academic career.

Perhaps this is Mowbray after all. The building that zooms past on the right seems familiar. I ought to know it but I am lost, hopelessly lost, and as my mind gropes for recognition I feel a feathery flutter in my womb, so slight I cannot be sure, and again, so soft, the brush of a butterfly, and under cover of my handbag I spread my left hand to hold my belly. The shaft of light falling across my shoulder, travelling this route with me, is the eye of God. God will never forgive me.

I must anchor my mind to the words of the women on the long seat opposite me. But they fall silent as if to protect their secrets from me. One of them bends down heavily, holding on to the jaws of her shopping bag as if to relieve pressure on her spine, and I submit to the ache of my own by swaying gently while I protect my belly with both hands. But having eyed the contents of her full bag carefully, her hand becomes the beak of a bird dipping purposefully into the left-hand corner and rises triumphantly with a brown paper bag on which grease has oozed light-sucking patterns. She opens the bag and her friend looks on in silence. Three chunks of cooked chicken lie on a piece of greaseproof paper. She deftly halves a piece and passes it to her thin friend. The women munch in silence, their mouths glossy with pleasure.

'These are for the children,' she says, her mouth still full as she wraps the rest up and places it carelessly at the top of the bag.

'It's the spiced chicken recipe you told me about.' She nudges her friend. 'Lekker hey!'

The friend frowns and says, 'I like to taste a bit more cardamom. It's nice to find a whole cardamom in the food and crush it between your teeth. A cardamom seed will never give up all its flavour to the pot. You'll still find it there in the chewing.'

I note the gaps in her teeth and fear for the slipping through of cardamom seeds. The girls at school who had their two top incisors extracted in a fashion that raged through Cape Town said that it was better for kissing. Then I, fat and innocent, nodded. How would I have known the demands of kissing?

why is she so insecure?

The large woman refuses to be thwarted by criticism of her cooking. The chicken stimulates a story so that she twitches with an irrepressible desire to tell.

'To think,' she finally bursts out, 'that I cook them this nice surprise and say what you like, spiced chicken can make any mouth water. Just think, it was yesterday when I say to that one as she stands with her hands on her hips against the stove saying, "I don't know what to give them today, I've just got too much organising to do to bother with food." And I say, feeling sorry for her, I say, "Don't you worry about a thing, Marram, just leave it all in cook's hands (wouldn't it be nice to work for really grand people where you cook and do nothing else, no bladdy scrubbing and shopping and all that) . . . in cook's hands," I said,' and she crows merrily before reciting: 'And I'll dish up a surprise / For Master Georgie's blue eyes.

'That's Miss Lucy's young man. He was coming last night. Engaged, you know. Well there I was on my feet all day starching linen, making roeties and spiced lentils and sweet potato and all the lekker things you must mos have with cardamom chicken. And what do you think she says?'

She pauses and lifts her face as if expecting a reply, but the other stares grimly ahead. Undefeated she continues, 'She says to me, "Tiena," because she can't keep out of my pots, you know, always opening my lids and sniffing like a brakhond, she says, "Tiena," and waits for me to say, "Yes Marram," so I know she has a wicked plan up her sleeve and

I look her straight in the eye. She smile that one, always smile to put me off the track, and she say looking into the fridge, "You can have this nice bean soup for your dinner so I can have the remains of the chicken tomorrow when you're off." So I say to her, "That's what I had for lunch today," and she say to me, "Yes I know but me and Miss Lucy will be on our own for dinner tomorrow," and she pull a face, "Ugh, how I hate reheated food." Then she draws up her shoulders as if to say, That's that.

'Cheek hey! And it was a great big fowl.' She nudges her friend. 'You know for yourself how much better food tastes the next day when the spices are drawn right into the meat and anyway you just switch on the electric and there's no chopping and crying over onions, you just wait for the pot to dance on the stove. Of course she wouldn't know about that. Anyway, a cheek, that's what I call it, so before I even dished up the chicken for the table, I took this,' and she points triumphantly to her bag, 'and to hell with them.'

The thin one opens her mouth, once, twice, winding herself up to speak.

'They never notice anyway. There's so much food in their pantries, in the fridge and on the tables; they don't know what's there and what isn't.' The other looks pityingly at her.

'Don't you believe that. My marram was as cross as a bear by the time I brought in the pudding, a very nice apricot ice it was, but she didn't even look at it. She know it was a healthy grown fowl and she count one leg, and she know what's going on. She know right away. Didn't even say, "Thank you Tiena." She won't speak to me for days but what can she do?' Her voice softens into genuine sympathy for her madam's dilemma.

'She'll just have to speak to me.' And she mimics,

putting on a stern horse face. '"We'll want dinner by seven tonight," then "Tiena the curtains need washing," then, "Please, Tiena, will you fix this zip for me, I've got absolutely nothing else to wear today." And so on the third day she'll smile and think she's smiling forgiveness at me.'

She straightens her face. 'No,' she sighs, 'the more you have, the more you have to keep your head and count and check up because you know you won't notice or remember. No, if you got a lot you must keep snaps in your mind of the insides of all the cupboards. And every day, click, click, new snaps of the larder. That's why that one is so tired, always thinking, always reciting to herself the lists of what's in the cupboards. I never know what's in my cupboard at home but I know my Sammie's a thieving bastard, can't keep his hands in his pockets.'

The thin woman stares out of the window as if she had heard it all before. She has finished her chicken while the other, with all the talking, still holds a half-eaten drumstick daintily in her right hand. Her eyes rove over the shopping bag and she licks her fingers abstractedly as she stares out of the window.

'Lekker hey!' the large one repeats, 'the children will have such a party.'

'Did Master George enjoy it?' the other asks.

'Oh he's a gentleman all right. Shouted after me, "Well done, Tiena. When we're married we'll have to steal you from madam." Dressed to kill he was, such a smart young man, you know. Mind you, so's Miss Lucy. Not a prettier girl in our avenue and the best-dressed too. But then she has mos to be smart to keep her man. Been on the pill for nearly a year now; I shouldn't wonder if he don't feel funny about the white wedding. Ooh, you must see her blush over the pictures of the wedding gowns, so pure and innocent she think I can't read the packet. "Get me my headache pills out of that drawer Tiena," she say sometimes when I take her cup of cocoa at night. But she play her cards right with Master George; she have to 'cause who'd have what another man has pushed to the side of his plate. A bay leaf and a bone!' and moved by the alliteration the image materialises in her hand. 'Like this bone,' and she waves it under the nose of the other who starts. I wonder whether with guilt, fear or a debilitating desire for more chicken.

'This bone,' she repeats grimly, 'picked bare and only wanted by a dog.' Her friend recovers and deliberately misunderstands, 'Or like yesterday's bean soup, but we women mos know that food put aside and left to stand till tomorrow always has a better flavour. Men don't know that hey. They should get down to some cooking and find out a thing or two.'

But the other is not deterred. 'A bone,' she insists, waving her visual aid, 'a bone.'

It is true that her bone is a matt grey that betrays no trace of the meat or fat that only a minute ago adhered to it. Master George's bone would certainly look nothing like that when he pushes it aside. With his fork he would coax off the fibres ready to fall from the bone. Then he would turn over the whole, deftly, using a knife, and frown at the sinewy meat clinging to the joint before pushing it aside towards the discarded bits of skin.

This bone, it is true, will not tempt anyone. A dog might want to bury it only for a silly game of hide and seek.

The large woman waves the bone as if it would burst into prophecy. My eyes follow the movement until the bone blurs and emerges as the Cross where the head of Jesus lolls sadly, his lovely feet anointed by sad hands, folded together under the driven nail. Look, Mamma says, look at those eyes molten with love and pain, the body curved with suffering for our sins, and together we weep for the beauty and sadness of Jesus in his white loincloth. The Roman soldiers stand grimly erect in their tunics, their spears gleam in the light, their dark beards are clipped and their lips curl. At midday Judas turns his face to the fading sun and bays, howls like a dog for its return as the darkness grows around him and swallows him whole with the money still jingling in the folds of his saffron robes. In a concealed leather purse, a pouch devoid of ornament.

The buildings on this side of the road grow taller but oh, I do not know where I am and I think of asking the woman, the thin one, but when I look up the stern one's eyes already rest on me while the bone in her hand points idly at the advertisement just above my head. My hands, still cradling my belly, slide guiltily down my thighs and fall on my knees. But the foetus betrays me with another flutter, a sigh. I have heard of books flying off the laps of gentle mothers-to-be as their foetuses lash out. I will not be bullied. I jump up and press the bell.

There are voices behind me. The large woman's 'Oi, I say' thunders over the conductor's cross 'Tickets please.' I will not speak to anyone. Shall I throw myself on the grooved floor of this bus and with knees drawn up, hands over my head, wait for my demise? I do not in any case expect to be alive tomorrow. But I must resist; I must harden my heart against the sad, complaining eyes of Jesus.

'I say, Miss,' she shouts and her tone sounds familiar. Her voice compels like the insistence of Father's guttural commands. But the conductor's hand falls on my shoulder, the barrel of his ticket dispenser digs into my ribs, the buttons of his uniform gleam as I dip into my bag for my purse. Then the large woman spills out of her seat as she leans forward. Her friend, reconciled, holds the bar of an arm across her as she leans forward shouting, 'Here, I say, your purse.' I try to look grateful. Her eyes blaze with scorn as she proclaims to the bus, 'Stupid these young people. Dressed to kill maybe, but still so stupid.'

She is right. Not about my clothes, of course, and I check to see what I am wearing. I have not been alerted to my own stupidity before. No doubt I will sail through my final examinations at the end of this year and still not know how I dared to pluck a fluttering foetus out of my womb. That is if I survive tonight.

I sit on the steps of this large building and squint up at the marble facade. My elbows rest on my knees flung comfortably apart. I ought to know where I am; it is clearly a public building of some importance. For the first time I long for the veld of my childhood. There the red sand rolls for miles, and if you stand on the koppie behind the house the landmarks blaze their permanence: the river points downward, runs its dry course from north to south; the geelbos crowds its banks in near straight lines. On either side of the path winding westward plump little buttocks of cacti squat as if lifting the skirts to pee, and the swollen fingers of vygies burst in clusters out of the stone, pointing the way. In the veld you can always find your way home.

I am anxious about meeting Michael. We have planned this so carefully for the rush hour when people storming home crossly will not notice us together in the crush.

'It's simple,' Michael said. 'The bus carries along the main roads through the suburbs to the City, and as you reach the Post Office you get off and I'll be there to meet you. At five.'

A look at my anxious face compelled him to say, 'You can't get lost in Cape Town. There,' and he pointed over his shoulder, 'is Table Mountain and there is Devil's Peak and there Lion's Head, so how in heaven's name could you get lost?' The words shot out unexpectedly, like the fine arc of brown spittle from between the teeth of an old man who no longer savours the tobacco he has been chewing all day. There are, I suppose, things that even a loved one cannot overlook.

Am I a loved one?

I ought to rise from these steps and walk towards the City. Fortunately I always take the precaution of setting out early, so that I should still be in time to meet Michael who will drive me along de Waal Drive into the slopes of Table Mountain where Mrs Coetzee waits with her tongs.

Am I a loved one? No. I am dull, ugly and bad-tempered. My hair has grown greasy, I am forgetful and I have no sense of direction. Michael, he has long since stopped loving me. He watched me hugging the lavatory bowl, retching, and recoiled at my first display of bad temper. There is a faraway look in his eyes as he plans his retreat. But he is well brought up, honourable. When the first doubts gripped the corners of his mouth, he grinned madly and said, 'We must marry,' showing a row of perfect teeth.

'There are laws against that,' I said unnecessarily.

But gripped by the idyll of an English landscape of painted greens, he saw my head once more held high, my lettuce-luscious skirts crisp on a camomile lawn and the willow drooping over the red mouth of a suckling infant.

'Come on,' he urged. 'Don't do it. We'll get to England and marry. It will work out all right,' and betraying the source of his vision, 'and we'll be happy for ever, thousands of miles from all this mess.'

I would have explained if I could. But I could not account for this vision: the slow shower of ashes over yards

of diaphanous tulle, the moth wings tucked back with
delight as their tongues whisked the froth of white lace. For
two years I have loved Michael, have wanted to marry him..
Duped by a dream I merely shook my head.

'But you love babies, you want babies some time or
other, so why not accept God's holy plan? Anyway, you're
a Christian and you believe it's a sin, don't you?'

God is not a good listener. Like Father, he expects
obedience and withdraws peevishly if his demands are not
met. Explanations of my point of view infuriate him so that
he quivers with silent rage. For once I do not plead and
capitulate; I find it quite easy to ignore these men.

'You're not even listening,' Michael accused. 'I don't
know how you can do it.' There is revulsion in his voice.

For two short years I have adored Michael.

Once, perched perilously on the rocks, we laughed
fondly at the thought of a child. At Cape Point where the
oceans meet and part. The Indian and the Atlantic,
fighting for their separate identities, roared and thrashed
fiercely so that we huddled together, his hand on my belly.
It is said that if you shut one eye and focus the other
carefully, the line separating the two oceans may rear
drunkenly but remains ever clear and hair-fine. But I did
not look. In the mischievous wind I struggled with the
flapping ends of a scarf I tried to wrap around my hair. Later
that day on the silver sands of a deserted beach he wrote
solemnly: Will you marry me? and my trembling fingers
traced a huge heart around the words. Ahead the sun
danced on the waves, flecking them with gold.

I wrote a poem about that day and showed Michael.
'Surely that was not what Logiesbaai was about,' he
frowned, and read aloud the lines about warriors charging
out of the sea, assegais gleaming in the sun, the beat of

tom-toms riding the waters, the throb in the carious cavities of rocks.

'It's good,' he said, nodding thoughtfully, 'I like the title, "Love at Logiesbaai (Whites Only)," though I expect much of the subtlety escapes me. Sounds good,' he encouraged, 'you should write more often.'

I flushed. I wrote poems all the time. And he was wrong; it was not a good poem. It was puzzling and I wondered why I had shown him this poem that did not even make sense to me. I tore it into little bits.

Love, love, love, I sigh as I shake each ankle in turn and examine the swelling.

Michael's hair falls boyishly over his eyes. His eyes narrow merrily when he smiles and the left corner of his mouth shoots up so that the row of teeth forms a queer diagonal line above his chin. He flicks his head so that the fringe of hair lifts from his eyes for a second, then falls, so fast, like the tongue of a lizard retracted at the very moment of exposure.

'We'll find somewhere,' he would say, 'a place where we'd be quite alone.' This country is vast and he has an instinctive sense of direction. He discovers the armpits of valleys that invite us into their shadows. Dangerous climbs led by the roar of the sea take us to blue bays into which we drop from impossible cliffs. The sun lowers herself on to us. We do not fear the police with their torches. They come only by night in search of offenders. We have the immunity of love. They cannot find us because they do not know we exist. One day they will find out about lovers who steal whole days, round as globes.

There has always been a terrible thrill in that thought.

I ease my feet back into my shoes and the tears splash on to my dress with such wanton abandon that I cannot believe they are mine. From the punctured globes of stolen days these fragments sag and squint. I hold, hold these pictures I have summoned. I will not recognise them for much longer.

With tilted head I watch the shoes and sawn-off legs ascend and descend the marble steps, altering course to avoid me. Perhaps someone will ask the police to remove me.

Love, love, love, I sigh. Another flutter in my womb. I think of moth wings struggling against a window pane and I rise.

The smell of sea unfurls towards me as I approach Adderley Street. There is no wind but the brine hangs in an atomised mist, silver over a thwarted sun. In answer to my hunger, Wellingtons looms on my left. The dried-fruit palace which I cannot resist. The artificial light dries my tears, makes me blink, and the trays of fruit, of Cape sunlight twice trapped, shimmer and threaten to burst out of their forms. Rows of pineapple are the infinite divisions of the sun, the cores lost in the amber discs of mebos arranged in arcs. Prunes are the wrinkled backs of aged goggas beside the bloodshot eyes of cherries. Dark green figs sit pertly on their bottoms peeping over trays. And I too am not myself, hoping for refuge in a metaphor that will contain it all. I buy the figs and mebos. Desire is a Tsafendas tapeworm in my belly that cannot be satisfied and as I pop the first fig into my mouth I feel the danger fountain with the jets of saliva. Will I stop at one death?

I have walked too far along this road and must turn back to the Post Office. I break into a trot as I see Michael in the distance, drumming with his nails on the side of the car. His sunburnt elbow juts out of the window. He taps with anxiety or impatience and I grow cold with fear as I jump into the passenger seat and say merrily, 'Let's go,' as if we are setting off for a picnic.

Michael will wait in the car on the next street. She had said that it would take only ten minutes. He takes my hand and so prevents me from getting out. Perhaps he thinks that I will bolt, run off into the mountain, revert to savagery. His hand is heavy on my forearm and his eyes are those of a wounded dog, pale with pain.

'It will be all right.' I try to comfort and wonder whether he hears his own voice in mine. My voice is thin, a tinsel thread that springs out of my mouth and flutters straight out of the window.

'I must go.' I lift the heavy hand off my forearm and it falls inertly across the gearstick.

The room is dark. The curtains are drawn and a lace-shaded electric light casts shadows in the corners of the rectangle. The doorway in which I stand divides the room into sleeping and eating quarters. On the left there is a table against which a servant girl leans, her eyes fixed on the blank wall ahead. On the right a middle-aged white woman rises with a hostess smile from a divan which serves as sofa, and pats the single pink-flowered cushion to assert homeliness. There is a narrow dark wardrobe in the corner.

I say haltingly, 'You are expecting me. I spoke to you on the telephone yesterday. Sally Smit.' I can see no telephone in the room. She frowns.

'You're not Coloured, are you?' It is an absurd question. I look at my brown arms that I have kept folded across my chest, and watch the gooseflesh sprout. Her eyes are fixed on me. Is she blind? How will she perform the operation with such defective sight? Then I realise: the educated voice, the accent has blinded her. I have drunk deeply of Michael, swallowed his voice as I drank from his tongue. Has he swallowed mine? I do not think so.

I say 'No,' and wait for all the cockerels in Cape Town to

crow simultaneously. Instead the servant starts from her trance and stares at me with undisguised admiration.

'Good,' the woman smiles, showing yellow teeth. 'One must check nowadays. These Coloured girls, you know, are very forward, terrible types. What do they think of me, as if I would do every Tom, Dick and Harry. Not me you know; this is a respectable concern and I try to help decent women, educated you know. No, you can trust me. No Coloured girl's ever been on this sofa.'

The girl coughs, winks at me and turns to stir a pot simmering on a primus stove on the table. The smell of offal escapes from the pot and nausea rises in my throat, feeding the fear. I would like to run but my feet are lashed with fear to the linoleum. Only my eyes move, across the room where she pulls a newspaper from a wad wedged between the wall and the wardrobe. She spreads the paper on the divan and smooths with her hand while the girl shuts the door and turns the key. A cat crawls lazily from under the table and stares at me until the green jewels of its eyes shrink to crystal points.

She points me to the sofa. From behind the wardrobe she pulls her instrument and holds it against the baby-pink crimplene of her skirt.

'Down, shut your eyes now,' she says as I raise my head to look. Their movements are carefully orchestrated, the manoeuvres practised. Their eyes signal and they move. The girl stations herself by my head and her mistress moves to my feet. She pushes my knees apart and whips out her instrument from a pocket. A piece of plastic tubing dangles for a second. My knees jerk and my mouth opens wide but they are in control. A brown hand falls on my mouth and smothers the cry; the white hands wrench the knees apart and she hisses, 'Don't you dare. Do you want the bladdy

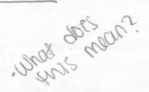

police here? I'll kill you if you scream.'

The brown hand over my mouth relaxes. She looks into my face and says, 'She won't.' I am a child who needs reassurance. I am surprised by the softness of her voice. The brown hand moves along the side of my face and pushes back my hair. I long to hold the other hand; I do not care what happens below. A black line of terror separates it from my torso. Blood spurts from between my legs and for a second the two halves of my body make contact through the pain.

So it is done. Deflowered by yellow hands wielding a catheter. Fear and hypocrisy, mine, my deserts spread in a dark stain on the newspaper.

'OK,' she says, 'get yourself decent.' I dress and wait for her to explain. 'You go home now and wait for the birth. Do you have a pad?'

I shake my head uncomprehendingly. Her face tightens for a moment but then she smiles and pulls a sanitary towel out of the wardrobe.

'Won't cost you anything lovey.' She does not try to conceal the glow of her generosity. She holds out her hand and I place the purse in her palm. She counts, satisfied, but I wave away the purse which she reluctantly puts on the table.

'You're a good girl,' she says and puts both hands on my shoulders. I hold my breath; I will not inhale the foetid air from the mouth of this my grotesque bridegroom with yellow teeth. She plants the kiss of complicity on my cheek and I turn to go, repelled by her touch. But have I the right to be fastidious? I cannot deny feeling grateful, so that I turn back to claim the purse after all. The girl winks at me. The purse fits snugly in my hand; there would be no point in giving it back to Michael.

Michael's face is drawn with fear. He is as ignorant of the

process as I am. I am brisk, efficient and rattle off the plan. 'It'll happen tonight so I'll go home and wait and call you in the morning. By then it will be all over.' He looks relieved.

He drives me right to the door and my landlady waves merrily from the stoep where she sits with her embroidery among the potted ferns.

'Don't look,' she says anxiously. 'It's a present for you, for your trousseau,' and smiling slyly, 'I can tell when a couple just can't wait any longer. There's no catching me out, you know.'

Tonight in her room next to mine she will turn in her chaste bed, tracing the tendrils from pink and orange flowers, searching for the needle lost in endless folds of white linen.

Semi-detached houses with red-polished stoeps line the west side of Trevelyan Road. On the east is the Cape Flats line where electric trains rattle reliably according to timetable. Trevelyan Road runs into the elbow of a severely curved Main Road which nevertheless has all the amenities one would expect: butcher, baker, hairdresser, chemist, library, liquor store. There is a fish and chips shop on that corner, on the funny bone of that elbow, and by the side, strictly speaking in Trevelyan Road, a dustbin leans against the trunk of a young palm tree. A newspaper parcel dropped into this dustbin would absorb the vinegary smell of discarded fish and chips wrappings in no time.

The wrapped parcel settles in the bin. I do not know what has happened to God. He is fastidious. He fled at the moment that I smoothed the wet black hair before wrapping it up. I do not think he will come back. It is 6 a.m. Light pricks at the shroud of Table Mountain. The streets are deserted and, relieved, I remember that the next train will pass at precisely 6.22.

HOME SWEET HOME

A lady must never be seen without her handbag. So Aunt Cissie always says. Which must be why she has wedged the unwieldy object between her stomach and the edge of the dinner table. Visibly relieved, she pushes back her chair and releases the bag in order to rummage for the letter. Her eyes caper at the secrets awakened by her touch in that darkness, secrets like her electricity bill, so boldly printed in words and figures, protected from their eyes by the thin scuffed leather. They wait with the patience of those who expect to hear nothing new while her fingers linger over something deep down in the bag before she draws out the blue envelope. Then she reads aloud from Uncle Hermanus's letter written in the careful English he never spoke:

'I haven't seen the ground for so many weeks now that I can't believe it's the same earth I'm walking on. Here is hard snow as far as the eyes can see. This really is the land for the white man.'

'That's Canada hey!' and she pats the folded letter before slipping it back into the bag on her lap.

Father licks his bone conscientiously and says, 'Ja-nee' with the sense of the equivocal born out of watching rainclouds gather over the arid earth and then disperse. 'Ja-nee,' he repeats, 'that's now a place hey!' and with a whistling extraction of marrow from the neck of the goat, he laughs the satisfied laugh of one who has come to see the hidden blessings of drought.

'And then they have to eat frozen meat as well,' he adds, and they all roar with laughter.

Uncle Gerrie shakes his head and points to Bakenskop in the distance. 'No man, there, just there you can bury me.' He turns abruptly to me. 'Sies! What you want to go to these cold places for?'

Father hangs his head. The silence squirms under the sound of clanking cutlery and the sucking of marrow bones. I herd the mound of rice on my plate, drawing into line the wayward grains so that Uncle Gerrie says, 'Just so foolish like Uncle Hermanus. What you eating like that with just a fork? Take your knife man; you were brought up decent.'

On this eve of my departure I will not invite discussion. I say nothing and think of Great Uncle Hermanus on the poop deck.

The horn sounded, a rumbling deep in the belly of the ship, and we searched among the white faces for that of the old man. When he had finally found his way to the deck it was not hard to spot the dark crumpled figure whose right hand signalled its staccato wave like the mechanism of a wind-up toy gone wrong.

Just before boarding he had said, 'Man, there's no problem; we're mos all Juropeens when we get to Canada.' His rough hand fluttered delicately to his mouth as if to screen a cough. And then he vomited. A watery stream with barely masticated meat and carrot splattered on Cousin Lettie's new patent-leather shoes and excited relatives in bestwear stood back and the old man, bewildered in the ring created by his own regurgitation, staggered a grotesque dance around the puddle, looking confusedly at us in turn so that Aunt Cissie stepped into the ring and pressed him to the eastern slope of her enormous bosom, mindful of the mess still clinging to his mouth.

'Ag Oompie, you're so lucky to be going to a decent place. Mary and Andrew are there waiting for you; you haven't seen Mary for three years now and shame, there's a new grandchild hey! The Cloetes are in Canada also; all those old faces waiting to see you,' consoled Cousin Lettie looking up from her once again shiny shoes. 'And the journey won't take long at all. I'm sure there's some nice Coloured person on the boat. Look out for the Van Stadens from Wynberg; I think they're also emigrating today.'

Uncle Hermanus lowered the left corner of his mouth in grim pursuit of a smile. Then he kissed his goodbyes to all of us who had now moved in curved formation, shielding him from the pool of vomit. One of the children who audibly muttered 'Sies' was smacked and sobbed all the while we waited for the final wave, so that an uncle said, 'Never mind, one day you can go and visit him in Canada.'

He made it to the deck where he peered from under a hand shading his eyes at the gay tangled streamers, the coloured fragility of the ties that would snap as the boat wriggled away. In his pocket Great Uncle Hermanus found the two neat rolls of streamers, fumbled with the perfectly secured edges and, fishing for meaning in the threadbare convention, flung the little rolls triumphantly to the quay where one was caught by a sixteen-year-old white girl in beatnik dress. Behind the stirring ship Table Mountain, whose back I have woken up to for so many years in the Southern suburbs, stood squarely.

'So we've sent you to college, your very own college that

this government's given you, just so you can go away and leave us to stew in ignorance. I know,' Uncle Gerrie continued, 'that here in the veld amongst the Griquas is no place for an educated person, but we all thought you liked Cape Town. The most beautiful city in the world you know, and the richest. There's a future for you here.'

I do not give a fig for the postcard beauty of the bay and the majesty of the mountain, the pretty white houses clinging to its slopes and the pines swaying to the Old Cape Doctor. A city of gleaming lavatories with the smell of disinfectant wafting from its pines. And the District Six I do not know and the bulldozers, impatient vultures, that hover about its stench. But I say nothing. At the base of this hollow edifice of guilt rattles the kernel of shame. I am grateful to Aunt Cissie who explains, 'Ag, Gerrie, you know this child's always been so. Everybody goes to Canada so she wants to go to England where there's nobody, not a soul from South Africa. She's stubborn as a mule; always pulls the other way.'

But she laughs her clear laugh of running water and pats my back. I note the alarm in Father's eyes and the lie comes effortlessly.

'Mrs Beukes, my landlady, has a cousin who lives in London. I've arranged to live with her. And her family. They're quite a large family.'

They are pleased at the thought of a family, comforted at the Beukeses' ability, in common with the rest of the animal kingdom, to reproduce themselves. But Uncle Gerrie is not prepared to let me off.

'And why are you sailing at the devilish hour of midnight? Respectable people are fast asleep in their beds by then.'

An image of Uncle Gerrie as a young man flickers before

me but I grope in vain for something to pin my dislike on.

'A good time to sail, New Year's Eve,' I say, attempting to sound gay. 'I think there might be one or two decent people still dancing at that hour.'

'Friedatjie,' Aunt Cissie says, and I stiffen under the gravity of her tone. 'You must be very careful, my child. Behave yourself at all times like a lady and remember honesty is always the best policy. Let me tell you, it's at dances that temptation comes in all sorts of disguises.' And dropping her voice in the interest of decency she adds, 'Mrs Karelse tells me in her letter how the people behave on the ship where there's no laws or police. Just poor whites, you know, so remember you're an educated girl. There are skollies amongst the English as well. And if you're good and careful, you'll always be happy. D.V. And remember to pray every day.'

Anxious to seal the topic of lust and temptation, Uncle Gerrie licks his fingers loudly and appeals to Aunt Cissie, 'You must cut us the piece about Boeta Sol Geldenhuys's daughter's wedding in Beaufort.' Aunt Cissie laughs her running-water laugh and launches into the story. They fill in the minor details while she develops a new theory on those events of three years ago. Father cannot resist pipping her at the post with the last line, 'And the bridegroom jumped into the motor car and was never seen again.'

They cut their stories from the gigantic watermelon that cannot be finished by the family in one sitting. They savour as if for the first time the pip-studded slices of the bright fruit and read the possibilities of konfyt in the tasteless flesh beneath the green. Their stories, whole as the watermelon that grows out of this arid earth, have come to replace the world.

I would like to bring down my fist on that wholeness and

watch the crack choose its wayward path across the melon, slowly exposing the icy pink of the slit. I would like to reveal myself now so that they will not await my return. But they will not like my stories, none of them, not even about the man in the train last night. When I should have said to the guard, 'Sir,' I should have said, 'Excuse me, sir, but this is a women's compartment.' But of course he knew. Deference at that midnight hour might have worked. But how my voice would have quivered ineffectually, quivered with reluctance and come out sounding matter-of-fact anyway.

I am wrenched out of sleep by the commotion outside my compartment door. A whining 'Please my baas,' and the Boer's, 'This way, you drunk bastard.' And the terror tightens in my chest as the key fumbles in the door and the long silver tongue of the lock flicks over. The blue-eyed guard holds the sliding door with his uniformed thigh while he turns on the light and beckons to someone outside.

'Come boy, and behave yourself; here's a woman up there.' But he does not as much as glance at me lying on the top bunk.

A young man stumbles in with a record player and drops it loud enough to drown Blue Eyes' key locking the door. I practise a number of sentences of protest and see myself charging after the guard in the corridor only to be met by the rebuff of ice-blue eyes staring through me uncomprehendingly. I do not choose to put up with the man in my compartment; fear of both men leaves me lying frozen in my bunk.

I keep a concealed eye trained on him slumped on the opposite seat. He has brought with him the sour smell of sweat and too much wine. He pulls out the foldaway table and carefully sets up his record player and the disc to which he hums, She wears my ring . . .

Under cover of the music the halted blood resumes its course through my veins. I manoeuvre my left elbow to support my body in readiness to defend myself against this man who will not leave me alone for long. I freeze again as he takes a bottle of brandy from his pocket and shouts, 'Heppy, Heppyyyy,' holding it out to the stiff rug-wrapped form that is me. A double swig to compensate for my failure to reply and he brings the bottle with such force on to the table that the needle shoots across to the last desperate notes of the song. He starts the record again, and having decided that I am a corpse sings along loudly the misheard words in fake American: To tell the world she die eternally. Over and over the record runs, reiterating its apology: That's why I sing, Because she wears my ring.

I cough and he looks up startled. He mimes the raising of a hat, greeting silently in order not to disturb the voice that etches its acid sentiment into my mind. As the song ends and he lifts the arm to start it yet again, I am driven to say, 'How about the other side?'

'No good, my goosie, a lot of rubbish that.'

And down drops the needle to scratch its melancholic message once again so that I scramble from my bunk and rush out into the corridor and stare into the darkness of the country. I do not know where we are until I watch the day break into contours of light and shade across the frilled peaks of the Koeivleiberg, the plain bathed in the even yellow light and the sky a marble wash. The man inside turns the volume up. The chopped tune stutters its lyrics in the quieter moments of the train's jicketty-can and I move further down the corridor. As we steam into Klawer I decide to take my seat again, but just as I reach the door it slides open and his body grows into the growing space as he stretches luxuriously. His trousers are slung low on his hips, not quite showing the crack of his buttocks, but the hat with the bouquet of feathers which he presses on to his head at a precarious angle is that of a countryman. When he gets off with the record player, which is his only luggage, he explains in the babyish diminutives of Afrikaans, 'Gotta little businessy here before I return to Town. Lekker ridie my little bridie.' And he winks, waving his single record merrily at me.

No, they will not like this story. I rise from the table saying, 'I must go down to the river. Where I spent so many happy hours of my childhood,' I add histrionically, for I know that sentiment will stem the insistent cries that I should have another portion of Christmas pudding before setting out. And perhaps I ought to stand upon that ground, lower my head deep into the gorra and whisper my guilty secret: I will not come back. I will never live in this country again.

In the six-monthly visits home over the past few years, I have not been down to the river. I have sat reading in the sun, anxious to return to the wet Cape Town winter. Or in the darkened room, fanning at the thick summer's heat, steeped in the bright green meadows of Hardy's England, a landscape anyone could love.

The right bank on which I theoretically stand has almost disappeared, so that the land slides imperceptibly into the depression. Ahead, two thin lines of water meander along an otherwise dry bed. Beyond, a gaping donga replaces the track that previously staggered up the left bank. Which means that this road to the dorp no longer exists. How the back of the lorry bobbed up and down like a swallow's tail in the shallow water as the men came home from work on Saturdays. Before the lorry it had been a tractor towing a trailerload of people, and before that, long ago, the dim memory of a wagon drawn by Oom Dawid's mules.

There must have been a flood and I wonder why Father did not write to tell me. Rainfall in the distant Bokkeveld mountains would have filled the river head with a swirling orange-brown water that raged its way for miles downstream. And here it surprised us on a morning as unremarkable as any other, without warning except for the muffled roar travelling a mile or more ahead, a sound by night that sleepers weave into their dreams. It would sweep along uprooted trees, monstrous swollen logs, a sheep or goat caught grazing in the river bed, and once there was the body of a woman. I had not seen her, the strange dead woman who passed so swiftly through the plains to be tossed under the eyes of fishermen into the sea at Papendorp. But at night in bed I saw her glassy eyes staring out of the blue-black face swollen with water. And the breasts like balloons bobbed on the water. She would have torn her clothes in the first struggle, and I buried my head in the pillow and squeezed my palms into my eardrums to fend off that death.

On the first day the water roared along Salt River, filling the bed, beating against the high banks so that the women roaming the veld in search of firewood tossed the bundles from their heads and rushed down, doekies in disarray, to the call of the water. On the bank they stood huddled together in wonder and awe, and recounted previous floods and always the dead woman whose glass eyes still glinted from every wave. For three days the flood raged, and when the water subsided children and grown-ups alike paddled knee-deep in abandonment, the orange-brown liquid lapping at their legs. But I squatted on the sun-cracked bank and stared at the orange growing red-brown and viscous in the sun. Then I would see her black body bobbing in blood.

But this flood must have been more forceful than anything I'd ever known as a child. For as far as I can see there is no real bank at all. Nothing more than a descent into the river. There is no point at which it could be said with certainty, this is where the river bed starts. For the bed and the right bank, quite unlike the left, lose themselves in each other. Even with a clearly defined bank the river presents difficulties. Not that anyone would argue about the three narrow ribbons of water or even the strips of wet sand between these. But on this side, where the sand seems dry, the possibility of a fourth ribbon of water cannot be altogether dismissed. Strips of blue-grey where dissolved salt glistens or patches of textured crust where salt crystals lie embedded in the sand suggest the possibility. I have known such strips to swell with water in a winter of rainfall and grow into yet more streams making up the river. Only where the sand lies in wind-wave patterns or rests in mounds at the bases of stunted dabikwa trees is there no doubt of the water remaining deep down in the earth. If there is any water at all. It seems more likely that a perpendicular sent down to the centre of the earth would erupt in a cloud of finest dust.

The goats that had settled down for the afternoon's rest stir as I approach the trees. I do not have a hat and sit down in the dappled shade where sparse leaves admit dancing flecks of sunlight. Birds flutter through the needle-leafed branches. A donkey brays from behind a further clump of trees, frogs croak and water, if only there were enough, would surely babble its protest from its separate brooks.

I spit and watch the gob sizzle on the hot sand. It is not only an act of exasperation; my sinuses are troublesome today. And what do I expect? Did I not hope that my senses would quiver with receptivity, that all these sights and sounds would scratch about in the memory like hens in the straw until they found the perfect place to nest. Where in feather-warm familiarity I could be the child once more, young and genderless as I roamed these banks alone, belonging without question to this country, this world.

In the ghanna bushes behind me there is a rustling sound I cannot identify. I remember the words, 'Beware of snakes,' the red letters of the warning label escaping from Father's lips. It is true that he stumbled over the first syllable in the way that people do when they search for something to say. And muffled by the sound of my chair pushed back, I pretended not to hear. Just as I did this morning when he said, 'It's no good being so touchy. Just shut yourself off against things around you, against everything, and you'll keep your self-respect. There's something for you to try when you come back.' When he raised his torso from the sawhorse the two suspended flaps of greased hair fell once again into their ordained places, adjacent, without a fraction of overlap, covering the shiny pate completely. If only there were no need to bend. Is it my fault that Father has grown so old?

My hand goes to the crown of my own head. If my hair should drop out in fistfuls, tired of being tugged and stretched and taped, I would not be surprised. Do my fingers run through the synthetic silk with less resistance than usual? What will I do in the damp English weather? I who have risked the bulge of a bathing suit and paddled in the tepid Indian Ocean, aching to melt in the water while my hair begged to keep dry. What will I do when it matts and shrinks in the English fog? Perhaps so far away where the world is reversed an unexpected shower will reveal a brand-new head of hair sprung into its own topiarian shape of one-eared dog.

A whip cracks through the silence. If I keep very still I might not be seen, but the foliage is too sparse. It is Oom Dawid in his ankle-hugging veldskoen and faded khaki shirt, flourishing his whip. My tongue struggles like a stranded fish in the dry cavity of my mouth. Why do I find it so hard to speak to those who claim me as their own? There is nowhere to hide so with studied casualness I walk towards him, but the old man, preoccupied, seems to stumble upon me, squinting before he greets. The stentorian voice has shrunk to a tired rumble and the eyes are milky in their intimate search of my face. The great rough hand shakes mine with faltering vigour and under his smile my mouth grows moist and my tongue pliant once more.

'Ja,' Oom Dawid says, 'about time you came home to see us. But I hear you're going over the waters to another world. Now don't stay away too long.'

'Yes, it's nice to be back. I'm going to England on New Year's Day,' I blurt.

'Still,' the old man persists, 'you're home now with your own people: it can't be very nice roaming across the cold water where you don't belong.'

I burrow the point of my shoe in the sand and giggle foolishly.

'Ja, Ja-nee . . .' Oom Dawid rumbles. 'So-o, so it goes,' which he repeats after a short silence with the ease of someone offering a fresh diversion in the face of flagging conversation. Then his face breaks out in a network of smiles as he remembers a request he has been nursing.

'About the Queen,' he announces, 'you must go and see if she's still young and beautiful.'

I remember the faded magazine picture of the Coronation stuck above his sideboard.

'Oh, I won't be seeing the Queen of England. I don't care two hoots about her.' I instantly regret the sharp words. But the old man laughs, unperturbed.

'Then I'll have to go and see for myself one day and tell the Queen about these Boers and how they treat us.'

He looks at me sharply. 'You have to put your heart with someone. Now you don't want to know about Vorster and you don't care about the Queen and our Griqua chief isn't grand enough for you. It's leaders we need. You young people with the learning must come and lead us.'

The old guilt rises and wrings the moisture from my tongue. Even though I know him to be committed to the slogan of Grown-ups Know Best, that he wouldn't dream of paying heed to anything I have to say.

'Ja . . . aa . . . so-o,' Oom Dawid reiterates and the old Namaqua eyes narrow amiably. 'Anyway, you're back with us now, here where you can always see the white stones of our mother's grave on the koppie. And he points to the hills in the distance. 'And your father grows grey. A man mustn't grow old without his children around him. Old Shenton must write a letter for me to Lizzie's madam in Cape Town. She's got a grand job in Town, a kind of housekeeper for English people, but she must come home now. We're getting too old. Antie Saartjie can't do much now – the legs you know. Ag, you young people are so grand in your motor cars,' he says inexplicably, and turns, deftly pinching his nostrils in turn to propel from each a neat arc of snot.

'I must go and find these damn mules. Do you remember Bleskop? Very old now, but still goes wandering off to plague me. Yes, I'm after them every day. Like you they've always got somewhere to go. More trouble than they're worth.'

He shakes my hand and walks off, saying, 'When you get back, come and tell me about the wonderful things across the water. I must tell you about the old days, of how the people trekked from Griqualand', and he stops for a moment, genuinely perplexed, to add, 'I don't know if the Queen knows about all that.'

I watch him stride across the water to the left bank where the new path winds tortuously around the donga. The crack of his whip echoes across the river bed. If I did not fear his scorn, I would have asked him where the gorra was. But he would have seen it as city affectation. 'Don't be silly,' he would snort, 'you've carried water all your life like the rest of us.'

Why did Father not ask me to take a bucket, I wonder, as I walk towards the gorra. I stop to tip the sand out of my shoes but the earth sizzles with heat and I can barely keep my balance hopping on each shod foot in turn. I must find it and get out of this heat.

The wide bank with a sprinkling of Jan Twakkie trees is surely the place. But the bank is a uniformly smooth stretch of sand with no trace of the well. I orientate myself by lining up the great dabikwa tree with the cavern on the left bank. Sitting down, I survey the shape of the gully, unfamiliar at this angle. And move to the left, and move again until the blinding light strikes the fissure where the crabs dig snug holes in the dove-blue clay.

With a twig I draw a circle which is unmistakably where the gorra had been, where it now lies buried under a layer of sand and mud from distant mountains. Or else they have removed it and the wet sand, according to kinetic law, has fallen in piece by piece as it shook off the years of restraint moulded by the cement walls. For the well had been just a six-foot cylinder of cement sunk into the sand and then evacuated. Here Oom Klonkies from Rooiberg trailed his forked stick, frowning, and pronounced that the water would be less salty. And he was right. The water was brack but thirst-quenching, unlike the bitter-salt running water of the river that parches the throat.

The mouth of the cylinder curved outward for nine inches above the sand level. Here as a child I lay on my stomach to watch my framed face in the water below. And bent down with the cement wedged under my left armpit, I would scoop up the still water with a tin mug and in that vast silence listen to the rhythms of water lilted into tin, hauled up against the cement wall, and warble into the metal bucket. Before the buckets were filled the water supply would run out. And as the level fell the framed portrait faded, grew darker so that I would clasp with both arms the fat cement mouth, straining to see through my mocking image the new growth of water. Unless you whispered, coaxed, the water refused to rise. With my head hanging deep down in the darkness and the blood rushing hither and thither in my veins, I sang my song of supplication until the water spirits gurgled with pleasure and the face framed in the circle of water grew whole once more.

If the well were here still, if I could feel the pitted cement pressing into my naked armpits and stare at my severed head in the water, it would come – the song of supplication that will rouse the appropriate feelings in me.

My head nods to the tune but the words loiter on the tip of my tongue, scratch as they try to scale my slippery throat, and then a bird screams so that they scurry back down. Instead another chant from childhood takes over:

Bucket in the hand
Bucket on the head

Feet in the sand
Wish I were dead. (There was nothing else to rhyme
with head.)

Over and over along the track as I balanced my way home
with the buckets, stopping only once to change hands.

The traffic of words is maddening. I am persecuted by a
body of words that performs regardless of my wishes,
making its own choices. Words will saunter in and vanish
in a flash, refusing to be summoned or expelled. Just as I
cannot summon my heart to beat faster or slower, so the
words in conversation could tumble out regardless or refuse
to be uttered, betraying or making a fool of me. Thus the
water song will not surface while the bucket chant will not
be banished.

I follow the track which was once the well-worn path to
our house. Half-way along I stop to look back. I can see the
old man across climbing the hill. The tops of trees pop up
above the straight line cut by the river. Across the river,
the hills swell abruptly into a ridge that meets the sky in a
straight line horizontal to the fissure of the river. The
glaring white pebble crust of the hill lifts pointillistically in
the sun, its squat succulents grey stipples in the distance.
The railway line at the foot of the ridge parallel to the river
has only just been built. I have not yet seen the ISCOR
train running along it, its hundred or more trucks a black
line of iron and steel drawn across the ridge. Or so Father
said in his last letter. That there were a hundred and nine
trucks that day, the longest ever to travel between Sishen
and Saldanha Bay. Which means that he runs out to the
train every other day to count the trucks, for how else
would he know and why would he write immediately, a
scribbled salutation and then the breathless news of a

hundred and nine trucks, before the guarded demand that I spend the last days at home where everybody, all the family, is coming to see me?

Empty-handed I carry on walking towards the house. They are sitting on the stoep waiting for the breeze that will cool the day. The wind is just rising. On the dead plain, circles of dust are spun and lifted, up, up, spiralling into fine cones that dance teasingly in my path. Grains of sand whirl past and sting my cheeks. The hot breath of this wind brings no relief.

The party on the stoep is watching, no doubt discussing me, my marriage prospects, my waywardness and my unmistakable Shenton determination. There is no point in lingering. There is no concealed approach to the house. A head-on collision with all that consanguinity cannot be avoided. The bosoms of the aunts are mountainous; the men are large like trees. Aunt Nettie has timed the coffee to be ready at my arrival.

'You've been a long time,' someone says.

I smile, unable to summon a reply.

'Ag, no,' Father says, 'let the girl be. She hasn't seen the old place for such a long time.'

'There's no place like home,' says Aunt Cissie.

'And home is where the heart is,' Father adds, and then he frowns for that is not quite what he means. *LOL*

I watch him pour the coffee into his saucer. With lips pouted for the purpose, the liquid is syphoned from saucer to throat. Coffee trickles from his old man's mouth. With the lower lip both protruding and sagging, the liquid has no choice but to drip on to his new crimplene trousers. He rubs the stain with the back of his hand.

'Ag ja,' Aunt Nettie sighs, 'a woman's work is never done.' She casts a significant but fruitless look at her older sister before rising with the tray, her rear following reluctantly.

A conversation buzzes about my ears while the silly bucket rhyme mills through my mind.

'What do you say, Frieda?'

There is no need to admit that I have not been listening. I do not have to say anything. The question is purely phatic. They have come to see me, to rest their eyes on me, reassured by the correctness of the family gathered here.

'A person of few words, our Frieda,' says Uncle Gerrie, 'a sure sign of wisdom.' I remember now, in his pre-gold-teeth days, Uncle Gerrie as a young man in a straw hat, trowel in his hand. 'Baboon,' he shouted at me. 'Why is this ugly child always in the way?' And he slap-slapped the cement, levelling off this very stoep. Not that this can really be called a stoep. Merely a two-foot-high block of cement on to which the kitchen door opens, keeping the dust at bay. There is no verandah, and without that protective structure the eyes cannot consume the land in the same way that the colonial stoep allows.

'So you've been down to the river?' he asks.

'Yes, eh . . .' and the dots of hesitation hang like a row of fireflies in the dark until I find my voice to continue. 'It must have been quite a flood. I barely recognised the place. I had some trouble trying to find the gorra but then I remembered the big tree and the gully.'

Father says, 'The gorra's been gone for nearly a year now. We even get our washing water from the dorp. Nice to get a good lather with soapsuds. I'm surprised you found the gorra; that whole bank's completely washed away. Did you go beyond Blouklip? From there you can just about recognise the old gully.'

'No.'

'Then you lined up the tree with the wrong gully, I think. Yours is the recent one made by last year's flood.'

Perhaps I ought to go to Blouklip now, but in this whirling dust I fear for my sinuses. It will be better indoors. I join Aunt Nettie in the kitchen where she dries the dishes but she clutches the dish towel to her chest when I offer to help.

'No, you have a rest today,' she says. 'But don't forget, my child, wherever you lodge – with a nice family of course – to always help with the work. Don't just sit in your room with your books. A girl should help to keep the house tidy. And when you meet a nice man you'll have the experience of housework.' She winks awkwardly.

'Yes,' I say, and wander off into the sitting room where dust lies thickly spread over all the surfaces, inviting the calligraphy that will expose the polished wood beneath. On which of these surfaces would I write my guilty secret? I would not dare. Not here where Mother sat in the late afternoons, after the wind had dropped, her voice rumbling distantly through the phlegm, her mouth opening and closing frog-like as she snapped up the air. Here she sat to recover her breath before dusting, her asthmatic breathing filling the room, her face uplifted as if God squatted just there, above, on the other side of the galvanised iron roof. And inside, below, always the tap-tap of the roof as the iron contracted, tap-tap like huge drops of rain falling individually, deliberately. But drops of rain would sizzle on the hot iron and roll off evaporating, hissing as they rolled. So merely the sound of molecular arrangement in the falling temperature of the iron. Even now that ceilings have been put in, still a tap-tap that stops and a silence followed by a tap-shudder-tap for all the world as if she were still sitting there gasping for breath with her God just on the other side.

Aunt Nettie bustles in with the duster.

'Unbelievable all this dust; how it gets in I'll never know. I don't know why your father doesn't move somewhere cool where there's also grass.'

She dusts well, with a practised hand – that is, if the criteria for dusting are indeed speed and agility. Her right wrist flicks the duster of dyed ostrich feathers across surfaces, the left hand moving simultaneously, lifting, before the duster flicks, and then replacing ornaments. Feathers flutter across the glazed faces of Jesus, the Queen Mother in her youth, Oupa Shenton and the picture of an English thatched cottage in the Karroo headed with the flourished scroll of Home Sweet Home. There is no hesitation in her hand. She removes dust just as she has removed from her memory the early years as a servant when she learned to dust with speed. Not that she would ever lose sight of those attributes that lifted her out of the madam's kitchen, the pale skin and smooth wavy hair that won her a teacher for a husband.

Aunt Nettie caresses her hair with her right hand as she passes with the duster into the bedroom. What will I do next? If I were to follow her, I'd land back on the stoep where they sit in the cooling afternoon.

'I think,' I shout after her, 'I'll go down to the river again.'

'Yes Meisie,' she agrees, 'and then come and rest with us on the stoep. The wind is lying down and soon it'll be lovely outside.'

I sprint past the others and Father shouts, 'Be careful of puff adders. They often come out when the wind drops.'

What nonsense! He did not stumble over the words. He has, after all, said it before. No doubt he will say it again. Or fabricate some other dangers: lions in the veld, man-eating plants, and perhaps it is not awkwardness at all, not simply a desire to drop sounds into the great silence between us. It is the father's assertion that he knows best.

Their words, all their words, buzz like a drove of persistent gnats about my ears. I no longer have any desire to find the gorra. I have done with sentimental nonsense about water spirits. They have long since been choked to death. The fissure of the river offers mere escape.

Ignoring the path, I scramble down the bank and remain sitting where the sliding earth comes to rest. Before me, between two trickles of water, a mule brays. It struggles in what must be a stretch of quicksand. Transformed by fear its ears alert into quivering conductors of energy. With a lashing movement of the ears, the bray stretches into an eerie whistle. It balances on its hind legs like an ill-trained circus animal, the front raised, the belly flashing white as it staggers in a grotesque dance. When the hind legs plummet deep into the sand, the front drops in search of equilibrium. Then, holding its head high, the animal remains quite still as it sinks.

Birds dart and swoop through the pliant Jan Twakkie branches, and a donkey stirs from its sleep, braying.

He did not say, 'Beware of the quicksand.' Not that I would ever tell what I have seen in the river today.

BEHIND THE BOUGAINVILLEA

The papery panicles of bougainvillea rustle in an unexpected play of breeze. From the top of the whitewashed wall it tumbles, armfuls of exuberant purple blossom. And below, the group of people stir, shift from one buttock to another, shake an ankle or ease a shoulder before settling back into a sprawling cluster of bodies. Except for the faces, turned to meet the scrunch of my shoes on the gravel.

I pull an ambiguous face so that it can be seen as either greeting or grimace. This is after all a doctor's surgery and I could well be in pain. I am abjectly grateful for the response, which I take in with a careless glance. Some purse their lips but nod, others mutter or grunt their greeting and smiling young child pipes a clear, 'Môre Antie' at me.

I hesitate. Father's words repeat in my ears. 'Oh you'll find it very different now. It's not the old business of waiting in the yard; there's even a waiting room for us now with a nice clean water lavatory. Not that these Hotnos know how to use it, but ja man, I think you'll find the Boers quite civilised now.'

Why are they sitting outside in the yard? I move past the

group to the open door at the end of the wall. With one foot on the raised threshold I crane my neck into the room. The walls are a brooding eggshell. Above a row of empty chairs a Tretchikoff Weeping Rose leans recklessly out of a slender glass to admire her new-born tear, perfect in plastic rotundity. Artfully the blue tint deepens into the parent blue of the plastic frame. My shoe scours the threshold in hesitation and my eyes rest on the smooth primrose crimplene suit of a woman motionless in her chair. Her hair flicks up above her ears in an iron-induced curl that will never bounce in the breeze, and she stares at the framed picture of a woman in yellow on the opposite wall. Her dress is a darker yellow, sunnier, and her hair, the colour of ripe corn, flies away in fear of being eaten by a heifer with amorous eyes. Has she seen me? She reverses the nylon-clad legs crossed at the ankles and her right hand starts to move up and down as she beats off the heat. Below her gaze a man studies the smoke ring he blows into the heat. A large briefcase stands clamped between his shoes. Under his trousers his calves bulge with the effort.

The floor is a highly polished parquet in which blurred reflections shudder portentously and I no longer care. It is in any case absurd to pretend that I have assumed this as my position for waiting. I turn and meet the thousand eyes of those squatting in the yard. They have been watching. They register the tension of the moment by shifting and scratching as people do who ease the discomfort of waiting. I settle on my haunches against the wall and open my bag for a book but cannot bring myself to haul it up. Such a display of literacy would be indecent. Instead I draw up a paper handkerchief and ostentatiously blow my nose.

A child starts whimpering and tugs at its mother's skirt but the mother stares resolutely before her, tracing with her eyes the untrammelled path of a red ant. A large woman in a blanket reaches over to the child. 'No, no,' her voice lulls, 'it's too hot to cry. You'll scare away the breeze.' But the breeze has already gone. A whimsical movement of air in a day so hot and still that it dropped in shame. Only the bougainvillea still whispers its fulsomeness as the blossoms settle into place.

An old man coughs and coughs, clutching at his chest with both hands. Eeeh, he wheezes, and Eeeh, a chorus of voices sigh in response, lifting him high so that his chest loosens and his head nods mechanically until the next bout of coughing.

Under Father's arm a Rhode Island Red hen squawked, her feathers fluffed with anxiety, her tilted head pressed against his chest. A darning needle gleamed in his right hand.

'Won't it hurt?' I asked, wincing. The orange eyes screamed a silent terror.

'Yes, but she'll feel so much better. You get to know the symptoms and it's just a question of picking off the horny growth at the tip of the tongue – kuikenpiep we call it – you just remove it and pour salt on the wound to disinfect and she'll be right as rain within a day. Only the females tend . . .' but his words were gobbled up by the hideous cry of the bird whose feathers turned to foam as she raged to escape.

'No man,' he reverted to my condition, 'you must see Dr van Zyl about that pain in your chest. A clever chap that van Zyl. He got you through rheumatic fever when you were only five or six. Then he was only a young man, fresh from school. Do you remember?'

I did. I remembered the silence, the half light of drawn curtains and the sunlight crowding into the sateen pattern.

Diamonds drifting into curlicues lifted with light from the dull pink of the fabric. Outside the chickens quarrelled or announced their eggs listlessly in the heat. On the bed like a stove, the heat pressed and seared my joints and Mamma dabbed with spirit lotion, cool as the voice of Jesus. Then the doctor came with creaking sandals and hairy legs.

'Don't stand there like a stuffed owl in the dark; get some light into this place,' he bellowed at Mamma, and hee-haw, he threw back his head in appreciation of his simile.

When he left with a screech of wheels, Mamma coaxed the curtains back across the window and the feverish diamonds glowed like rubies in the afternoon sun. I drifted off to the sound of the turkey cock dragging his boastful wing in the dust. Otherwise such silence that I knew the hens had resolutely tucked their heads under their wings.

'Yes, I'll make an appointment,' I agreed.

Father looked up startled and his arm slackened so that the fowl leapt down with a deafening cackle.

'I don't think you can make appointments, not yet. This isn't Cape Town, you know. You just go along and wait. But there's a lovely waiting room with a modern water lavatory.'

'Oh, I don't know that I want to spend the day waiting for Dr van Zyl to tell me that I have bronchitis.'

'Why not? You're on holiday and no one minds waiting for a doctor. Your health, my girlie, is as important as your books. Anyway, you can always take something along to read. Doctor will make a proper diagnosis and give you some antibiotics to clear it up. And the waiting room's nice and clean and modern, no need to spoil your best clothes sitting in the dust.'

I heard again Mamma's voice as she slapped the sewing out of my hands. 'No backstitching on a hem, you careless child. You'll just have to start again; nice girls don't do slovenly needlework.' And the snip-snip of the scissors as they lifted a square from the perfectly new dress she drew out of the trunk. Sprigs of yellow mimosa, the furry edges of pollen dust drifting into the cream of the muslin.

'Start on the plain edge,' she snapped and sat down with her hawk's eye trained on my stitches. But the stuff, a heap of crushed mimosa, rilled under her rings as her fingers plucked nervously at it. So that I dared to say, 'It's nice, why don't you want it any more?'

'I wore it once,' she said, 'spent the whole day making it and wore it the very next day when I woke with an asthma attack. I couldn't stand there waiting, felt too bad, so I lay down right there in Dr van Zyl's yard.' She pushed the dress away. 'It's stained, all along the right side,' and her mouth twisted into lines of disgust as she tossed the dress into the trunk. 'A decent chap, van Zyl, said, "Make way for the old girl," and saw me first that afternoon.'

So we alighted on the same scene of Mamma's heaving chest and the articulated pride of her lowered eyes as she sank to the ground.

I had been home a week, a whole week in which we struggled like tourists in a market place. Now those words that trailed off in tentative dots melted in the moment of a shared past. So fragile a moment that I snapped.

'I don't want antibiotics and I dress entirely for my own pleasure. If I had best clothes I would certainly not reserve them for an uncouth old white man.'

He blinked, once, twice, uncomprehendingly, and I should have explained that there was no point in pampering a memory embedded in lies. Perhaps he winced at the rehearsed quality of my words. But so sadly did he clutch the salt container with both hands, and replaced it

so gingerly that it toppled in the dust and the little blue
Cerebos man's demented smile grew wise in the somersault,
so that I said, 'Oh, I'll go and see van Zyl tomorrow.' He
smiled gratefully, a child placated by a parent's exasperated,
Yes, all right.

I watch two girls sharing a photo-story. Their practised eyes
meet as they reach the end of the page simultaneously. It
will take no time at all to finish the book but I note a
further supply poking out of a bag; they have come well
armed for waiting. So far there has been no indication that
anyone is aware of our presence in the yard. Have the two
in the waiting room been receiving whispered messages
from a nurse whose starched head would just pop around a
door with an earnest, 'Doctor won't be long'?
    I toy again with the idea of reading my book but my hand
in the bag is arrested by the faltering sound of a young man
limping into the yard. He takes no care in avoiding the
bougainvillea so that the blossoms tremble afresh in his
wake. He stops and only his eyes move to register the
group, scooping up even the stragglers in a single swivelled
beam. His face is covered with dust so evenly spread as to
beguile the casual observer. He jerks his shoulder to adjust a
green khaki strap and he pats the bag briefly as if to
ascertain the contents. Then he walks briskly into the
waiting room. I hear the stuff of his trousers on the plastic
chair as he settles into a position of comfort. The silence of
the room swallows him. Where will he be sitting? Next to
the man whose feet will clench suspiciously around the
briefcase; whose eyes will accuse him of dissembling? For
what has become of his limp? Will the woman's nostrils curl
at the acrid smell of perspiration? The roots of my hair
tingle as the stranger's face grows before me, the close-up

magnified into a distorted mountain of flesh. Into the great caverns of the flared nostrils I, an awe-struck Gulliver, peer and tremble at the fire that the inhalations promise. Waves of heat skid in silver sign-curves across the black flesh and I must blink, no, rub my fists into my eyes to clear the screen.

As if to recover his place, the stranger stumbles out of the waiting room. His lips move in a mutter of inarticulate sounds as he swings his body down on to the ground, almost blocking the doorway. From his right pocket he draws a pair of dark glasses and simultaneously from the left a dazzling white handkerchief with which he carefully polishes the lenses. He puts them on and, as if to test their efficacy, aims straight at me. In the round mirror glass I see my face bleached by an English autumn, the face of a startled rabbit, and I drop my eyes. I burrow in my bag for a book and allow it to fall open. Under that gaze I cannot allow my hands to tremble while searching for the correct page.

I read, 'The right side was browner than a European's would be, yet not so distinctly brown as to type him as a Hindu or Pakistani and certainly he was no Negro, for his features were quite as Caucasian as Edward's own.'

These words are sucked off the page by the mirrors and I flush with shame and put my arm across the print. I know that the cover is safely pressed against my lap but I fear for the reflection of light, beams criss-crossing and back-tracking and depositing their upside-down images God knows where. The mirrors twitch knowingly. Had I been careless in taking the book out?

The parched soul will be nourished by literature, say the moral arbiters. And I have become their willing slave. Nevertheless I ought to challenge this man who stares so unashamedly. Am I not here precisely because I am tired of being stared at by the English? Please God, I can bear no more scrutiny. Guiltily I stuff the novel back into my bag and drop my head on to my knees.

Last winter it rained and rained. From the window I had been watching the lurid yellow of oil-seed rape sag like sails under squalls of rain. On the beam in the kitchen drops of rain lined up at regular intervals, the bright little drops meeting their destruction in an ache for perfection, growing to roundness that the light from the bare electric bulb would catch, so that the star at the base grew into a hard bright point of severance and for a second was the perfect crystal sphere before it fell, ping, into the tin plate and splattered into mere wetness. But then, just then, before the fall, the star would spread into an oval of reflected light, pale and elliptical on the shadowed beam, an opal ghost escaping.

I watched them in turn, knees hugged, and listened to the symphony of perfect drops splattering into the receptacles arranged in a line below the beam. Individual drops tapped a morse message of conciliation that belied the slanted drone of rain outside.

Curled up on the table, the cat fixed a suspicious eye on her tin plate catching the water under the beam.

So much rain Kitty, I addressed the cat, allowing the brine in my eyes to reach perfect roundness before the drops tumbled and splattered ignominiously on my cheeks. The water gurgled in the sinkpipes, the drone outside grew deeper and the cat, encouraged by the noise and my unusually friendly tone, purred loudly. So much rain, I concluded, and I'm in the wrong bloody hemisphere.

But heroines must cry, so I allowed the tears to flow freely although I had just lost interest in crying. Another drop on the beam pearled into perfection and in that second of the spreading light I came to a decision which, after all, followed logically from my remark to the cat. I would go home. I could no longer avoid a visit.

I shut my eyes and under the purr of Kitty travelled south where the African sun swelled visibly in the sky and in kinship curling waves of heat bounced off the galvanised-iron roof. But oh, when it rained the roof sang in clear soprano. On the floor the enamelled pots caught the leaks from the roof in concert. Out we ran to feel the silver trails of fine-grained sand between our toes so that new puddles grew a crushed orange under our feet. So many children clad in the peaked hoods of sugar sacks folded into capes, our bodies bent to the slant of the rain. The rain warbled on our jute-woven backs. On the next day, with the sky rinsed blue and the red earth washed, the sun shot beams of bright yellow to swell the brittle sticks of vine. We lifted our faces to God's spread hands. And he muttered through his beard, Honour thy mother and thy father so that thy days may be lengthened . . .

I do not, dear God, wish to lengthen my days. I wish to be turned into a drop of water now, before these very mirror eyes.

I start at a cry, 'Mholo Boeti,' behind me and turn to a woman whose face is eagerly lifted to the leafy entrance some yards away. Across the road, hovering on his bicycle like a bird on the wing, a Black man shouts through the foliage a long message in his language to her. The bicycle wobbles as he gesticulates, but he pedals furiously, back and forth to the sing-song of his tale. Fortunately the wire basket attached for the delivery of meat – for the sign on the basket declares Andries Brink to be the best butcher in the village – is empty.

The woman interjects with appreciative Ewe's, but her face grows puzzled as the narrative unfolds. The messenger stops abruptly at the sound of a Boer's voice calling from the stoep of the butcher's on the corner. We turn to the flame-red hibiscus chalices that hide the form of the proprietor. 'Kosie, gebruik jy alweer my tyd om to skinder. Waarom moet julle kaffers tog so skree. So 'n geraas in die hitte gee 'n beskawe mens 'n kopseer.'

Kosie wheels off on his bike with an unrestrained, 'Ewe Sisi, Ewe,' and leaves the woman and her friends to take up the matter in loud dispute. Someone argues passionately, gravely, so that I speculate on topics like the death of the doctor or the assassination of the magistrate. But then a woman from the group rises, for the debaters have moved together. She twists her buttocks in a mocking dance, throws back her head and projects malt-dark laughter into the heat. I stare unashamedly into the pink flesh of her mouth rimmed by the polished plum of her lips. The mouth remains open as the sound dribbles away and I pull vigorously at the tips of my fingers until the joints crack.

I do not know what they are saying. Their gestures, the careless laughter and the pensive nods, tell me less than nothing.

The girls immersed in the romance of a blonde heroine shut their book with theatrical exasperation. 'Such a noise gives you a headache,' one whispers loudly. The other traps me with her eyes and inclines her head with a twitch in the direction of the woman who has just stopped laughing. My facial muscles tighten, but the girl's eyes persist. Am I drawn into the kraal of complicity? The stranger's glasses are trained on me. I think of jumping up, protesting, when he calmly addresses the group in Zulu. The argument gains new momentum; the dancer looks chastened and beats her chest while others shout simultaneously. So that a head pops over the wall behind us and says cheekily in Afrikaans, 'Shut up you lot. This is a surgery, not a shebeen.' Someone shouts back, 'To hell with that; where's the old bugger?' and an old woman complains, 'Don't you speak to your elders like that,' but the girl throws her head back and laughs raucously and drops behind the high wall. There must be a step-ladder on the other side for her poise is perfect. She does not disturb the unripe bunches of tight green grapes hanging lightly like ornaments above her shoulder.

A woman addresses a remark in Zulu to the dust-covered stranger and he replies, itemising on his five fingers, and as he strikes his thumb in final iteration, I see who he is. Does he recognise me?

I am once again engulfed by the loneliness of childhood and must swallow hard to prevent the tears from beading in the corners of my eyes. How I hugged my knees and listened to the afternoon wind piping mournfully through the cracks in the old school door. There, alone, I repossessed the ignominious day. There the yearning stretched with the sound of the wind, grew wide as the world and the random words in my head jostled just beneath the surface of clarity.

There I found the letter. He had placed it conspicuously in a crack in the door, presumably just before I crept in. Yes, the letter said, as I had probably guessed, he, Henry Hendrikse, loved me. Surprise swiftly converted into prescience . . . yes, that was what the wind had murmured through the cracks. He would like, he wrote, to press his lips against mine which were soft as velvet. I was surprised at his ability to think of love in such concrete terms. Could he imagine his hands travelling over my folds of fat? But he did not mention my fat, my squishy breasts. Instead he said my breasts were two fawns, twins of a gazelle, that feed among the lilies. But that I think came later, weeks later, in a letter, for we never spoke. (Except the last time, but I do not want to think about that.) All through that summer we composed delicious letters of love. Secret, for Father said I was too young to think of boys; besides, Henry Hendrikse, I had heard him say many times, was almost pure kaffir. We, the Shentons, had an ancestor, an Englishman whose memory must be kept sacred, must not be defiled by associating with those beneath us. We were respectable Coloureds.

It was a summer's evening, days before we were both to leave for high school. Henry went to the nearest Afrikaans school at Nuwerus, a place of waving grass, or so his letters said. The heat had dropped and the sky was a washed purple of dying light when he found me behind the chicken run. He said nothing but placed his hands on either side of my head and pressed his lips on mine. Then with his tongue he forced open my lips with such a rush of saliva that I thought he had spat in my mouth, that his contempt for me could no longer be contained. I drew away and ran off pressing my palms against my ears lest he say something offensive.

At home Father had laid the table. I lingered over the Sunday bowl of tinned peaches and cream, thick cream that Father stole from the butter churn for me. The cream curled through the clear syrup making its marbled pattern around the island of peach halves. In my mouth they fused exquisitely into a fountain of pleasure so that I held each mouthful with cheeks bulging indecently. Should a kiss not have been like that? I sank my teeth into the flesh of the peach. Perhaps we hated each other; perhaps that was why the kiss had been a failure. But no, his letter said the next day, the kiss was divine ambrosia, and so stirring the memory of peach syrup and cream, I was once again in love.

Will he today take the opportunity to retract those words? Has he too tired of the hyperboles of love? He will find so many reasons to spit at me.

But that was a very long time ago. Now his contempt will be a grown-up silence. Or his words, in a language I ought to know, will fall on my uncomprehending ears. Or perhaps I, sealed off from the eloquent world around me, will not be worthy of his notice.

I look up and meet myself in his glasses which tell me that I must leave. But my right leg that had been tucked under the left thigh tingles with pins and needles. I rise, wobble, reach out for the wall but find my hand landing in his firm grip.

'Are you all right?' he asks in English, and takes off his glasses. An empty gesture since his face retains the anonymity that sunglasses so mercifully bestow. I am still not sure whether he recognises me: my hair is no longer straightened, my clothes are carefully chosen from jumble sales and I have a vegetarian diet to thank for my not altogether unbecoming plumpness. An alternative bourgeois, European style. Perhaps my voice.

'Yes, it's just that . . .' but my legs give way as I withdraw my hand. How has he managed to get my own body to rebel against me in this way? He reclaims my hand.

'You need water,' and he leads me with the confidence of those acquainted with emergencies to a tap almost hidden by the tarnished orange of tattered cannas.

Someone says, 'You'd better not. That tap is for the flowers. The old man will let thunder loose on us.'

Upon which a woman with several doekies wrapped around her head produces from under her bundles a gallon can of water.

'Here,' she says, 'I fill my can wherever I go. Our water in Moedverloor is salt enough to shrink the innards. Here, have a drink but don't splash. As long as there's no splashing he won't know a thing.'

The can passes round in an infectious thirst. The woman parts the cannas and just turns the tap on when the starched cap of the servant girl pops over the wall.

'My God,' she exclaims indignantly, 'your mama won't know you when doctor finishes with you – pulp,' and she pummels and moulds with her hands an imaginary ball of flesh. The woman listens composedly, with cocked head, but does not stop the tap. 'There,' pointing into the distance, 'across those blue mountains lies my mama, a box of bones under an antheap,' she says irrelevantly. So that the girl laughs and says, lowering her voice, 'He'll be here soon. Just doing the last sick white.' The green grapes twitch as she drops behind the wall.

I have found a cushion for my dizzy head in the cleft of bougainvillea branches. I stare at the crushed confetti of mauve blossoms at my feet and note for the first time the tiny yellow trumpets in the centre. I do not realise that I look ridiculous until he draws me out of the shrub.

'You ought to have a walk,' and he puts his dark glasses back on. Surely he is seeking my death. Exercise seems an unusual remedy for faintness which he thinks I suffer from. But I do not resist. I do not tell this tokolos of a man to piss off. And I find no comfort in the thought of going home to Father and a cup of Rooibos tea.

We stumble along past the butcher's where the man in the white polystyrene hat packs his parcels of meat into the bicycle basket in readiness for the afternoon delivery. Henry shouts something to him in his language but the man looks puzzled and Henry repeats, enunciating more carefully. Do I imagine his words echoing? The street is so still; only the shopkeepers are left, turning their keys as they retreat from the afternoon heat. The man in the hat smiles and lets loose a volley of grunts and Ewe's so that I assume the exchange to be purely phatic. Just showing off. But I want him to know where my allegiance lies. Shame and vanity produce the words, 'You speak Zulu?' I keep my voice flat, matter-of-fact.

'No,' and he waits for the word to take effect before he continues, 'Xhosa.' His reply induces faintness, an alternating light- and heavy-headedness. I feel the thrill of an adolescent wish coming to pass. How I hoped that I would sink into a faint and be carried along the corridor by the science teacher whose impatience at my stupidity would melt into solicitude. But I was always big, robust; it is unlikely that I will lose consciousness for even one delicious second.

We walk slowly and in silence. Which I break. 'Where did you learn?'

'Karasburg,' another pause, 'Namibia,' as if I would not know.

'All the way up there?'

'Yes all the way up there.' He will not be enticed into explaining. Unless it is simply a lie, since Xhosa is not spoken that far north.

We turn into the Main Road lined with dusty trunks of eucalyptus trees. The remote grey-green foliage has forged ahead into cooler regions way above the single-storey buildings. The still midday rays of the sun become molten globules of metal that fall plop into my thick black hair. My neck bulges under the weight. I reach with my free hand towards the trunk of a tree and he says with a trace of impatience, 'What's the matter?' I have to hold on to his heavy rural 'metter, metter, metter,' before I manage to say that I feel faint. He looks up and down the deserted Main Road, quickly, anxiously, and I wonder whether he thinks of Father appearing from around a corner.

He says, 'I have a friend just a few yards away. You could sit down there and rest.' I would rather go back to the surgery, but he assumes my assent and leads me down an affluent white residential street. 'It's so hot,' I say apologetically; I am dimly aware of the fact that I do not want to be here. It is clear that he is irritated by me.

We turn into a lane lined with hibiscus blossoms that bellow their well-being from flame-red trumpets, and enter at a side gate. Behind the house, after the beds of dahlias and obedient rows of pink gladioli, we come to a flat-roofed building. Its door faces away from the house, clearly the servant's room. The occupant, still wearing her white apron, sits on the step, her door ajar. She has kicked off her shoes and the bunion on her right foot looks bruised.

'Middag,' she says moodily. He explains hurriedly in Afrikaans that he needs the room, that I, Mr Shenton's daughter from England, feel faint.

She puts on her shoes and from her apron pocket takes a key which she throws at him. She walks off without a word towards the house.

There is a single bed with a candy-striped cotton cover against the far wall. A door leading into a cramped lavatory stands ajar. He is familiar with this room. He takes a plastic mug from the cupboard, fills it with water and passes it to me. I drink greedily. The bed is soft. My body sinks into it and I drift off to a faint lullaby of rain dripping from a beam.

Kitty miaows plantively but darkness falls, and I am drawn into, dwindle, in the dark pupils narrowing to night.

When I come to he is on the floor, hurriedly replacing the spilled contents of his bag. I note a revolver, a map and a hipflask.

'You were out cold for a couple of minutes,' he says.

'What,' I ask, 'do you need a revolver for?'

I do not expect a reply, but he answers earnestly, 'In the bush there's a war going on that you know nothing of, that no newspaper will tell you about.'

'I know,' and I look out at the bougainvillea pressing against the window. He says pleasantly, 'Surprising that you lose your resistance to the heat so soon. Only ten years you've been away, actually eleven in January.' So he had been checking my movements in those last years when I had neither seen him nor thought about him. He waits in vain for me to betray my surprise before he continues, 'Tell me about the green and pleasant land.'

I reel off the words. 'In autumn the trees lose their leaves so that camouflage gear would be as conspicuous as party dress. I collect leaves from Sherwood forest, beech, oak, bracken, and soak them in glycerine.'

His first smile, wry. 'Why?' he asks.

'To heighten the colour, preserve them, before pressing for ornamental use.'

It is true that I once pressed some leaves but then I did not know about the preserving qualities of glycerine. I found the leaves months later in the Yellow Pages but the urgency of my search for a plumber made me drop them and they crushed under my feet.

'Hm,' he says, 'your breasts are as lovely as they were fifteen years ago.'

Propped up on my right elbow, my blouse has slipped

down that shoulder. The top button has come undone and
what can be seen of my breasts is moulded to their
advantage by the supporting pillow. I sit up briskly,
appalled by his presumption. But he jumps up to sit next to
me, his hand smoothing the stripes of the fabric between
us. He soothes with his voice.

'I'm sorry. I shouldn't have said that. I've forgotten how
shy you are.'

I see no advantage in pointing out that his regret is
ill-focused; I do not necessarily believe his regret.

His hand moves to my ankle and a finger hovers over a
scratch that I had not noticed before.

'How did it happen?'

I am grateful for the provision of something to focus on.
The scratch is deeper than it appears and I am surprised
that I do not know its origin. I concentrate until the neat
line of dried blood knitted purlwise into the healed flesh
unravels under the insistent movement of his thumb. So
that the blood seeps afresh from the gash. A crisp winter's
morning cracks open to reveal a uniform world encased in
fire-white frost. I pick a sprig of parsley and twirl it between
my fingers. Shit, shit, shit, I shout. I have come to expect
parsley to survive the English winter. I kick the stems of
the plants into the frozen ground, angry as a child.

'Nice morning,' a voice breaks from the neighbouring
rooftop. I look up into the face of a man in white overalls
watching me with a rooftile held in his raised hand. He
grins maliciously. I retreat, back into the hoary hawthorn
hedge. The thorn drags through the flesh of my right ankle
but I press against the untrimmed hedge. The man repeats,
'Nice morning,' then incomprehensibly, 'Gonna get the
kettle on love?' I bolt. I cannot hear what he shouts. Drops
of blood glow for a moment on the grubby kitchen floor

before they disappear into the dirt of the tiles.

'Tell me,' he says again, 'about England.'

His hand has travelled the length of my leg, my thigh. I keep still. I do not understand the source of his confidence. His eyes swivel on stalks as they travel the perimeter of my body. Dark as a reptile's they dart about my still outline, as if following the frantic flight of a trapped fly.

'England,' he says musingly, by way of encouragement, 'sounds green and peaceful.'

'The telly will give you a better idea than I can. Mine will always be the view of a Martian.' He composes his face for pleasantries so that I add, 'I don't want to talk.'

He would like to fuck me without my noticing. I will not allow him that luxury; my cowardice does not stretch to that. Fear seeps into the striped cotton cover crossed by the dark imprint of my sweating body. Somehow, I expect, it will be translated into desire, the assuagement of guilt. I follow his movements carefully. His hand creeps up my thigh. He leans over me and I do not draw away. But he merely wipes the sweat from my forehead. The profusion of sweat unnerves him. Or perhaps it is the urgency of the bulge as he deftly unzips his trousers and flicks out the terrifying thing of which I catch a glimpse only. I relax at his haste and correctly predict that it will not take long. My body registers a fleeting disappointment so that I have every reason to be pleased with the transaction.

He rests his head on my chest for a while before I go to the lavatory to clean up the mess. On the seat I inhale deeply and contract my stomach muscles to expel the stubborn semen. His voice is soft against the crackle of cheap toilet paper. 'Have you seen your friend, Olga?'

'Who?'

'Olga Simson.'

Then I remember. I assume he has done his trousers up, that he is leaning against the wall, toying perhaps with his mirror shades.

Adolescent Olga, who had giggled upon meeting him, said too loudly, 'That's not the Henry who writes those letters?'

'No,' I whispered, 'don't be silly. Would I be writing to a native?' and looked round for the last time into the wounded eyes that had seen it all.

When I come out of the lavatory I look into his mirrors and say briskly, 'No, I lost touch with that set when I started college, long before I even left this country. All that was a long time ago.' I can do no more. I have always miscalculated the currency of sex.

Father stoops over a young peach tree. Its leaves have curled up into stubborn little funnels. He puts down the spray can and beams, 'Just in time for a nice cup of coffee hey.'

The kitchen is hot. The gingham curtains are drawn against the wrath of the afternoon sun. He bangs the gauze door to and asks, 'What does van Zyl say?'

Why does he have to shout? I answer quietly under the clatter of cups and coffeepot. 'Didn't wait in the end. I met this bloke, Henry Hendrikse, you may remember him. He beat me a few times at primary school, came top of the class. Anyway I met him and went for a walk when I got fed up of waiting. Hmm,' I conclude with a cry of delight as he produces a little pot of cream, 'this is heaven.'

'Yes,' he says, 'that boy turned up out of the blue about six months ago and then just disappeared again. People say that he works for the government, that he gets paid a lot of money for being a spy. People talk such blinking nonsense; what would the government need spies for?'

A FAIR EXCHANGE

The wood and tin of the door, held together by nails now brittle with rust, creaked and rattled independently. Skitterboud stepped out in time to see the crest of a blood-red sun buckle the horizon.

'Ooh,' he crowed, 'in a hurry this morning, there's time enough old girl, time enough to do the blue climb today.'

He liked to rise just before the sun. His hands fumbled with the buttonholes of his shirt. The button must have come off in the night and he remembered dimly a hard disc probing his dreams. Or was it the spear of her elbow as her wiry body turned away from him.

'Meid,' he called, 'Meid, the sun's up.'

She clasped her hands behind her head and from the bedclothes followed the slow swell of sun. Now young and fiery, it stuck out its chest to battle against the timid morning. She did not move. Later, when the sun grew pale and quivered with rage, she would not be able to look it in the eye. She knew of a girl in the Kamiesberg who had summoned her eyes to meet the midday sun and something so terrible did she see that no words ever crossed her lips again and the day grew black with thunder. That's how things happen: not blinded but struck dumb. The next day the sun rose as if nothing had gone wrong.

Meid drew the blanket over her head so that the infant
on her right murmured and rolled closer to the smell of
milk. It tugged lazily at the nipple, its eyelids sealed with
sleep. She could hear him outside, still chattering to the
sun, to the chickens that tumbled noisily out of the pen,
coaxing the fire in the cooking shelter with sweet talk.
That was Skitterboud all right with his sweet talk, his
chatter to keep the world smiling.

The child rolled the nipple like a boiled sweet in his
mouth and complained loudly.

'Shsht, shsht,' she said, 'you'll wake the others.' The
trickle of milk had dried up and the child opened an eye to
question the source. She smiled, rubbing the thick matting
of his head.

'I told you it would dry up in the summer. You're a big
boy now, nearly two, you can't go on for ever.' The
uncomprehending eye dropped its shutter and the child
rolled back, bleating. She thought of the lambs in the veld
wagging their tails in vain for milk as their dams stormed off
in irritation. Soon they would find a use for that wagging
after all, use it to fan away the summer flies until their tails
grow heavy with the storage of fat. By then they would
have forgotten the udder.

'Meid, Meid,' he called, 'what can the matter be with
this woman?' as if he could not address her directly
through the reeds of the house. Where the mud had flaked
off the reeds with heat, the smoke crept through the crevices
making her stomach heave. But she sprang out of bed
lightly, slipped on the dress which hung from a nail and
fumbled for her doekie amongst the bedclothes. In the
summer she slept bareheaded but during the day the doekie
kept the sun from burrowing into the thick black hair, from
worrying at her scalp like lice.

He was mending a wooden stool by the fire. The steel triangle stood stoically over the flames and the flat black pot on it sang. By its side the sound of hissing coffee water issued from the round belly of the three-legged pot brooding over the coals.

'Where's the mealiemeal?' he asked. Her hands hung limp and her eyes scanned the veld as she replied, 'Yes I'll get it.' But he jumped up impatiently, 'I'll go and I'll get the children up as well.' He moved like lightning and for a moment her body was kindled by a smile turned inward. Still Skitterboud, and she thought of how she had walked all those days from the Kamiesberg and arrived on this farm on the night of a dance. How rare such days with a reward at the end of the road, when he laid down his guitar and danced. Under the yellow moon the earth breathed gold dust and she the stranger whispered, 'Who is he?' His eyes were on her, Skitterboud, the man of shimmering thighs who spun like a top, his thin legs studded with stars.

She sprinkled a film of yellow mealiemeal on to the steaming circle and watched the boiling centre draw in the flour in greedy spirals, down, down, until the circles grew outward once again.

'You must stir it in,' he said. 'You're in a dream today. There's nothing worse than lumpy mealiepap.'

Pimples of maize lazing in the slush, she could almost feel them captured between tongue and teeth, and her hand flew to her stomach to stem the nausea. He took the spoon from her. Stirring all the while, 'I'll bring you some kambroo from Dipkraal. I saw some in the valley last week; some tubers should be ready by now.'

So he knew. After three children he could not fail to detect that she was with child. The kambroo would steady her stomach.

'Tata, Tata,' the little girl called, 'I want to come to Dipkraal.' He swung her on to his hip and the leather of his face cracked into so wide and relieved a smile that she turned to her brother and from the lofty position chanted, 'Eehee, Eehee, I'm going to Di-ipkraal.' For a moment he thought of taking her. She would cool the hours in the stony hills stretching before him, but the sun was already paling with heat and the day would be very long. So like her mother little Blom, his favoured second born, and he put her down to explain to the coalblack eyes how Baas Karel wanted the sheep rounded up for a count. He, Skitterboud, had not seen the merinos for a few days; they may well have been impounded by Baas Coetzee. Stony hills then miles of red sand to cover, through the knee-high bushes dripping their sticky milk. And nowhere to hide from the sun.

'Boohoo,' she cried, 'boohoo, you took Dapperman to Dipkraal.' He packed the bread and filled the canvas bag with water from the bucket.

'But that was in spring and Dapperman is older and stronger.' He patted her head.

'Yes,' said the steam engine that was Dapperman, puffing energetically, his cheeks blown taut with concentration as he snaked spitefully around her, puffing, puffing through her amplified boohoos. He narrowly missed his mother's clout and leapt deftly over the pressed thornbush wall that formed the circle of the cooking shelter. The little one inside had woken up and his cries fiddled to Blom's boohoos, thickening the morning air, spreading into the vast expanse of open veld around her so that she dug recklessly into the jute sack hanging above their reach for the new enamel plates that she had meant to save for later that day. Pretty plates to catch the tears. What did it matter which set of tears, there would be plenty that day; there would always be snot and tears until the bodies grow strong enough to stifle the sobs and the sun dries up those wells.

'Blom, Blom,' she reprimanded, dishing with her back to them the mealie porridge into the new dish and, turning, saw the scrunched face first slacken then light up with pleasure. Blom's finger circled the white enamel edge around the steaming porridge. 'And white sugar,' she crowed. They waited for Meid to explain these luxuries but her face was locked as she reached for the baby on Skitterboud's knee.

'You should be going.' But he held on to the child; he did not want to go. He would give the little one his porridge today. The child flailed its arms wildly and kicked at the proffered plate. 'No,' it shrieked, 'my dish,' so that the porridge had to be transferred to the old dented tin plate. Now he was happy; he murmured in accompaniment to the beat of the spoon on tin.

'Ooh,' cried Dapperman and Blom together and, laughing, they shoved down the porridge to complete the picture that peeped in brilliant flashes of red and green from the brief paths made by the spoons. And there it was. A full-blown rose and a train painted on the white enamel. Dapperman, the steam engine, puffed and snaked once again around her, she crosslegged with face of bursting rosebud. 'And now my turn,' so that he collapsed, rose head lolling as Blom beat out a train-dust around him. Neither had ever seen a rose or a train. Dapperman said that roses were printed on, no, grew between the carriages.

The dishes had newly arrived in the shop. Last week on the monthly outing to the village she watched the boy stacking them on the counter and she strained to see the colour shifting under the tissue paper in which they were wrapped. The picture leapt out at her from the last plate. In his haste to unpack, the boy had pulled the paper right off.

With her provisions packed carefully in a bag for balancing on her head she held on to the concrete pillar on the stoep of Baas Piet's store. She could not leave. Round and round she swung so that her body stretched like toffee in the heat, wrapped itself around the pillar, wanting what she could not have. It was then that she felt the new life twitch in her belly so that she swung the bag defiantly over her shoulder and went back into the shop. Baas Piet, who had long since despaired of discouraging the farm workers from colonising his stoep, looked eager and read aloud from the back of the plate: Made in China. A rose and a train made so far away in China for her children. She wished that she could take them far, far away. Someone had once told her that Chinese people did not look so unlike them, the Namaquas, except of course for the hair, long straight black hair, smooth as a horse's tail. And Baas Piet? People say that once there were no white people in these parts, that they too came from far, far away, but then she knew that people say all sorts of things as they wait for the purpling hills to swallow up the last of the light. She looked at the Boer as if his face would tell the truth but his eyes were fixed with such intent on the knot she was undoing in her handkerchief that she fumbled with the coin and remembered that he had of course not addressed the Made in China to her.

On that long walk home with the month's mealiemeal swaying on her head she squirmed at her extravagance. Skitterboud would be angry. She tried to be a good wife but there were so many people a woman had to please that she no longer knew what to do. As for the children – and she smiled as she thought of the enamel plates – they had seen neither train nor rose.

Ounooi Annie had a rose bush, right there in the middle of the veld, so that when she arrived at the big white house she had not minded so much after all. That was what a woman had to do. Baas Karel said shortly after she had come to stay that the place for his shepherd's new woman was in Ounooi Annie's kitchen. She knew that that was right, but oh, how she had hoped that Skitterboud's smile and sweet talk would keep her out of that farmhouse so far away from their own pondok.

But as she approached, there was the rose blazing red in the sun so that she smiled as she pored over it, its breath on her cheek until she looked up to see Ounooi Annie smiling at her and yes, she thought, it would not be so bad after all, not so bad surrounded by these pretty things. For the curtains flapping in the window sent their printed pink posies spilling out on to the veld. Ounooi smiled, 'Pretty roses hey! You can look after them if you like.' And she, Magriet, plunged both hands into the rosebush to cup for a second the scented redness so that the Ounooi shrieked, 'Meid, Meid, pasop!' and she watched red blood trickle through her fingers thinking, That is my new name, baptised in blood.

Once her mother had told her of the name Magriet, a flower in the garden of Ounooi Visser whom she worked for until her death. White with a yellow-sun centre. How fervently she had whispered those words to the wind. Seeds, she had been taught at mission school, could travel for miles in the wind and she waited for the stray marguerite to root in the veld. But the wind whistled by in a flurry of dust; the name did not sound real. It was bound to be reclaimed some day. And so she became Meid.

Ounooi was sorry but she had plenty grounds for complaint. Cleanliness was next to godliness and Meid did not clean with the thoroughness expected in a Boer house. She was too often caught dreaming and she neglected even to water the rose. This was true. On the gleaming sideboard in the parlour she lavished all her care on a brass bowl of artificial carnations. She wrapped the cloth tightly around her little finger and, wetting it with spittle, carefully crept into the crevices of the waxy pink petals with their impossibly frilled edges. They made her smile. Whatever will these Boers have next? She could stare for hours into the glass front of the sideboard but best of all were the carnations. She wondered what would happen if she watered them.

Ounooi said to Skitterboud as he waited in the kitchen for his wages and the weekly bottle of wine, 'She's lazy, you'll have to take her away and train her and then perhaps we could try her again some time.' Lowering her voice she added, 'She'll be better, more willing to learn, if you married her. It's not right, you know, even if you Bushmen will not think of God, He doesn't forget you. He looks upon your sins and weeps.'

Meid could swear that Skitterboud wiped away a tear as Ounooi gave details of the document that would console God. She watched him crumple his hat in both hands and dimly did she hear the sound of his tin guitar twang out of tune. She could not remember the excuse she made for going back to the parlour where under their very noses she plucked a plastic carnation from its brass bowl. A ridiculously long stem but she would weave it through her doekie, for a marriage surely meant dressing up as for a dance.

Was it the marriage that brought all the children? God's

blessing? Her girl was to be named after a flower, but a flower she would know, something she could shout to the wind: the Namaqua daisy that breaks out of the stones washed white by winter rain, so that the hills hum with colour in the sun. Just Blom, plain flower, a name that no one could take away from her. She would never take her to the big white house.

She went back from time to time when Ounooi needed her. But as soon as the children filled out with food she lapsed and shamefully disappointed Ounooi whose self-respect could not allow Meid to stay. Not that Meid did not keep her eyes lowered or keep her voice from rising into a question mark, but the tell-tale dust pressed against a white finger trailed along the sideboard; her quiet yes to all Ounooi's questions curdled in the blandness of the mutton bredie she served up – always a few minutes late.

Back home there were the children, hers again, and the patch of mealies she kept alive with buckets of brack water they carried from the river. The cobs were stunted, but in autumn she listened to the tall stalks rustling like paper in the wind. Then the marriage brought another child and she found herself once again standing at Ounooi's back door, her head bowed.

Skitterboud's figure was a black dot in the distance but little Blom still waved. Meid had gathered clothes in bundles and was now ruining a see-through doekie by weaving through the delicate stuff the thick stem of a faded plastic flower. She had not been allowed to wear it on the day of her marriage. Skitterboud said that it was wrong, that the magistrate would know by just looking that it was stolen. She snorted at the memory. The red-nosed man did not even look at them. His pale eyes were fixed at some point above their heads, taking instruction from God. Oh, she had not expected him to smile at them, but how could the sin be put right by Him if he, the intermediary, did not know what they looked like? She knew right from the start that the certificate had no power over her; that it was a useless piece of paper and certainly no match for the tokolos. She knew the tokolos would win in the end. She was the first to see him. On a summer's night when they escaped from the heat of the house and the restless children to lie under a white moon, the stunted figure scuttled by, stared boldly and disappeared into thin air as she screamed. Skitterboud, who fortunately had a full bladder, pissed a wide circle around the house to protect them for the night. It was the very next day that Giel arrived.

The children shrieked with delight and she had to bend down for them to touch the frilled edges of the carnation now faded with age.

'It's horrible like you, like you, like you,' chanted Dapperman at Blom.

'No it's not, it's beautiful,' said Blom, whose voice quivered uncertainly at the dirty pink of years of dust.

And they were off again, wringing each other dry with taunts. She would leave them to fight it out, wait until Blom, ashen with spent rage, should collapse on her for comfort. Meid waited, propped in the shade against the house. Around her the strange damp circles of just-darkened earth crimped at the edges. The tears of the earth, she thought, the stifled tears that rise mistily by night leaving the grey stain of salt. She watched the shafts of heat sucking up the moisture as the shadow of the house was shoved along by the sun. She burrowed a hand into the delicious cool sand. It crumbled through her fingers and fell into an untidy heap. She should not have disturbed this shadow of moisture. But things will happen without your consent just as Giel arrived and things could no longer be the same.

She had heard of him, the smart nephew who worked at a garage in the town. He arrived with wonderful tales which he told after much clearing of the throat as everyone gathered around Oompie Piet's fire in the evenings. Of how he had driven cars, of trains with green leather seats and of three months spent in gaol for a crime which he could not tell about or had not yet ascertained. But when he described the red shirts and khaki shorts of the convicts lined up with their sickles to harvest wheat for Baas van Graan, his eyes blazed with anger. He tugged at the spotted neckerchief and looked into the distance and his eyes scaled the hills and seemed to land in the town from where his words came oven fresh.

He had come to shear, then stayed to plough for Baas Karel – there were not many who had learnt to drive a tractor. One day he returned with a sheep from Baas Karel's flock. It was simple, he said, the sheep had collapsed in the heat and they were hungry.

'Hungry, are we not?' he challenged, but they all remained silent and Skitterboud narrowed his eyes and shook his head and shifted on his haunches saying, 'It isn't right. Baas Karel will shoot every one of us. The sheep are sacred to him.'

Giel looked at him musingly then waved a reckless hand, 'Fuck Baas Karel.' He sharpened a knife on a slab of blue stone and she, Meid, was the first to rise. She held a bucket under the animal's throat and watched the hot blood foam into it. She built a fire; the offal had to be scraped that night. Fat from the roasting ribs spluttered on the coals and with the woodsmoke sent a maddening smell into the night air. No one could resist, and the children asked quietly for more. Later, as she helped him to hang out the meat for drying, their eyes met and clung to the moment. He rubbed his head shyly as if to check that the convict's skull had not reappeared.

Meid rose.

The sand had dried out prematurely with all that raking, leaving the grey stain of salt.

Shit shit shit, she cried into her empty hands. For once the children were quiet, watching her with awe.

Skitterboud's story is yellow with age. It curls without question at the edges. Many years have passed since the events settled into a picture which then was torn in sadness and rage so that now reassembled the cracks remain all too clear. They soften a facial line here and pinch into meanness a gesture elsewhere. A few fragments are irretrievably lost. Or are they? If I pressed even further . . .

Such, however, is my excuse for having constructed this portrait: the original has long since ceased to exist for him; only here is the story given its coherence. I am after all responsible for reassembling the bits released over the days that I sought him out as he moved with the winter sun around the pondok. We shouted above the sound of Boeremusiek crackling from a radio with tired batteries.

I am uneasy. He knows that I am after the rest of the story and there is of course my original reason for seeking him out. I can see no other way of getting through this visit after years away from the place of my birth. The silence of the veld oppresses me. I need dagga. In spite of his crumpled Sunday tie and talk of going to church, I suspect him of rolling a regular dagga pil. On a Saturday afternoon he would strum his tin guitar and beat out a dust outside his pondok with a truly remarkable shudder of the legs and he would sink down, pooped, saying, 'Skitterboud, that's what they call me,' his pupils dilated in narcotic bliss. These legs will go on shimmering for years. But you have to dance on your own these days, no one has time to dance anymore, or makes a decent guitar. I don't know what these Namaquas are coming to.

I do not have the courage to ask about the dagga. I am content with the story.

Today he looks tired. His face is a nicotine brown and pillow-down waves helplessly in his hair. I ought to leave him alone; besides, he is wary and will be on the lookout for leading questions.

We measure the efficiency of our eyes. I am amazed at how well he sees from those slits, banked up with wrinkles and sunken behind the high cheekbones that threaten to pierce through the skin. Yes, he can see the blue megalithic outcrop in the distance and the lone thorn tree on the horizon and the clump on the right which he tells me is a flock of sheep. And then I realise that he knows the veld as he does the lines of his hand; no degree of myopia or astigmatism can blur the topography. He had driven the sheep towards Bloukrans himself; he knows from the position of the sun that they will now be resting in the sparse shade of the dabikwa trees. He does not know how much he actually sees. I hand him my spectacles and his face cracks with surprise. Clearly his vision is improved and he mutters with wonderment as he steps around the house to gaze about the veld. He will not tell me of the things he discovers, of how the veld has aged. Have I ruined it for him? This, he says, tapping at the frames, is just precisely what I want. Then he whips them off and balances on his heels as he tells.

'Those merinos were the death of me. The short-tailed Dorper, that's the sheep for this veld, or even the fat-tailed Afrikaner, but the merino is as wayward as a young woman. No doubt sweating under that hot coat she is always restless, disobedient, leading the others astray. You should see them on shearing day trying to scale the walls like monkeys, even though they like nothing better than losing those heavy expensive coats. Ooh, I may be rickety now, but yes, I was the prize shearer in my day. All of us Septembers of Rooiberg, all the brothers and uncles and cousins, were good shearers, but I was the best, the chief shearer. The Boers would travel miles in their shiny motor cars in search of me.'

He puts on the spectacles and with the right hand shading his eyes he scans the horizon in a pantomime search.

'Did you find the merinos?' I ask.

'Which?' He bores a stick into the ground.

'You know,' I insist, 'the Boer's.'

'Which Boer's?' he repeats stubbornly.

I swallow. I will have to use his term. There is no getting round it.

'Baas Karel's.' And the word Baas drowns in my mouth, flooded with gall. I will not be foxed by him. He is amused by my repugnance at the word Baas. I retaliate with a direct question.

'I mean the day you were asked to round up the sheep for a count. Did you find the merinos?'

He drags the stick to and fro in the dust before he looks up to say, 'Yes, it was a long day. I didn't get home till late, and in my bag the puniest piece of kambroo you have ever seen. It was too dry that spring.'

'And Meid?' I pressed.

'Gone. They had all gone. Filled the buckets with water and left. That night they all slept under Giel's new roof.'

'And she had really said nothing?'

'No, there was no need. But I had hoped. She was a smart one that Meid, nothing could stop her. I think you had better leave these glasses with me. They'll be of greater use here in the veld. If you put your mind to it you could see right over a hill with these, and if that's no good, through the clouds into heaven.'

'No, they've been made specially for my eyes. You should go and see the doctor and get him to make up a pair to suit you. Pensioners get concessions on such things so it shouldn't cost much.'

'I saw Dr van Zyl last year. You know Dr van Zyl, always a joke and a slap on the back. Well, he said to me, "Skittie you need a nose to wear glasses. Next time you'll be asking me to replace your baboon's nose." And that was it. Anyway, I don't have any papers and you need certificates before you're given pension. They say I'm too young, see I move too fast for pension, and the young baas poked about in my mouth and said I had too many teeth left. Now my mamma and tata knew we were there without any papers from a magistrate. They told us to keep away from magistrates, said magistrates bring nothing but trouble. As a young man I thought I knew better, but you should pay heed, my child, to the elders. They know what's right,' and as I snorted he came to the point. 'I see you'll have to leave these with me.'

'It's not that I don't want you to have them, they're just no good to you. It will damage your eyes wearing glasses not specially prescribed for you.'

'But I can see better with them.'

'That's not the point.'

'But it is precisely the point.' He looks at me sympathetically. 'You've been to school for so many years and you still believe everything they tell you. It's those magistrates again, they'll be behind this nonsense for sure. Who can know better than myself whether these glasses are good for me or not?'

'Well, I can't pretend to know better than you do but there are experts who know,' I insist, placing the glasses firmly on my nose.

'Yes,' he says pensively, 'the longer they sit on school benches with chalk and slate, the less they know. Look, I believed all that because they're supposed to be so clever – until I heard what the cleverest man of all had to say. The magistrate. He's supposed to know right from wrong and it was he who said it . . . filth.'

Skitterboud spits vigorously.

'He knows nothing of right and wrong. All those people he locks up, you can be sure they know more than he does. Oh, they think they know so much but they know nothing, nothing. When I take off my hat and say, "Yes Baas, yes my grootbaas," and hold my hat to my chest, I have to squint and chew my cheeks to keep from laughing out loud.'

He mimics in a grave voice: '"Spend your pay carefully, Skitterboud. Here's your bottle of wine, now you won't need any more, and I know you people dance all night but get to church on Sunday, the sheep won't need you then."

'I say, "Yes Baas," and I don't say that no one dances any more, that the young people have left. Ag man, they don't know anything, even with all those important bits of paper. They remember nothing,' and his Afrikaans slows down according to his idea of posh, 'need to peer over their glasses to check their papers all the time. I was afraid of him all right, of the magistrate who married us. And it was

Ounooi's idea when Meid went with the children. She said, "Skittie, you're a legally married man, a respectable Bushman. This is a case for the court. The Baas-magistrate will get the children back, he'll settle this business for you."'

'So it was the children you wanted,' I interrupt.

His tone is defensive. 'You miss the laughing and the crying and the fighting of the children. You don't always notice them when they're there but when they're gone the silence lurks in the corners like a sulking tokolos.'

The stick in his right hand sweeps careful arcs, clearing away the larger pebbles that fly off beyond its range. It is a young Jan Twakkie shoot, pliant, so that he is able to flatten some of its length on the ground and widen the clearing.

'I shouted for them across the veld and Meid leaned over the latched lower door (Giel was flash; he had built a lower and upper door out of old planks) and she said, "Skittie, they won't come. They live here now with me. They'll see you tomorrow, they'll see you every day, but first they must get used to sleeping here." And all the while she was flicking with a nail at one of the panels of the door where old green paint had been flaking off for years, and only at the end of her speech did she look up.'

He grinds his heels into the ground and shifts his haunches as he orders away the face, the burrowing nails.

'Eeh,' he sighs, 'I didn't need glasses in those days,' and he holds out his hand to have another look. I oblige. 'Mine were the best eyes in Namaqualand.' I look dubiously into the faded pupils, dull like old marbles scratched over the years by boys who play rough and cheating games.

'I had,' he insists. 'Never a missing sheep.' But even this route betrays him into the story. 'Except that once when

Baas Karel knew, but I didn't say a word, not a word about Giel.'

Skitterboud wrinkles his nose to adjust the glasses. He is resigned to telling the story. His Namaqua vowels dip sharply, angrily.

'I said to the magistrate – his nose you know had disappeared by then. Funny that was, he ended up with quite a small nose for a white man, but his ears had grown, limp soutslaai leaves that fell from the close-clipped back and sides of his head like those of a freshly shorn merino. I could swear that he wasn't the magistrate but of course he was and anyway I had seen him only the once before, and I said to him, "It's Dapperman and Blom, the baby doesn't count, he's still drinking at his mamma." And as before the magistrate looked up to the back of the courtroom and said in a voice of thunder to the wooden beam, "Magriet September is the lawfully wedded wife of Johannes" (that's my real name) "and has no right to take away with her anything from his house. Everything, from the children to the last scrap of underclothing she is wearing, belongs to him and is his right to retrieve."

'Now yes, at that point I shut my ears and listened no more and when I came out I spat out those words into the hot red sand and watched it sizzle. And there was nothing to do about my shame. I just had to wear it like the tie and jacket I bought from Baas Karel for the court. Everyone knew where I had been that day, the whole of Rooiberg knew of the filthy words of the magistrate. That he should want me to make her undress and keep all her clothes and send her running across to Giel naked under the roasting sun. Well, I shut my door when I got home and didn't go down to Oompie Piet's where a huge fire burned in the shelter and lit the faces of those listening to Oompie Piet's stories. No, I went to sleep on those shameful words.'

'Skittie,' I say, breaking the silence, 'perhaps you had better keep the glasses. I expect they will be more useful to you.'

His face cracks with a cock-a-doodle-doo of laughter so that I jump at the opportunity.

'So you and Meid became good neighbours?'

'Yes,' he replies tersely. 'I stayed in town till the evening and brought back a flagon of wine which I finished behind that closed door. So I found my way over to Giel's house and dragged her out and slapped her once, twice, before Giel stopped me. It was a bitter day of shame for me, but you see when I woke up the next morning in the ditch where Giel had dropped me I knew that under the red eye of the sun we could drink a cup of coffee together. Meid always knew things. She wouldn't have allowed me to hit her if it wasn't for the baby in her belly. She said straight away that it was the fault of the magistrate; that the tokolos lurking about Rooiberg had an uncommonly large nose.'

Skitterboud walks off without further explanation. His chin is raised in recognition of the glasses he wears so that his last words whirl off in a gust of wind. I watch the slight figure lean hare-like as he makes his way across the veld.

ASH ON MY SLEEVE

Desmond is a man who relies on the communicative powers of the handshake. Which renders my hand, a cluster of crushed bones, inert as he takes a step back and nods approvingly while still applying the pressure. He attempts what proves impossible in spite of my decision to co-operate. That is to stand back even further in order to inspect me more thoroughly without releasing my hand. The distance between us cannot be lengthened and I am about to point out this unalterable fact when his smile relaxes into speech.

'Well what a surprise!'

'Yes, what a surprise,' I contribute.

It is of course no longer a surprise. I arranged the meeting two months ago when I wrote to Moira after years of silence between us, and yesterday I telephoned to confirm the visit. And I had met Desmond before, in fact at the same party at which Moira had been struck by the eloquence of his handshake. Then we discussed the role of the Student Representative Council, he, a final year Commerce student, confidently, his voice remaining even as he bent down to tie a shoe-lace. And while I floundered, lost in subordinate clauses, he excused himself with a hurried, 'Back in a moment.' We have not spoken since.

'You're looking wonderful, so youthful. Turning into something of a swan in your middle age hey!'

I had thought it prudent to arrange a one-night stay which would leave me the option of another if things went well. I am a guest in their house; I must not be rude. So I content myself with staring at his jaw where my eyes fortuitously alight on the tell-tale red of an incipient pimple. He releases my hand. He rubs index finger and thumb together, testing an imagined protuberance, and as he gestures me to sit down the left hand briefly brushes the jaw.

It always feels worse than it looks, he will comfort himself, feeling its enormity; say to himself, the tactual never corresponds with the appearance of such a blemish, and dismiss it. I shall allow my eyes at strategic moments to explore his face then settle to revive the gnathic discomfort.

Somewhere at the back of the house Moira's voice has been rising and falling, flashing familiar stills from the past. Will she be as nervous as I am? A door clicks and a voice starts up again, closer, already addressing me, so that the figure develops slowly, fuzzily assumes form before she appears: '. . . to deal with these people and i just had to be rude and say my friend's here, all the way from England, she's waiting . . .'

Standing in the doorway, she shakes her head. 'My God Frieda Shenton, you plaasjapie, is it really you?'

I grin. Will we embrace? Shake hands? My arm hangs foolishly. Then she puts her hands on my shoulders and says, 'It's all my fault. I'm hopeless at writing letters and we moved around so much and what with my hands full with children I lost touch with everyone. But I've thought of you, many a day have I thought of you.'

'Oh nonsense,' I say awkwardly. 'I'm no good at writing letters either. We've both been very bad.'

Her laughter deals swiftly with the layer of dust on that old intimacy but our speech, like the short letters we exchanged, is awkward. We cannot tumble into the present while a decade gapes between us.

Sitting before her I realise what had bothered me yesterday on the telephone when she said, 'Good heavens man I can't believe it . . . Yes of course I've remembered . . . OK, let me pick you up at the station.'

Unease at what I now know to be the voice made me decline. 'No,' I said. 'I'd like to walk, get to see the place. I can't get enough of Cape Town,' I gushed. For her voice is deeper, slowed down eerily like the distortion of a faulty record player. Some would say the voice of a woman speaking evenly, avoiding inflection.

'I bet,' she says, 'you regretted having to walk all that way.'

She is right. The even-numbered houses on the left side of this interminable street are L-shaped with grey asbestos roofs. Their stoeps alternate green, red and black, making spurious claims to individuality. The macadamised street is very black and sticky under the soles, its concrete edge of raised pavement a virgin grey that invites you to scribble something rude, or just anything at all. For all its neat edges, the garden sand spills on to the pavement as if the earth were wriggling in discomfort. It is the pale porous sand of the Cape Flats pushed out over centuries by the Indian Ocean. It does not portend well for the cultivation of prizewinning dahlias.

I was so sure that it was Moira's house. There it was, a black stoep inevitably after the green, the house inadequately fenced off so that the garden sand had been swept along the pavement in delicately waved watermark by the previous afternoon's wind. A child's bucket and spade had been left in the garden and on a mound of sand a jaunty strip of astroturf testified to the untameable. I knocked without checking the number again and felt foolish as the occupier with hands on her hips directed me to the fourth house along.

Moira's is a house like all the others except for the determined effort in the garden. Young trees grow in bonsai uniformity, promising a dense hedge all around for those who are prepared to wait. The fence is efficient. The sand does not escape; it is held by the roots of a brave lawn visibly knitting beneath its coarse blades of grass. Number 288 is swathed in lace curtains. Even the glass-panelled front door has generously ruched lengths of lace between the wooden strips. Dense, so that you could not begin to guess at the outline approaching the door. It was Desmond.

'Goodness me, ten, no twelve years haven't done much to damage you,' Moira says generously.

'Think so Moi,' Desmond adds. 'I think Frieda has a contract with time. Look, she's even developed a waistline,' and his hands hover as if to describe the chimerical curve. There is the possibility that I may be doing him an injustice.

'I suppose it's marriage that's done it for us. Very ageing, and of course the children don't help,' he says.

'It's not a week since I sewed up this cushion. What do the children do with them?' Moira tugs at the loose threads then picks up another cushion to check the stitching.

'See,' Desmond persists, 'a good figure in your youth is no guarantee against childbearing. There are veins and sagging breasts and of course some women get horribly fat; that is if they don't grow thin and haggard.' He looks

sympathetically at Moira. Why does she not spit in his eye? *LOL*
I fix my eye on his jaw so that he says, 'Count yourself lucky
that you've missed the boat.'

Silence. And then we laugh. Under Desmond's stern eye
we lean back in simultaneous laughter that cleaves through
the years to where we sat on our twin beds recounting the
events of our nights out. Stomach-clutching laughter as we
whispered our adventures and decoded for each other the
words grunted by boys through the smoke of the braaivleis.
Or the tears, the stifled sobs of bruised love, quietly, in
order not to disturb her parents. She slept lightly, Moira's
mother, who said that a girl cannot keep the loss of her
virginity a secret, that her very gait proclaims it to the
world and especially to men who will expect favours from
her.

When our laughter subsides Desmond gets a bottle of
whisky from the cabinet of the same oppressively carved
dark wood as the rest of the sitting-room suite.

'Tell Susie to make some tea,' he says.

'It's her afternoon off. Eh . . .' Moira's silence asserts
itself as her own so that we wait and wait until she explains,
'We have a servant. People don't have servants in England,
do they? Not ordinary people, I mean.'

'It's a matter of nomenclature I think. The middle classes
have cleaning ladies, a Mrs Thing, usually quite a
character, whom we pretend to be in awe of. She does for
those of us who are too sensitive or too important or
intelligent to clean up our own mess. We pay a decent
wage, that is for a cleaner, of course, and not to be
compared with our own salaries.'

Moira bends closely over a cushion, then looks up at me
and I recall a photograph of her in an op-art mini-skirt,
dangling very large black and white earrings from delicate

lobes. The face is lifted quizzically at the photographer, almost in disbelief, and her cupped hand is caught in movement perhaps on the way to check the jaunty flick-ups. I cannot remember who took the photograph but at the bottom of the picture I recognise the intrusion of my right foot, a thick ankle growing out of an absurdly delicate high-heeled shoe.

I wish I could fill the ensuing silence with something conciliatory, no something that will erase what I have said, but my trapped thoughts blunder insect-like against a glazed window. I who in this strange house in a new Coloured suburb have just accused and criticised my hostess. She will have seen through the deception of the first-person usage; she will shrink from the self-righteousness of my words and lift her face quizzically at my contempt. I feel the dampness crawl along my hairline. But Moira looks at me serenely while Desmond frowns. Then she moves as if to rise.

'Don't bother with tea on my account,' I say with my eye longingly on the whisky, and carry on in the same breath, 'Are you still in touch with Martin? I wouldn't mind seeing him after all these years.'

Moira's admirers were plentiful and she generously shared with me the benefits of her beauty. At parties young men straightened their jackets and stepped over to ask me to dance. Their cool hands fell on my shoulders, bare and damp with sweat. I glided past the rows of girls waiting to be chosen. So they tested their charm – 'Can I get you a lemonade? Shall we dance again?' – on me the intermediary. In the airless room my limbs obeyed the inexorable sweep of the ballroom dances. But with the wilder Twist or Shake my broad shoulders buckled under a young man's gaze and my feet grew leaden as I waited for the casual enquiry after Moira. Then we would sit out a dance chatting about Moira and the gardenia on my bosom meshed in maddening fragrance our common interest. My hand squeezed in gratitude with a quick goodnight, for there was no question about it: my friendship had to be secured in order to be considered by Moira. Then in the early hours, sitting cross-legged on her bed, we sifted his words and Moira unpinned for me the gardenia, crushed by his fervour, when his cool hand on my shoulder drew me closer, closer in that first held dance.

Young men in Sunday ties and borrowed cars agreed to take me with them on scenic drives along the foot of Table Mountain, or Chapman's Peak where we looked down dizzily at the sea. And I tactfully wandered off licking at a jumbo ice-cream while they practised their kissing, Moira's virginity unassailable. Below, the adult baboons scrambled over the sand dunes and smacked the bald bottoms of their young and the sunlicked waves beckoned at the mermaids on the rocks.

Desmond replies, 'Martin's fallen in love with an AZAPO woman, married her and stopped coming round. Shall we say that he finally lost interest in Moi?'

The whisky in his glass lurches amber as he rolls the stem between his fingers.

'Would you like a Coke?' he asks.

I decline but I long to violate the alcohol taboo for women. 'A girl who drinks is nothing other than a prostitute,' Father said. And there's no such thing as just a little tot because girls get drunk instantly. Then they hitch up their skirts like the servant girls on their days off, caps scrunched into shopping bags, waving their Vaaljapie bottles defiantly. A nice girl's reputation would shatter with a single mouthful of liquor.

'The children are back from their party,' Moira says.

There is a shuffling outside and then they burst in blowing penny whistles and rattling their plastic spoils. Simultaneously they reel off the events of the party and correct each other's versions while the youngest scrambles on to his mother's lap. Moira listens, amused. She interrupts them, 'Look who's here. Say hallo to the auntie. Auntie Frieda's come all the way from England to see you.' They compose their stained faces and shake hands solemnly. Then the youngest bursts into tears and the other two discuss in undertones the legitimacy of his grievance.

'He's tired,' Desmond offers from the depths of his whisky reverie, 'probably eaten too much as well.'

This statement has a history, for Moira throws her head back and laughs and the little boy charges at his father and butts him in the stomach.

'Freddie, we've got a visitor, behave yourself hey,' the eldest admonishes.

I smile at her and get up to answer the persistent knock at the back door which the family seem not to hear. A man in overalls waiting on the doorstep looks at me bewildered but then says soberly, 'For the Missus,' and hands over a bunch of arum lilies which I stick in a pot by the sink. When I turn round Moira stands in the doorway watching me. She interrupts as I start explaining about the man.

'Yes, I'll put it in the children's room.'

I want to say that the pot is not tall enough for the lilies but she takes them off hurriedly, the erect spadices dusting yellow on to the funnelled white leaves. Soon they will droop; I did not have a chance to put water in the pot.

I wait awkwardly in the kitchen and watch a woman walk past the window. No doubt there is a servant's room at the far end of the garden. The man must be the gardener but from the window it is clear that there are no flowers in the garden except for a rampant morning glory that covers the fence. When Moira comes back she prepares grenadilla juice and soda with which we settle around the table. I think of alcohol and say, 'It's a nice kitchen.' It is true that sunlight sifted through the lace curtains softens the electric blue of the melamine worksurfaces But after the formality of the sitting room the clutter of the kitchen comes as a surprise. the sink is grimy and harbours dishes of surely the previous day. The grooved steel band around the table top holds a neat line of grease and dust compound.

'Yes,' she says, 'I like it. The living room is Desmond's. He has no interest in the kitchen.'

And all the while she chops at the parsley, slowly chops it to a pulp. Then beneath the peelings and the spilled contents of brown paperbags she ferrets about until she drags out a comb.

'Where the hell are the bay leaves?' she laughs, and throws the comb across the worksurface. I rise to inspect a curious object on the windowsill from which the light bounces frantically. It is a baby's shoe dipped into a molten alloy, an instant sculpture of brassy brown that records the first wayward steps of a new biped. I tease it in the sunlight, turning it this way and that.

'Strange object,' I say, 'whose is it?'

'Ridiculous hey,' and we laugh in agreement. 'Desmond's idea,' she explains, 'but funnily enough I'm quite attached to that shoe now. It's Carol's, the eldest; you feel so proud of the things your child does. Obvious things, you know, like walking and talking you await anxiously as if they were man's first steps on the moon and you're so absurdly pleased at the child's achievement. And so we ought to be, not proud I suppose, but grateful. I'm back at work, mornings only, at Manenberg, and you should see the township children.

Things haven't changed much, don't you believe that.'

She picks up the shoe.

'Carol's right foot always leaned too far to the right and Desmond felt that that was the shoe to preserve. More character, he said. Ja,' she sighs, 'things were better in those early days. And anyway I didn't mind his kak so much then. But I'd better get on otherwise dinner'll be late.'

I lift the lace curtain and spread out the gathers to reveal a pattern of scallops with their sprays of stylised leaves. The flower man is walking in the shadow of the fence carrying a carrierbag full of books. He does not look at me holding up the nylon lace. I turn to Moira bent over a cheese grater, and with the sepia light of evening streaming in, her face lifts its sadness to me, the nutbrown skin, as if under a magnifying glass, singed translucent and taut across the high cheekbones.

'Moira,' I say, but at that moment she beats the tin grater against the bowl.

So I tug at things, peep, rummage through her kitchen, pick at this and that as if they were buttons to trigger off the mechanism of software that will gush out a neatly printed account of her life. I drop the curtain still held in my limp hand.

'What happened to Michael?' she asks.

'Dunno. There was no point in keeping in touch, not after all that. And there is in any case no such thing as friendship with men.' I surprise myself by adding, 'Mind you, I think quite neutrally about him, even positively at times. The horror of Michael must've been absorbed by the subsequent horror of others. But I don't, thank God, remember their names.'

Moira laughs. 'You must be kinder to men. We have to get on with them.'

'Yes,' I retort, 'but surely not behind their backs.'

'Heavens,' she says, 'we were so blarry stupid and dishonest really. Obsessed with virginity, we imagined we weren't messing about with sex. Suppose that's what we thought sex was all about: breaking a membrane. I expect Michael was as stupid as you. Catholic, wasn't he?'

I do not want to talk about Michael. I am much more curious about Desmond. How did he slip through the net? Desmond scorned the methods of her other suitors and refused to ingratiate himself with me. On her first date Moira came back with a headache, bristling with secrecy no doubt sworn beneath his parted lips. We did not laugh at the way he pontificated, his hands held gravely together as in prayer to prevent interruptions. Desmond left Cape Town at the end of that year and I had in the meantime met Michael.

There was the night on the bench under the loquat tree when we ate the tasteless little fruits and spat glossy pips over the fence. Moira's fingers drummed the folder on her lap.

'Here,' she said in a strange voice, 'are the letters. You should just read this, today's.'

I tugged at the branch just above my head so that it rustled in the dark and overripe loquats fell plop to the ground.

'No, not his letters, that wouldn't be right,' I said. And my memory skimmed the pages of Michael's letters. Love, holy love that made the remembered words dance on that lined foolscap infused with his smell. I could not, would not, share the first man to love me.

'Is he getting on OK in Durban?' I asked.

'Yes, I expect he still has many friends there. I'm going up just after the finals and then perhaps he'll come back to

Cape Town. Let's see if we can spit two pips together and hit the fence at the same time.'

So we sat in the dark, between swotting sessions, under the tree with yellow loquats lustrous in the black leaves. Perhaps she mimicked his Durban voice, waiting for me to take up the routine of friendly mockery. I try in vain to summon it all. I cannot separate the tangled strands of conversation or remembered letters. Was it then, in my Durban accent, that I replied with Michael's views about the permanence and sanctity of marriage?

'Ja-ja-ja,' Moira sighs, pulling out a chair. And turning again to check a pot on the stove, her neck is unbecomingly twisted, the sinews thrown into relief. How old we have grown since that night under the loquat tree, and I know that there is no point in enquiring after Desmond.

'Do you like living here?' I ask instead.

'It's OK, as good as anything.'

'I was thinking of your parents' home, the house where I stayed. How lovely it was. Everything's so new here. Don't you find it strange?'

'Ag Frieda, but we're so new, don't we belong in estates like this? Coloureds haven't been around for that long, perhaps that's why we stray. Just think, in our teens we wanted to be white, now we want to be full-blooded Africans. We've never wanted to be ourselves and that's why we stray . . . across the continent, across the oceans and even here, right into the Tricameral Parliament, playing into their hands. Actually,' and she looks me straight in the eye, 'it suits me very well to live here.'

Chastened by her reply I drum my fingertips on the table so that she says gently, 'I don't mean to accuse you. At the time I would have done exactly the same. There was little else to do. Still, it's really nice to see you. I hope you'll be able to stay tomorrow.' Her hand burns for a moment on my shoulder.

It is time for dinner. Moira makes a perfunctory attempt at clearing the table, then, defeated by the chaos, she throws a cloth at me.

'Oh God, I'll never be ready by seven.'

I am drawn into the revolving circle of panic: washing down, screwing lids back on to jars, shutting doors on food that will rot long before discovery. Moira has always been hopeless in a kitchen so that there is really no point in my holding up the bag of potatoes enquiringly.

'Oh stick it in there,' and with her foot she deftly kicks open a dank cupboard where moisture tries in vain to escape from foul-smelling cloths. In here the potatoes will grow eyes and long pale etiolated limbs that will push open the creaking door next spring.

Her slow voice does not speed up with the frantic movements; instead, like a tape mangled in a machine, it trips and buzzes, dislocated from the darting sinewy body.

The children watch television. They do not want to eat, except for the youngest who rubs his distended tummy against the table. We stand in silence and listen to the child, 'I'm hungry, really hungry. I could eat and eat.' His black eyes glint with the success of subterfuge and in his pride he tugs at Moira's skirt, 'Can I sit on your knee?' and offers as reward, 'I'll be hungry on your knee, I really will.'

Something explodes in my mouth when Desmond produces a bottle of wine, and I resolve not to look at his chin, not even once.

'I've got something for you girls to celebrate with; you are staying in tonight, aren't you? Frieda, I promise you this is the first Wednesday night in years that Moira's been in.

Nothing, not riots nor disease will keep her away from her Wednesday meetings. Now that women's lib's crept over the equator it would be most unbecoming of me to suspect my wife's commitment to her black-culture group. A worthy affair, affiliated to the UDF you know.' The wine which I drink too fast tingles in my toes and fingertips.

'So how has feminism been received here?' I ask.

'Oh,' he smiles, 'you have to adapt in order to survive. No point in resisting for the sake of it, you have to move with the times . . . but there are some worrying half-baked ideas about . . . muddled women's talk.'

'Actually,' Moira interjects, 'our group has far more pressing matters to deal with.'

'Like?' he barks.

'Like community issues, consciousness raising,' but Desmond snorts and she changes direction. 'Anyway, I doubt whether women's oppression arises as an issue among whites. One of the functions of having servants is to obscure it.'

'Hm,' I say, and narrow my eyes thoughtfully, a stalling trick I've used with varying success. Then I look directly at Desmond so that he refills my glass and takes the opportunity to propose a toast to our reunion. This is hardly less embarrassing than the topic of servants. The wine on my tongue turns musty and mingles with the smell of incense, of weddings and christenings that his empty words resurrect.

Desmond is in a cooperative mood, intent on evoking the halcyon days of the sixties when students sat on the cafeteria steps soaking up the sun. Days of calm and stability, he sighs. He reels off the names of contemporaries. Faces struggle in formation through the fog of the past, rise and recede. Rita Jantjes detained under the Terrorism act. 'The Jantjes of Lansdowne?' I ask.

'It's ridiculous of them to keep Rita. She knows nothing; she's far too emotional, an obvious security risk,' Moira interjects.

'No,' Desmond explains, 'not the Lansdowne Jantjes but the Port Elizabeth branch of the family. The eldest, Sammy, graduated in Science the year before me.'

I am unable to contribute anything else, but he is the perfect host. There are no silent moments. He explains his plans for the garden and defers to my knowledge of succulents. There will be an enormous rockery in the front with the widest possible variety of cacti. A pity, he says, that Moira has planted those horrible trees but he would take over responsibility for the garden, give her a bit more free time, perhaps I didn't know that she has started working again?

Moira makes no effort to contribute to the conversation so diligently made. She murmurs to the little one on her knee whose fat fingers she prevents from exploring her nostrils. They giggle and shh-ssht each other, marking out their orbit of intimacy. Which makes it easier for me to conduct this conversation. Only once does he falter and rub his chin but I avert my eyes and he embarks smoothly on the topic of red wine. I am the perfect guest, a deferential listener. I do not have the faintest interest in the production of wine.

When we finish dinner Desmond gets up briskly. He returns to the living room and the children protest loudly as he switches off the television and puts on music. Something classical and rousing, as if he too is in need of revival.

'Moi,' he shouts above the trombones, 'Moi, the children are tired, they must go to bed. Remember it's school tomorrow.'

'OK,' she shouts back. Then quietly, 'Thursdays are always schooldays. But then Desmond isn't always as sober as I'd like him to be.'

She lifts the sleeping child from her lap on to the bench. We rest our elbows on the table amongst the dirty dishes.

'He gets his drink too cheaply; has shares in an hotel.' Moira explains how the liquor business goes on expanding, how many professional people give up their jobs to become liquor moguls.

'Why are the booze shops called hotels? Who stays in them? Surely there's no call for hotels in a Coloured area?'

'Search me, as we used to say. Nobody stays in them, I'm sure. I imagine they need euphemisms when they know that they grow rich out of other people's misery. Cheap wine means everyone can drown his sorrows at the weekends, and people say that men go into teaching so that they have the afternoons to drink in as well. I swear the only sober man to be found on a Saturday afternoon is the liquor boss. The rest are dronkies, whether they loaf about on street corners in hanggat trousers or whether they slouch in upholstered chairs in front of television sets. And we all know a man of position is not a man unless he can guzzle a bottle or two of spirits. It's not surprising that the Soweto kids of '76 stormed the liquor stores and the shebeens. Not that I'd like to compare the shebeen queen making a miserable cent with the Coloured "elite" as they call themselves who build big houses and drive Mercedes and send their daughters to Europe to find husbands. And those who allow themselves to be bought by the government to sit in Parliament . . .'

She holds her head. 'Jesus, I don't know. Sometimes I'm optimistic and then it's worth fighting, but other times, here in this house, everything seems pointless. Actually that wine's given me a headache.'

I stare into the dirty plate so hard that surely my eyes will drop out and stare back at me. Like two fried eggs, sunny-side-up. Then I take her hand.

'Listen, I know a trick that takes headaches away instantly.' And I squeeze with my thumb and index finger deep into the webbed V formed by the thumb of her outstretched hand. 'See? Give me the other hand. See how it lifts?' Like a child she stares in wonderment at the hand still resting in mine.

The back door bursts open and Tillie rushes in balancing on her palm a curious object, a priapic confection.

'Look,' she shouts, 'look, isn't it lovely? It's the stale loaf I put out for the birds and they've pecked it really pretty.'

The perfectly shaped phallus with the crust as pedestal has been sculpted by a bird's beak. Delicately pecked so that the surface is as smooth as white bread cut with a finely serrated knife. We stare wanly at the child and her find, then we laugh. Tears run down Moira's face as she laughs. When she recovers her voice is stern. 'What are you doing outside at this hour? Don't you know it's ten o'clock? Where's Carol?'

Carol bursts in shouting, 'Do you know what? There are two African men in the playhouse, in our playhouse, and they've got our sleeping bags. Two grown-ups can't sleep in there! And I went to tell Susie but she won't open the door. She spoke to me through the window and she said it's time to go to bed. But there's other people in her room. I heard them. And Susie shouldn't give people my sleeping bag.'

Moira waves her arm at Carol throughout this excited account, her finger across her lips in an attempt to quieten the child.

'Ssht, ssht, for God's sake, ssht,' she hisses. 'Now you are not to prowl around outside at night and you are not to interfere in Susie's affairs. You know people have problems with passes and it's silly to talk about such things. Daddy'll be very cross if he knew that you're still up and messing about outside. I suggest you say nothing to him, nothing at all, and creep to bed as quietly as you can.'

She takes the children by the hands and leads them out of the room. Moments later she returns to carry off the little one sleeping on the bench. I start to clear the table and when she joins me she smiles.

'Aren't children dreadful? They can't be trusted an inch. I clean forgot about them, and they'll do anything not to go to bed. When adults long to get to bed at a reasonable hour which is always earlier than we can manage . . . Of course sleep really becomes a precious commodity when you have children. Broken nights and all that. No,' she laughs, looking me straight in the eye, 'I can't see you ever coping with children.'

The dishes are done. There is a semblance of order which clearly pleases Moira. She looks around the kitchen appreciatively then yawns. 'We must go to bed. Go ahead, use the bathroom first. I'll get the windows and doors shut. Sleep well.'

I have one of the children's bedrooms. For a while I sit on the floor; the little painted chair will not accommodate me, grotesque in the Lilliputian world of the child. Gingerly I lay my clothes across the chair. It is not especially hot, but I open the window. For a while. I lie in my nightdress on the chaste little bed and try to read. The words dance and my eyes sting under heavy lids. But I wait. I stretch my eyes wide open and follow a mad moth circling the rabbit-shaped lamp by the side of the bed. I start to the mesmerising scent of crushed gardenia when the book slips and slips from under my fingers. In this diminutive world it does not fall with a thud. But I am awake once more. I wait.

You've always loved your father better.

That will be her opening line.

The chair she sits in is a curious affair, crude like a crate with armrests. A crate for a large tough-skinned vegetable like hubbard squash which is of course not soft as its name suggests.

I move towards her to adjust the goatskin karos around her shoulders. It has slipped in her attempt to rise out of the chair. I brace myself against the roar of distaste but no, perhaps her chest is too tight to give the words their necessary weight. No, she would rather remove herself from my viperous presence. But the chair is too low and the gnarled hands spread out on the armrests cannot provide enough leverage for the body to rise with dignity. ('She doesn't want to see you,' Aunt Cissie said, biting her lip.)

Her own words are a synchronic feat of syllables and exhalations to produce a halting hiss. 'Take it away. I'll suffocate with heat. You've tried to kill me enough times.' I drop the goatskin on to the ground before realising that it goes on the back of the chair.

I have never thought it unreasonable that she should not want to see me. It is my insistence which is unreasonable. But why, if she is hot, does she sit here in the last of the sun? Her chair stands a good twenty yards from the house, beyond the semi-circle of the grass broom's vigorous expressionistic strokes. From where I stand, having made the predicted entrance through the back gate, she is a painterly arrangement alone on the plain. Her house is on the very edge of the location. Behind her the Matsikamma Range is interrupted by two swollen peaks so that her head rests in the cleavage.

Her chair is uncomfortable without the karos. The wood must cut into the small of her back and she is forced to lean forward, to wriggle. Our eyes meet for a second, accidentally, but she shuts hers instantly so that I hold in my vision the eyes of decades ago. Then they flashed coal-black, the surrounding skin taut across the high cheekbones. Narrow, narrow slits which she forced wide open and like a startled rabbit stared entranced into a mirror as she pushed a wave into the oiled black hair.

'If only,' she lamented, 'if only my eyes were wider I would be quite nice, really nice,' and with a snigger, 'a princess.'

Then she turned on me. 'Poor child. What can a girl do without good looks? Who'll marry you? We'll have to put a peg on your nose.'

And the pearled half moon of her brown fingertip flashed as she stroked appreciatively the curious high bridge of her own nose. Those were the days of the monthly hairwash in the old house. The kitchen humming with pots of water nudging each other on the stove, and afterwards the terrible torments of the comb as she hacked with explorer's determination the path through the tangled undergrowth, set on the discovery of silken tresses. Her own sleek black waves dried admirably, falling into place. Mother.

Now it is thin, scraped back into a limp plait pinned into

a bun. Her shirt is the fashionable cut of this season's muttonleg sleeve and I remember that her favourite garments are saved in a mothballed box. Now and then she would bring something to light, just as fashion tiptoeing out of a dusty cupboard would crack her whip after bowing humbly to the original. How long has she been sitting here in her shirt and ill-matched skirt and the nimbus of anger?

She coughs. With her eyes still closed she says, 'There's Jantjie Bêrend in an enamel jug on the stove. Bring me a cup.'

Not a please and certainly no thank you to follow. The daughter must be reminded of her duty. This is her victory: speaking first, issuing a command.

I hold down the matted Jantjie Bêrend with a fork and pour out the yellowish brew. I do not anticipate the hand thrust out to take the drink so that I come too close and the liquid lurches into the saucer. The dry red earth laps up the offering of spilled infusion which turns into a patch of fresh blood.

'Clumsy like your father. He of course never learned to drink from a cup. Always poured it into a saucer, that's why the Shentons all have lower lips like spouts. From slurping their drinks from saucers. Boerjongens, all of them. My Oupa swore that the English potteries cast their cups with saucers attached so they didn't have to listen to Boers slurping their coffee. Oh, he knew a thing or two, my Oupa. Then your Oupa Shenton had the cheek to call me a Griqua meid.'

Her mouth purses as she hauls up the old grievances for which I have no new palliatives. Instead I pick up the bunch of proteas that I had dropped with my rucksack against the wall. I hand the flowers to her and wonder how I hid my revulsion when Aunt Cissie presented them to me at the airport.

'Welcome home to South Africa.' And in my arms the national blooms rested fondly while she turned to the others, the semi-circle of relatives moving closer. 'From all of us. You see everybody's here to meet the naughty girl.'

'And Eddie,' I exclaimed awkwardly as I recognised the youngest uncle now pot-bellied and grey.

'Ag no man, you didn't play marbles together. Don't come here with disrespectful foreign ways. It's your Uncle Eddie,' Aunt Cissie reprimanded. 'And Eddie,' she added, 'you must find all the children. They'll be running all over the place like chickens.'

'Can the new auntie ride in our car?' asked a little girl tugging at Aunt Cissie's skirt.

'No man, don't be so stupid, she's riding with me and then we all come to my house for something nice to eat. Did your mammie bring some roeties?'

I rubbed the little girl's head but a tough protea had pierced the cellophane and scratched her cheek which she rubbed self-pityingly.

'Come get your baggage now,' and as we waited Aunt Cissie explained. 'Your mother's a funny old girl, you know. She just wouldn't come to the airport and I explained to her the whole family must be there. Doesn't want to have anything to do with us now, don't ask me why, jus turned against us jus like that. Doesn't talk, not that she ever said much, but she said, right there at your father's funeral – pity you couldn't get here in time – well, she said, "Now you can all leave me alone," and when Boeta Danie said, "Ag man sister you musn't talk so, we've all had grief and the Good Lord knows who to take and who to leave," well you wouldn't guess what she said' . . . and Aunt Cissie's eyes roved incredulously about my person as if a good look would offer an explanation . . . 'she said plainly, jus like that, "Danie," jus dropped the Boeta there and then in front of everybody, she said . . . and I don't know how to say it because I've always had a tender place in my heart for your mother, such a lovely shy girl she was . . .'

'Really?' I interrupted. I could not imagine her being described as shy.

'Oh yes, quite shy, a real lady. I remember when your father wrote home to ask for permission to marry, we were so worried. A Griqua girl, you know, and it was such a surprise when he brought your mother, such nice English she spoke and good features and a nice figure also.'

Again her eyes took in my figure so that she was moved to add in parenthesis, 'I'll get you a nice step-in. We get good ones here with the long leg, you know, gives you a nice firm hip-line. You must look after yourself man; you won't get a husband if you let yourself go like this.'

Distracted from her story she leaned over to examine the large ornate label of a bag bobbing by on the moving belt.

'That's not mine,' I said.

'I know. I can mos see it says Mev. H.J.Groenewald,' she retorted. Then, appreciatively as she allowed the bag to carry drunkenly along, 'But that's now something else hey. Very nice. There's nothing wrong in admiring something nice man. I'm not shy and there's no Apartheid at the airport. You spend all that time overseas and you still afraid of Boers.' She shook her head reproachfully.

'I must go to the lavatory,' I announced.

'OK. I'll go with hey.'

And from the next closet her words rose above the sound of abundant pee gushing against the enamel of the bowl, drowning my own failure to produce even a trickle.

'I made a nice pot of beans and samp, not grand of course but something to remind you you're home. Stamp-en-stoot we used to call it on the farm,' and her clear nostalgic laughter vibrated against the bowl.

'Yes,' I shouted, 'funny, but I could actually smell beans and samp hovering just above the petrol fumes in the streets of London.'

I thought of how you walk along worrying about being late, or early, or wondering where to have lunch, when your nose twitches with a teasing smell and you're transported to a place so specific and the power of the smell summons the light of that day when the folds of a dress draped the brick wall and your hands twisted anxiously, Is she my friend, truly my friend?

While Aunt Cissie chattered about how vile London was, a terrible place where people slept under the arches in newspapers and brushed the pigeonshit off their brows in the mornings. Funny how Europeans could sink so low. And the Coloured people from the West Indies just fighting on the streets, killing each other and still wearing their doekies from back home. Really, as if there weren't hairdressers in London. She had seen it all on TV. Through the door I watched the patent-leather shoes shift under the heaving and struggling of flesh packed into corsets.

'Do they show the riots here in South Africa on TV?'

'Ag, don't you start with politics now,' she laughed, 'but I got a new TV you know.'

We opened our doors simultaneously and with the aid of flushing water she drew me back, 'Yes, your father's funeral was a business.'

'What did Mamma say?'

'Man, you mustn't take notice of what she says. I always say that half the time people don't know what they talking about and blood is thicker than water so you jus do your duty hey.'

'Of course Auntie. Doing my duty is precisely why I'm here.' It is not often that I can afford the luxury of telling my family the truth.

'But what did she say?' I persisted.

'She said she didn't want to see you. That you've caused her enough trouble and you shouldn't bother to go up to Namaqualand to see her. And I said, "Yes Hannah it's no way for a daughter to behave but her place is with you now."' Biting her lip she added, 'You mustn't take any notice. I wasn't going to say any of this to you, but seeing that you asked . . . Don't worry man, I'm going with you. We'll drive up tomorrow.'

'I meant what did she say to Uncle Danie?'

'Oh, she said to him, "Danie," jus like that, dropped the Boeta right there in the graveyard in front of everyone, she said, "He's dead now and I'm not your sister so I hope you Shentons will leave me alone." Man, a person don't know what to do.'

Aunt Cissie frowned.

'She was always so nice with us you know, such a sweet person, I jus don't understand, unless . . .' and she tapped her temple, 'unless your father's death jus went to her head. Yes,' she sighed, as I lifted my rucksack from the luggage belt, 'it never rains but pours; still, every cloud has a silver lining,' and so she dipped liberally into her sack of homilies and sowed them across the arc of attentive relatives.

'It's in the ears of the young,' she concluded, 'that these thoughts must sprout.'

She has never seemed more in control than at this moment when she stares deep into the fluffy centres of the proteas on her lap. Then she takes the flowers still in their cellophane wrapping and leans them heads down like a broom against the chair. She allows her hand to fly to the small of her back where the wood cuts.

'Shall I get you a comfortable chair? There's a wicker one by the stove which won't cut into your back like this.'

Her eyes rest on the eaves of the house where a swallow circles anxiously.

'It won't of course look as good here in the red sand amongst the thornbushes,' I persist.

A curt 'No.' But then the loose skin around her eyes creases into lines of suppressed laughter and she levers herself expertly out of the chair.

'No, it won't, but it's getting cool and we should go inside. The chair goes on the stoep,' and her overseer's finger points to the place next to a tub of geraniums. The chair is heavy. It is impossible to carry it without bruising the shins. I struggle along to the unpolished square of red stoep that clearly indicates the permanence of its place, and marvel at the extravagance of her gesture.

She moves busily about the kitchen, bringing from the pantry and out of the oven pots in advanced stages of preparation. Only the peas remain to be shelled but I am not allowed to help.

'So they were all at the airport hey?'

'Not all, I suppose; really I don't know who some of them are. Neighbours for all I know,' I reply guardedly.

'No you wouldn't after all these years. I don't suppose you know the young ones at all; but then they probably weren't there. Have better things to do than hang about airports. Your Aunt Cissie wouldn't have said anything about them . . . Hetty and Cheryl and Willie's Clint. They'll be at the political meetings, all UDF people. Playing with fire, that's what they're doing. Don't care a damn about the expensive education their parents have sacrificed for.'

Her words are the ghostly echo of years ago when I stuffed my plaits into my ears and the sour guilt rose dyspeptically in my throat. I swallow, and pressing my back against the cupboard for support I sneer, 'Such a poor investment children are. No returns, no compound interest, not a cent's worth of gratitude. You'd think gratitude were inversely proportionate to the sacrifice of parents. I can't imagine why people have children.'

She turns from the stove, her hands gripping the handles of a pot, and says slowly, at one with the steam pumping out the truth,

'My mother said it was a mistake when I brought you up to speak English. Said people spoke English just to be disrespectful to their elders, to You and Your them about. And that is precisely what you do. Now you use the very language against me that I've stubbed my tongue on trying to teach you it. No respect! Use your English as a catapult!'

I fear for her wrists but she places the pot back on the stove and keeps her back turned. I will not be drawn into further battle. For years we have shunted between understanding and failure and I the Caliban will always be at fault. While she stirs ponderously, I say, 'My stories are going to be published next month. As a book I mean.'

She sinks into the wicker chair, her face red with steam and rage.

'Stories,' she shouts, 'you call them stories? I wouldn't spend a second gossiping about things like that. Dreary little things in which nothing happens, except . . . except . . .' and it is the unspeakable which makes her shut her eyes for a moment. Then more calmly, 'Cheryl sent me the magazine from Joburg, two, three of them. A disgrace. I'm only grateful that it's not a Cape Town book. Not that one could trust Cheryl to keep anything to herself.'

'But they're only stories. Made up. Everyone knows it's not real, not the truth.'

'But you've used the real. If I can recognise places and people, so can others, and if you want to play around like that why don't you have the courage to tell the whole truth? Ask me for stories with neat endings and you won't have to invent my death. What do you know about things, about people, this place where you were born? About your ancestors who roamed these hills? You left. Remember?' She drops her head and her voice is barely audible.

'To write from under your mother's skirts, to shout at the world that it's all right to kill God's unborn child! You've killed me over and over so it was quite unnecessary to invent my death. Do people ever do anything decent with their education?'

Slumped in her chair she ignores the smell of burning food so that I rescue the potatoes and baste the meat.

'We must eat,' she sighs. 'Tomorrow will be exhausting. What did you have at Cissie's last night?'

'Bobotie and sweet potato and stamp-en-stoot. They were trying to watch the television at the same time so I had the watermelon virtually to myself.'

She jumps up to take the wooden spoon from me. We eat in silence the mutton and sousboontjies until she says that she managed to save some prickly pears. I cannot tell whether her voice is tinged with bitterness or pride at her resourcefulness. She has slowed down the ripening by shading the fruit with castor-oil leaves, floppy hats on the warts of great bristling blades. The flesh is nevertheless the colour of burnt earth, a searing sweetness that melts immediately so that the pips are left swirling like gravel in my mouth. I have forgotten how to peel the fruit without perforating my fingers with invisible thorns.

Mamma watches me eat, her own knife and fork long since resting sedately on the plate of opaque white glass. Her finger taps the posy of pink roses on the clean rim and I am reminded of the modesty of her portion.

'Tomorrow,' she announces, 'we'll go on a trip to the Gifberge.'

I swallow the mouthful of pips and she says anxiously, 'You can drive, can't you?' Her eyes are fixed on me, ready to counter the lie that will attempt to thwart her and I think wearily of the long flight, the terrible drive from Cape Town in the heat.

'Can't we go on Thursday? I'd like to spend a whole day in the house with the blinds drawn against the sun, reading the *Cape Times*.'

'Plenty of time for that. No, we must go tomorrow. Your father promised, for years he promised, but I suppose he was scared of the pass. Men can't admit that sort of thing, scared of driving in the mountains, but he wouldn't teach me to drive. Always said my chest wasn't good enough. As if you need good lungs to drive.'

'And in this heat?'

'Don't be silly, child, it's autumn and in the mountains it'll be cool. Come,' she says, taking my arm, and from the stoep traces with her finger the line along the Matsikamma Range until the first deep fold. 'Just there you see, where the mountains step back a bit, just there in that kloof the road goes up.'

Maskam's friendly slope stops halfway, then the flat top rises perpendicularly into a violet sky. I cannot imagine little men hanging pegged and roped to its sheer sides.

'They say there are proteas on the mountain.'

'No,' I counter, 'it's too dry. You only find proteas in the Cape Peninsula.'

'Nonsense,' she says scornfully, 'you don't know everything about this place.'

'Ag, I don't care about this country; I hate it.'

Sent to bed, I draw the curtains against huge stars burning into the night.

'Don't turn your light on, there'll be mosquitoes tonight,' she advises.

My dreams are of a wintry English garden where a sprinkling of snow lies like insecticide over the stubbles of dead shrub. I watch a flashing of red through the wooden fence as my neighbour moves along her washing line pegging out the nappies. I want to call to her that it's snowing, that she's wasting her time, but the slats of wood fit closely together and I cannot catch at the red of her skirt. I comfort myself with the thought that it might not be snowing in her garden.

Curtains rattle and part and I am lost, hopelessly tossed in a sharp first light that washes me across the bed to where the smell of coffee anchors me to the spectre of Mamma in a pale dressing gown from the past. Cream, once primrose seersucker, and I put out my hand to clutch at the fabric but fold it over a saucer-sized biscuit instead. Her voice prises open the sleep seal of my eyes.

'We'll go soon and have a late breakfast on the mountain. Have another biscuit,' she insists.

At Van Rhynsdorp we stop at the store and she exclaims appreciatively at the improved window dressing. The wooden shelves in the window have freshly been covered with various bits of patterned fablon on which oil lamps, toys and crockery are carefully arranged. On the floor of blue linoleum a huge doll with blonde curls and purple eyes grimaces through the faded yellow cellophane of her box. We are the only customers.

Old Mr Friedland appears not to know who she is. He leans back from the counter, his left thumb hooked in the broad braces while the right hand pats with inexplicable pride the large protruding stomach. His eyes land stealthily, repeatedly, on the wobbly topmost button of his trousers as if to catch the moment when the belly will burst into liberty.

She has filled her basket with muddy tomatoes and takes a cheese from the counter.

'Mr Friedland,' she says in someone else's voice, 'I've got the sheepskins for Mr Friedland in the bakkie. Do . . . er . . . does Mr Friedland want them?'

'Sheepskins?'

His right hand shoots up to fondle his glossy black plumage and at that moment, as anyone could have predicted, at that very moment of neglect, the trouser button twists off and shoots into a tower of tomato cans.

'Shenton's sheepskins.' She identifies herself under cover of the rattling button.

The corvine beak peck-pecks before the words tumble out hastily, 'Yes, yes, they say old Shenton's dead hey? Hardworking chap that!' And he shouts into a doorway, 'Tell the boy to get the skins from the blue bakkie outside.'

I beat the man in the white polystyrene hat to it and stumble in with the stiff salted skins which I dump at his fussy directions. The skin mingles with the blue mottled soap to produce an evil smell. Mr Friedland tots up the goods in exchange and I ask for a pencil to make up the outstanding six cents.

'Ugh,' I grunt, as she shuffles excitedly on the already hot plastic seat, her body straining forward to the lure of the mountain, 'How can you bear it?'

'What, what?' She resents being dragged away from her

outing. 'Old Friedland you mean? There are some things you just have to do whether you like it or not. But those people have nothing to do with us. Nothing at all. It will be nice and cool in the mountains.'

As we leave the tarred road we roll up the windows against the dust. The road winds perilously as we ascend and I think sympathetically of Father's alleged fear. In an elbow of the road we look down on to a dwarfed homestead on the plain with a small painted blue pond and a willow lurid against the grey of the veld. Here against the black rock the bushes grow tall, verdant, and we stop in the shadow of a cliff. She bends over the bright feathery foliage to check, yes it is ysterbos, an infallible remedy for kidney disorders, and for something else, but she can't remember other than that the old people treasured their bunches of dried ysterbos.

'So close to home,' she sighs, 'and it is quite another world, a darker, greener world. Look, water!' And we look up into the shaded slope. A fine thread of water trickles down its ancient worn path, down the layered rock. Towards the bottom it spreads and seeps and feeds woman-high reeds where strange red birds dart and rustle.

The road levels off for a mile or so but there are outcroppings of rock all around us.

'Here we must be closer to heaven,' she says. 'Father would've loved it here. What a pity he didn't make it.'

I fail to summon his face flushed with pleasure; it is the stern Sunday face of the deacon that passes before me. She laughs.

'Of course he would only think of the sheep, of how many he could keep on an acre of this green veld.'

We spread out our food on a ledge and rinse the tomatoes in a stone basin. The flask of coffee has been sweetened with condensed milk and the Van Rhynsdorp bread is crumbly with whole grains of wheat. Mamma apologises for no longer baking her own. I notice for the first time a slight limp as she walks, the hips working unevenly against a face of youthful eagerness as we wander off.

'And here,' I concede, 'are the proteas.'

Busy bushes, almost trees, that plump out from the base. We look at the familiar tall chalice of leathery pink and as we move around the bush, deciding, for we must decide now whether the chalice is more attractive than the clenched fist of the imbricated bud, a large whirring insect performs its aerobatics in the branches, distracting, so that we linger and don't know. Then the helicopter leads us further, to the next bush where another type beckons. These are white protea torches glowing out of their silver-leafed branches. The flowers are open, the petals separated to the mould of a cupped hand so that the feathery parts quiver to the light.

'I wonder why the Boers chose the protea as national flower,' I muse, and find myself humming mockingly:

Suikerbossie'k wil jou hê,
Wat sal jou Mamma daarvan sê . . .

She harmonises in a quavering voice.

'Do you remember,' she says, 'how we sang? All the hymns and carols and songs on winter evenings. You never could harmonise.' Then generously she adds, 'Of course there was no one else to sing soprano.'

'I do, I do.'

We laugh at how we held concerts, the three of us practising for weeks as if there would be an audience. The mere idea of public performance turns the tugging condition of loneliness into an exquisite terror. One night at the power of her command the empty room would become a packed auditorium of rustles and whispers. And around the pan of glowing embers the terror thawed as I opened my mouth to sing. With a bow she would offer around the bowl of raisins and walnuts to an audience still sizzling with admiration.

'And now,' she says, 'I suppose you actually go to concerts and theatres?'

'Yes. Sometimes.'

'I can't imagine you in lace and feathers eating walnuts and raisins in the interval. And your hair? What do you do with that bush?'

'Some perfectly sensible people,' I reply, 'pay pounds to turn their sleek hair into precisely such a bushy tangle.'

'But you won't exchange your boskop for all the daisies in Namaqualand! Is that sensible too? And you say you're happy with your hair? Always? Are you really?'

'I think we ought to go. The sun's getting too hot for me.'

'Down there the earth is baking at ninety degrees. You won't find anywhere cooler than here in the mountains.'

We drive in silence along the last of the incline until we reach what must be the top of the Gifberge. The road is flanked by cultivated fields and a column of smoke betrays a hidden farmhouse.

'So they grow things on the mountain?'

'Hmm,' she says pensively, 'someone once told me it was fertile up here, but I had no idea of the farm!'

The bleached mealie stalks have been stripped of their cobs and in spite of the rows lean arthritically in the various directions that pickers have elbowed them. On the other side a crop of pumpkins lies scattered like stones, the foliage long since shrivelled to dust. But the fields stop abruptly where the veld resumes. Here the bushes are shorter and less green than in the pass. The road carries on for two miles until we reach a fence. The gate before us is extravagantly barred; I count thirteen padlocks.

'What a pity,' she says in a restrained voice, 'that we can't get to the edge. We should be able to look down on to the plain, at the strip of irrigated vines along the canal, and the white dorp and even our houses on the hill.'

I do not mind. It is mid-afternoon and the sun is fierce and I am not allowed to complain about the heat. But her face crumples. For her the trip is spoiled. Here, yards from the very edge, the place of her imagination has still not materialised. Nothing will do but the complete reversal of the image of herself in the wicker chair staring into the unattainable blue of the mountain. And now, for one brief moment, to look down from these very heights at the cars crawling along the dust roads, at the diminished people, at where her chair sits empty on the arid plain of Klein Namaqualand.

Oh, she ought to have known, at her age ought not to expect the unattainable ever to be anything other than itself. Her disappointment is unnerving. Like a tigress she paces along the cleared length of fence. She cannot believe its power when the bushes disregard it with such ease. Oblivious roots trespass with impunity and push up their stems on the other side. Branches weave decoratively through the diamond mesh of the wire.

'Why are you so impatient?' she complains. 'Let's have an apple then you won't feel you're wasting your time. You're on holiday, remember.'

I am ashamed of my irritation. In England I have learnt to cringe at the thought of wandering about, hanging about idly. Loitering even on this side of the fence makes me feel like a trespasser. If someone were to question my right to be here . . . I shudder.

She examines the padlocks in turn, as if there were a possibility of picking the locks.

'You could climb over, easy,' she says.

'But I've no desire to.'

'Really? You don't?' She is genuinely surprised that our wishes do not coincide.

'I think I saw an old hut on our way up,' she says as we drive back through the valley. We go slow until she points, there, there, and we stop. It is further from the road than it seems and her steps are so slow that I take her arm. Her fluttering breath alarms me.

It is probably an abandoned shepherd's hut. The reed roof, now reclaimed by birds, has parted in place to let in shafts of light. On the outside the raw brick has been nibbled at by wind and rain so that the pattern of rectangles is no longer discernible. But the building does provide shelter from the sun. Inside, a bush flourishes in the earth floor.

'Is it ghanna?' I ask.

'No, but it's related, I think. Look, the branches are a paler grey, almost feathery. It's Hotnos-kooigoed.'

'You mean Khoi-Khoi-kooigoed.'

'Really, is that the educated name for them? It sounds right doesn't it?' And she repeats Khoi-Khoi-kooigoed, relishing the alliteration.

'No, it's just what they called themselves.'

'Let's try it,' she says, and stumbles out to where the bushes grow in abundance. They lift easily out of the ground and she packs the uprooted bushes with the one indoors to form a cushion. She lies down carefully and mutters about the heat, the fence, the long long day, and I watch her slipping off to sleep. On the shaded side of the hut I pack a few of the bushes together and sink my head into the softness. The heat has drawn out the thymish balm that settles soothingly about my head. I drift into a drugged sleep.

Later I am woken by the sun creeping round on to my legs. Mamma starts out of her sleep when I enter the hut with the remaining coffee.

'You must take up a little white protea bush for my garden,' she says as we walk back to the bakkie.

'If you must,' I retort. 'And then you can hoist the South African flag and sing "Die Stem."'

'Don't be silly; it's not the same thing at all. You who're so clever ought to know that proteas belong to the veld. Only fools and cowards would hand them over to the Boers. Those who put their stamp on things may see in it their own histories and hopes. But a bush is a bush; it doesn't become what people think they inject into it. We know who lived in these mountains when the Europeans were still shivering in their own country. What they think of the veld and its flowers is of no interest to me.'

As we drive back we watch an orange sun plummet behind the hills. Mamma's limp is pronounced as she gets out of the bakkie and hobbles in to put on the kettle. We are hungry. We had not expected to be out all day. The journey has tired her more than she will admit.

I watch the stars in an ink-blue sky. The Milky Way is a smudged white on the dark canvas; the Three Kings flicker, but the Southern Cross drills her four points into the night. I find the long axis and extend it two and a half times, then drop a perpendicular, down on to the tip of the Gifberge, down on to the lights of the Soeterus Winery. Due South.

When I take Mamma a cup of cocoa, I say, 'I wouldn't be surprised if I came back to live in Cape Town again.'

'Is it?' Her eyes nevertheless glow with interest.

'Oh, you won't approve of me here either. Wasted education, playing with dynamite and all that.'

'Ag man, I'm too old to worry about you. But with something to do here at home perhaps you won't need to make up those terrible stories hey?'

G L O S S A R Y

assegai	spear
bakkie	small truck
bobotie	spiced dish of meat and fruit
Boerjongens	country bumpkins
Boeta	addressed respectfully to a brother
boskop	frizzy head of hair
braaivleis	barbecue
brakhond	mongrel dog
bredie	stew
canna	flowering plant
crimplene	inexpensive synthetic fabric
dagga pils	marijuana joint
Dankie Meneer	Thank you, sir
'Die Stem'	Afrikaner national anthem
doekie	headscarf
dominee	minister of the Dutch Reformed Church
donga	ravine
dorp	small town
D.V.	*Deo volente* (Latin), God willing (common pious expression)
Ewe	greeting (Hello)
geelbos	type of bush
gelyk	simultaneously
gemake	made (Afrikaans prefix ge- forming the past tense)

goggas	insects
gorra	well
grenadilla	passion fruit
Hotnos	abbreviation of Hottentots
Hottentots	derogatory name for the Khoi-Khoi Cape aboriginals
Jantjie Bêrend	medicinal herb
kak	shit
kambroo	wild root vegetable
karos	blanket or shawl of animal skin
Khoi-Khoi	Cape aboriginals
klawerjas	card game
kloof	ravine
koeksisters	doughnuts
konfyt	melon preserve
kooigoed	bedding
koppie	small hill
kyk	look
lekker	nice, good
mealie	corn
mebos	dried-apricot confection
meid	girl (derogatory)/servant
melktert	custard tart
miskien	perhaps
moffies	homosexuals (derogatory)
Môre	Good morning
Old Cape Doctor	southeasterly wind
Oom/Oompie	Uncle (respectful form of address)
ounooi	female employer; white madam
oupa	grandpa
ousie	respectful term for older woman
pasop	watch out; be careful
plaasjapie	country bumpkin
platteland	rural areas
pondok/pondokkies	shack/little shacks

roeties	unleavened Indian bread
shebeen	unlicensed drinking place
sies	expression of disgust
skollie	hooligan
Slamse	derogatory term for Muslim
sousboontjies	stewed bean dish
soutslaai	a succulent (ice plant)
stamp-en-stoot	dish of beans and mealies (colloquial)
stoep	a small platform with verandah at the entrance to a building
tokolos	evil mythical creature
Vaaljapie	cheap locally produced white wine
veldskoen	stout shoe made of crude leather
vetkoek	flat bread fried in oil
vygies	a succulent related to the fig
ysterbos	bush, shrub

p. 114: 'Kosie, gebruik jy alweer my tyd om to skinder. Waarom moet julle kaffers tog so skree. So 'n geraas in die hitte gee 'n beskawe mens 'n kopseer.'

'Kosie, don't use my time for your gossiping. Why do you kaffirs have to shout like this. Such a racket in the heat gives a civilised person a headache.'

p. 177: 'Suikerbossie'k wil jou hê/Wat sal jou Mamma daarvan sê . . .'

A popular folk song in which a girl is affectionately called a protea

LITERARY AFTERWORD

I

You Can't Get Lost in Cape Town is remarkable both for its high literary achievement and for its unique status within South African and, indeed, world literature: it is the first book-length work of fiction set in South Africa by a coloured woman writer.[1] Although the book is not autobiographical in any but a superficial sense, the background of the protagonist, Frieda Shenton, is that of her creator, Zoë Wicomb, whose brave imagination has set before us a discomfiting heroine—frank, sometimes amused, often uncertain. Through ten connected stories, Wicomb offers a portrait of her protagonist's coming of age as a coloured woman and as a writer. Race and gender, shaped by the historical complexities of South Africa, profoundly affect Frieda's experiences and perspective, as well as her development as a writer.

This essay explores the unstable nature of Wicomb's narrative and the shifting identities of her characters as it traces Frieda's development from a sharp-eyed child eluding her mother's control to a mature woman capable of re-visioning her mother and her world. The little Frieda whom we first glimpse crouching under a kitchen table is a keen observer, too young perhaps to feel burdened by the weight of history, yet already aware of the politics of class and color that shape her family and community. Frieda-the-writer, wryly refracting her thirty-year-old memories through the lenses of her adult self, never loses touch with the naïve and revealing vision with which her child self once observed the world.

Frieda's world is a violent world, in a violent state of flux, even though violence as such is only glimpsed. The cumulative effects of centuries of oppression mark her from the very year of her birth, 1948, the year that the National Party took power under the slogan of apartheid, the doctrine of a forcibly maintained "apartness" of races. Wicomb's amused interest in the varieties and oddities of her characters' attitudes tempers the inherent grimness of her subject matter. Her mingled tones are evident the title of the first story, "Bowl Like Hole," which calls attention to the twin absurdities of apartheid and the English language. "Bowl" is pronounced like "hole," not like "howl"; and no one howls with grief in this nonetheless deeply painful book.

No one should miss Wicomb's astringent wit. Little Frieda peeking "through the iron crossbars of the table" sees her mother's "two great buttocks" as representing "the opposing worlds she occupied" (4). No child would draw such a comparison, of course; it is the adult narrator who amuses herself with the interpretation, at the same time hinting at the profoundly oppositional nature of life in South Africa. Other early examples of humor are situational, as when Mr. Shenton and the driver battle to open the car door for Mr. Weedon (3); or when Mr. Shenton gamely carries on a two-way conversation by assuming responses from his silent cousin, Jan Klinkies (18); or when Tamieta, at the memorial for the assassinated Prime Minister Hendrik Frensch Verwoerd, listens to the rector's "Ladies and gentlemen" and thinks: "Yes, it is only right that she should be called a lady. And fancy it coming from the rector. Unless he hasn't seen her" (59).[2] Wicomb satirizes such pretensions, but at the same time suggests what lies beneath them—a desire for dignity and recognition in a world that renders most of its inhabitants invisible.

Wicomb also makes sure to alert her readers even before page one to a dominant tone of seriousness. Epigraphs warn that "trouble" lies ahead in this "history of unfashionable families" and signal as well Wicomb's multiple intellectual origins, for she chooses the coloured South African poet Arthur Nortje[3] and the English novelist George Eliot. Like Nortje himself, Wicomb disregards the warning in the second epigraph; she takes us "beyond / . . . the intimate summer light / of England" to the barren landscape of Little (or Klein) Namaqualand. In Eliot's ironic words, these stories about "respectable" people disregard "the tone of good society." On the very first page, we observe a group of children engaged in "unfashionable" activities: they "empt[y] their bowels and bladders" in the bushes or gape with "their fingers plugged into their nostrils."

As the children gaze "with wonder and admiration" at "the magnificence" of Mr. Weedon's Mercedes—representing the routinely exercised power of the minority whites—the adult Frieda, in a characteristic narrative attitude, allows us to understand her characters' perceptions, even as we are distanced from them. Conflicting points of view mark the narrative from the start, as Frieda endeavors to become independent of the debilitating class and social stereotypes, perpetuated by apartheid, that deform coloured vision. The Shentons' belief that their single English ancestor raises them higher than other Afrikaans-speaking coloureds painfully illustrates the internalization of white values. English-speaking Mr. Weedon is, in Mrs. Shenton's whispered words, "a true gentleman," from whom the contemptible Afrikaans-speaking Boers "could learn a few things" (3). The Boers, or Afrikaners, are the whites to hate; and because history made Afrikaans the mother tongue of most coloureds, to speak English is, in part, to defy Afrikaner authority. As noted in the historical introduction, both language and constructions of ethnicity are deeply tied to class. In her regard for the English, Mrs. Shenton is expressing such class distinctions, as we see when she praises "civilised" Mr. Weedon because he employs a "registered Coloured" driver so light-skinned as to appear white (4).

A good deal of Wicomb's wit emerges from slyly contrasting points of view; her skill lies in creating various points of view, while permitting Frieda to move gradually toward increasingly aware and more consistent adult perceptions. As "Bowl Like Hole" proceeds, the narrative expands beyond Frieda's immediate realm, moving beyond the schoolyard and from beneath the kitchen table, to follow Mr. Shenton's and Mr. Weedon's trip to the mines. Wicomb creates Mr. Weedon's point of view—his "deep fear of appearing foolish" before the coloured miners, his awareness of the "disgust" that lies behind their apparent deference—as well as Mr. Shenton's temporizing as he omits translations of Weedon's more foolish comments (7–8). Certainly there is humor in Mr. Shenton's omissions and in the Shentons' puzzlement over the inconsistencies of English pronunciation. The imperfection of their understanding calls into doubt the rightness of any single point of view, including Frieda's.

You Can't Get Lost in Cape Town details Frieda's coming of age, revealing the impact of Frieda's experiences on her maturing consciousness. Part of what is narrated is Frieda's changing perspective; in the course of the book, her own point of view undergoes profound transformations. Wicomb's brilliant command of this shifting narrative ground is revealed in "A Clearing in the Bush" and "A Fair Exchange." "A Clearing in the Bush" alternates between Tamieta's story and Frieda's, illuminating the class differences that separate these two coloured women, both from the country and now both at the university: Tamieta as a canteen worker, Frieda as a student. Tamieta knows Frieda and her "father who drives a motor car" (46)—his material triumph underlining his middle-class status, however uncertain it may be. To Tamieta, Frieda is "the Shenton girl" (48), her social class making her too remote to matter much. To Frieda, Tamieta is barely noticeable, and the story demonstrates the young Frieda's failure of imaginative sympathy. But when the mature Frieda returns from her alienating residence in England with a more developed social consciousness and a more capacious imagination, she listens so well to Skitterboud, an unschooled Griqua shepherd, that she can tell his story and even submit to his reproof. The humility of her submission is another kind of triumph; we learn only toward the end of "A Fair Exchange" that she herself has written this account, and her listening and questions become part of the story.

Throughout *You Can't Get Lost in Cape Town*, as the South African scholar Dorothy Driver writes, "there is rarely a moment at which any one judgment rests without being nudged or more directly interrogated by another."[4] The very title of the book, which draws on a sentence spoken by Frieda's white boyfriend (73), throws out a challenge: to say *you* implies a speaking *I*, and in the title story, Michael's *you* excludes Frieda's *I*. Michael's breezy assurance betrays the fault of white liberalism in South Africa: the dominant minority group controls assertions of "fact," denying the felt experience of the dominated majority. The moment likewise reflects a male dismissal of female experience. Although Frieda is not literally lost, for she does get off the bus at the prearranged spot, she remains lost in a world without clear psychic navigational guides, left to form her own sense of direction by seeking—and questioning—truths.

Wicomb's readers, too, may sometimes feel lost in a book requiring constant reassessment of what they thought they knew. Words like *ambivalence* and *ambiguity* characterize critical writing about Wicomb's work; they also characterize her own fiction and essays. Even the question of genre—a novel? stories?—is difficult to settle. Frieda is the "focal character" in most stories, so the book is indeed, as Wicomb says in an interview with Eva Hunter, "novel-like";[5] yet "the gaps *between* the stories" preclude calling it a novel, for Wicomb has deliberately created what she describes as "chaos on the page" in order to unmask "the camouflage of coherence that socio-political structures are about."[6] Like much other twentieth-century literature that reflects the incoherent quality of history, this postmodern book challenges its readers to make tentative sense out of its gaps and inconsistencies—to search for patterns of meaning in its revisionary fabric and, in doing so, to question our definitions of literature and of "truth."

II

Wicomb's readers will recognize right away that she is out to challenge them, just as she challenges her protagonist, and just as she challenges herself. She shares with her flawed heroine a stubborn independence of mind and a hard-won courage to look steadily at what remains when a "fastidious" God flees humankind (81). The most obvious example of the courage to change one's mind comes at the very end of the book—and for that reason, anyone who relishes surprise should finish the book before reading the present paragraph. We may think we know that Mrs. Shenton dies while Frieda is a child; we may even have admired her widower-father's valiant, if awkward, efforts to raise his motherless child. But the final story challenges and undermines our understanding. Resurrecting a supposedly dead mother, Wicomb forces us to acknowledge that Frieda is a fictional character distinct from Wicomb herself.

Near the end of *You Can't Get Lost in Cape Town*, Mrs. Shenton angrily suggests that because Frieda has "used the real" for some of her details, people will suppose her stories to be autobiography (172). Wicomb has, at times, suffered the same fate at the hand of reviewers and critics. "In a sense," Wicomb has confessed, "I deliberately flirted with autobiography, almost maliciously catching my reviewers out."[7] In reality, as in the book, the process is considerably more complex. Like many writers, Wicomb has "drawn extensively on [her] own experience" for such details as dung-smeared floors, for characters who are "amalgams of various people [she has] known," and for elements of family stories.[8] Born, like Frieda, on the edge of Namaqualand in 1948, Wicomb grew up in a Griqua village with "a little school but no shop," so remote that "there were still old people who spoke the old Khoi language." The men were employed as laborers in the gypsum mines or on farms, the women as domestic servants in nearby towns.[9] Wicomb's parents, like Frieda's, were Afrikaans-speakers who "identified English as a way

out of oppression," her mother encouraging Wicomb
and her brothers to speak in the imported BBC accents of
South African radio newsreaders.[10]

Wicomb, like Frieda, studied English literature at the
Afrikaner-dominated coloured University of the Western
Cape (B.A. 1968) and in 1973 left for exile in Britain.
Enrolling for an honours degree in English at Reading
University (B.A., 1979), she discovered that a graduate
of the University of the Western Cape was worse educated than a student who had completed the college
preparatory course at a British secondary school.[11] During
the next ten years, Wicomb taught in schools and in adult
education, worked in the anti-apartheid movement,
wrote *You Can't Get Lost in Cape Town*, and took a
master's degree in literary linguistics (1989) at Strathclyde
University in Glasgow. Then, in 1991, feeling herself "an
alien in Britain,"[12] she returned to South Africa to teach
at her greatly transformed alma mater. Moving back to
Scotland in 1994, she now teaches in the Department
of English Studies at Strathclyde University. She has
recently completed her second full-length work of fiction,
a novel entitled *David's Story*, forthcoming from The
Feminist Press in fall 2000.

Whether in South Africa or in exile, Wicomb has contributed to the revitalization of South African intellectual
life. She was a founding editor of the *Southern Africa
Review of Books*, a journal initially produced by exiles in
Britain, to which she has contributed reviews and essays.
In trenchant essays, she trains an unflinching eye not only
on the "new" South Africa but also on the inescapable
legacy of the old. One element of her nonfiction relevant
to *You Can't Get Lost in Cape Town* is her feminism.
Wicomb credits "black consciousness" and "feminism"

equally in giving her the courage to write, and she calls herself "a black feminist."[13]

Apartheid has affected not only Wicomb's mind and imagination but also the publication history of *You Can't Get Lost in Cape Town*. When, in 1987, the book first appeared in Britain and the United States, official South African censorship made publication at home impossible, and there is still no South African edition. Despite the work's watershed status as the first book of fiction by a coloured South African woman set in South Africa,[14] critical reception in South Africa has been slow, although certain South African critics, like Driver, have recognized that the book offers "a new mode in South African writing."[15] That the work is written by a coloured woman and features a coloured woman protagonist may, in fact, help to explain the relative lack of notice, as does the date of publication. Annemarié van Niekerk, in her review of the book in the South African journal *Staffrider*, describes how male dominance of South African intellectual life has marginalized black and coloured women writers.[16] In the late 1980s, the final convulsions of the apartheid era produced oppositional reductive binaries described by André Brink as "us and them, black and white, good and bad, male and female."[17] With South African ears deafened by literal and figurative explosions, few could hear Wicomb's quiet complexities. Yet another reason for neglect may be that as an exile, Wicomb was what South Africans call an "outside" writer.

Meanwhile, in the United States, critical reception has been so warm as to disconcert the author herself.[18] Reviewers couched their praise in terms common in Western intellectual response to literature from the so-called

Third World: the book was read not so much as fiction
but as a useful report from an "exotic" land. No doubt, as
Lee Lescaze writes in the *Wall Street Journal*, "Americans
can learn a good deal about South Africa" from this
book,[19] but such benefits are a byproduct rather than the
purpose of reading good literature. Writers like Wicomb
must send their works out to an international readership,[20]
some of whom experience discomfort in encountering the
unfamiliar. This Feminist Press edition seeks to encour-
age a more subtle reading of Wicomb's restrained and oblique
stories, in which even the tiniest detail may hint at the
emotional valences created by apartheid. A homely milk
separator may become an emblem: "Out of the left arm
the startled thin bluish milk spurted, and seconds later
yellow cream trickled confidently from the right" (5).

III

You Can't Get Lost in Cape Town at once encapsulates particular moments of apartheid South Africa and, given the
still-present legacy of apartheid, remains relevant to
the country as it exists today. In both her fiction and her
essays, Wicomb strives to make the reader aware "not
only of power but of the equivocal, the ambiguous,
and the ironic . . . embedded in power."[21] The proper function of literature, as she argues, is to offer the reader "the
experience of discontinuity, ambiguity, [a] violation of
our expectations."[22]

   A country so long riven by multiple and institu-
tionalized divisions cannot reconstitute itself as a unity
simply by adopting a constitution and running democratic elections. As indicated in the historical introduction,
apartheid legislation deprived most South Africans of

benefits of citizenship that are taken for granted in democracies. As a result, until recently, writers from disenfranchised groups have tended to produce "protest" literature aimed at displaying the effects of apartheid upon those excluded from participation in civil society.[23]

By the early 1980s, however, protest literature and the wider anti-apartheid movement had successfully informed the world, freeing the imaginations of post-protest writers like Wicomb and Njabulo Ndebele to offer the subtle details of their "intimate knowledge" in what Ndebele calls a "rediscovery of the ordinary" that will foster "the growth of consciousness."[24] In fact, despite obvious differences in subject matter and perspective, many aspects of Wicomb's stories can be described in the same terms as Ndebele's own: they are, as Lokangaka Losambe notes, "internal and deeply rooted in the daily life of the oppressed,"[25] manifesting, as Ndebele himself writes, a "dialogue with the self" that features "the sobering power of contemplation, of close analysis, and the mature acceptance of failure, weakness, and limitations."[26]

For all these similarities, there is a radical difference between Ndebele's subject matter and Wicomb's—differences stemming from Ndebele's black identity and Wicomb's coloured identity. While the characters in works by Ndebele and other black contemporaries strive to recuperate black collective history, Wicomb's characters find their "roots in shame" about coloured historical origins in miscegenation and slavery.[27] From these roots grew "coloured complicity" in hiding their "Xhosa, Indonesian, East African, or Khoi origins," as well as their enslavement.[28] This led in turn to a shameful coloured "history of collaboration with Apartheid."[29] The effect of Wicomb's work is to condemn this complicity by coloured

people, especially those with more education and power.
But she is not without compassion for the characters who
seek a modicum of power and "respectability" at the
expense of blacks and "inferior" coloureds; the trap
they have fallen into is one set by apartheid.

In "Shame and Identity," Wicomb signals her own complex attitude: she uses *our* to characterize coloured
complicity with apartheid. In so doing, she asserts
imaginative sympathy with attitudes that she con-
demns intellectually—sympathy in its root meaning
of "suffering with." Such sympathy is the essential
ground of her ability to imagine, without condemning,
Skitterboud's obedience to his "baas" (master) and
Tamieta's baffled presence at the memorial for Verwoerd.
The adult Frieda who narrates the book recognizes her
student self as too limited to perceive Tamieta as *ours*; by
the time she returns from England, *us* and *them* are close
enough for her to hear the rich nuances of Skitterboud's
story.

In *You Can't Get Lost in Cape Town*, Frieda's task is to
work toward an ability to accept *our* rather than *their* as
a pronoun for coloured people—and in the end, her black
compatriots as well. This task requires a humility at
variance with the superiority inculcated by her anglophile
relatives. Frieda's conflict with her mother makes *our* even
more problematic; for, in addition to the expectable
mother-daughter competition, she must contend with a
mother who encapsulates the social snobbery of upward-
striving coloured people. The young Frieda follows her
mother's dictates, but at the same time she uses *they* and
their to distance her own family: she wants to destroy the
"wholeness" of "their stories, whole as the watermelon"
(87). Until the final story, the mother stands for every-

thing that the adult Frieda reviles, teaching her child what Judith L. Raiskin has described as "English and the cosmetics of self-hatred."[30]

Wicomb has a surprise in store for readers who think they have sorted out *our* and *their* and *my*, who think they know the mother depicted in "Bowl Like Hole" and "Behind the Bougainvillea." When Mrs. Shenton apparently dies of respiratory illness, and Little Namaqualand offers the child no alternative female role models of appropriate education and status, Frieda must depend on her father's judgment. Echoing her mother's insistence on rising above her station, Mr. Shenton presses his daughter to leave home and further her education: "'You must, Friedatjie, you must. There is no high school for us here and you don't want to be a servant. How would you like to peg out madam's washing and hear the train you once refused to go on rumble by?'"(24). Ensuring Frieda against sexual advances that might compromise her future, Mr. Shenton stuffs her with delicacies "marbled" with fat; compliant, she "eat[s] everything he offers" (24). Small wonder that Frieda-the-writer kills him off in the same story, "A Trip to the Gifberge," in which she takes a drive with her newly appreciated mother, tracing a route laid out—but never taken—by the father.

The final story suggests that knowledge of Griqua history may help an unashamed Frieda to identify in the future with the plight of coloured people, and even identify with black resistance. Shame has driven both her exile and her return to face her mother's challenge to embrace her people's history. Such an embrace, as the historical introduction explains, was made possible by the Black Consciousness movement, which took place during Frieda's years in England and which enabled

the renewed alliance across racial lines represented by
the United Democratic Front.[31] Coloured intellectuals
like Nortje and Wicomb could find encouragement in
the view of black intellectuals like Ndebele that "history will always clean your soul," as a wise uncle tells his
nephew in one of Ndebele's stories.[32] The prerequisite
for such a cleansing exists in Wicomb's unblinkered vision.
If coloured South Africans accept their own "multiple
belongings" with pride, Wicomb proposes in "Shame and
Identity," their shame will dissipate.[33]

IV

In tracing the story of Frieda's development, which
she tells both pitilessly and sympathetically, Wicomb shows
how deeply Frieda has been affected by her inescapable
heritage of race, class, and gender. Equally important,
Wicomb explores Frieda's choices: her choice to leave
and return to South Africa, her choice to become a writer.
It is the adult Frieda, a writer, who narrates the story of
her own development and who, in contrast with Wicomb
herself, publishes her stories in magazines before assem-
bling them into the book that we read (written, of
course, by Wicomb). In the first six stories, up to her departure for England, the writer-to-be at once yearns for
self-expression in words and rejects them as "mere escape"
or, worse, as "betraying or making a fool of me" so that
she cannot "ever tell" the horror she has seen (103, 98,
103)—the horror reflected in the very stories that we are
reading. Frieda-the-writer speaks the unspeakable in
stories superseding while incorporating the sad ano-
dynes of family stories that "have come to replace the
world" (87). By using the first person, "writ[ing] from under

[her] mother's skirts" (172), Frieda refuses "to be nice" and use the third person, a requirement that has so often silenced black South African women.[34] Frieda, and Wicomb behind her, invades what Brink calls those "territories of historical consciousness silenced by the power establishments" and their collaborators.[35]

Frieda pays a heavy cost in self-conscious misery for her awareness of issues of gender. She knows exactly what is meant when her father talks of resmearing the dusty floors: "he meant I should, since I am a girl" (18). She also knows that she "should be pleased" that she is "not the kind of girl whom boys look at" (21); but boys whistle at her anyhow. Mr. Shenton warns Frieda that servant-hood is the fate of the uneducated; but for educated women there are subtler forms of servitude. While the educated Moira, whom boys do look at, isn't a servant in the literal sense, she suffers confinement as the subservient wife of a man of inferior mind.

Earlier in the book, in the 1960s, Frieda's fellow students endorse the argument, openly scorned by Wicomb in her critical writing, that "the gender issue ought to be subsumed by the national liberation struggle."[36] As the male students huddle in the back of the cafeteria, planning the boycott of the memorial service for Verwoerd and whistling at the women,[37] they assume (justifiably) that they can exclude the women from the conversation and still obtain their compliance (49–55). Wicomb's explicitly feminist rejection of such behavior in an essay published three years after *You Can't Get Lost in Cape Town* is already implicit in her fiction: "I can think of no reason," she writes in "To Hear the Variety of Discourses," "why black patriarchy should not be challenged alongside the fight against apartheid."[38]

Wicomb's independence of mind regarding gender par-
allels her rejection of coloured timidity and acquiescence.
Frieda belongs to a racial category whose ambivalence
has often led to denial and self-betrayal. Frieda fears that
she will be "drawn into the kraal of complicity" (114)
and led to defend the "play-white" behavior that she
abhors (4).

But it will take time for Frieda to assert her independence from dominant racial and gender definitions. In "A
Clearing in the Bush," Frieda self-consciously "tug[s] at
the crinkly hairshaft" of her "otherwise perfectly straight"
hair (49)—hair texture being a potent racial and political signifier—and struggles to write an essay on Thomas
Hardy's *Tess of the D'Urbervilles*. But she fails to summon
up the moral or intellectual strength to contest her
professor's condemnation of Tess. Attracted to Tess's affir-
mation of her own moral code in the face of a hostile and
denigrating society, and warmed by the "amiable hum"
of coloured cafeteria workers, Frieda "wantonly move[s]
toward exonerating Tess" (48–49), but she cannot (yet)
write subversively. In the end, Frieda's essay parrots the
Afrikaner professor, Retief, who in turn parrots material that he has received from the University of South Africa.
By echoing Retief's party line, Frieda has "branded
[Tess] guilty and betrayed [her] once more" (56). She com-
mits this intellectual betrayal—of herself as well as of
Tess—at a significant moment in contemporary South
African history, on the day after Verwoerd's assassination.
Equally impure, Frieda's motive for observing the boy-
cott of the memorial service is to gain time to write her
overdue essay on Tess.

Frieda's relationship with Michael, a highly unusual
contravention of both custom and law, signals her capac-

ity for social and political rebellion—a capacity barely
realized while she remains in South Africa. On one of
her "stolen" days with Michael, they go to "Cape Point,
where the oceans meet and part. . . . fighting for their separate identities" (75). Out of this emblem of South
African race relations Frieda writes a cliché-ridden
poem "about warriors charging out of the sea, assegais
gleaming in the sun, the beat of tom-toms riding the waters"
(75–76). Resembling an exoticizing movie, the poem that
"did not even make sense to me [Frieda]" (76) is patron-
izingly admired by Michael as if it were an art film. In
the end, they can neither understand nor liberate one
another, and the relationship ends painfully, with Frieda's
abortion.

Several years later, recognizing that she must literally go far in order to achieve self-understanding and
self-expression, Frieda resolves to emigrate, despite her
family's disapproval. In the ironically titled departure narrative, "Home Sweet Home," she mocks the family
icons and tells two stories that she must conceal from her
family. The story about a mule caught in quicksand con-
nects with the social and political themes of the book.
Under the pretext of a sentimental visit to the landscape
of her childhood, Frieda leaves the family gathering in
order to escape their words of self-betrayal and complicity.
Her protective father, warning predictably against puff
adders, is oblivious to the impalpable sociopolitical
danger symbolized by the quicksand that fatally sucks in
the unwary. The story ends with a terrifying emblem of
a sterile people doomed by its inability to resist. Its
hind legs sinking into the quicksand, the mule brays, struggles, and then

balances on its hind legs like an ill-trained circus
animal, the front raised, the belly flashing white as it
staggers in a grotesque dance. When the hind legs plummet deep into the sand, the front drops in search of equilibrium. Then, holding its head high, the animal
remains quite still as it sinks. (103)

The dignified acquiescence of the mule as it dies
vainly seeking equilibrium suggests the attitude of
Frieda's family and the reason for her exile. She must distance herself from their acceptance of the fate imposed
by South African history. She also leaves to escape the
apocalypse hinted at in the changed landscape, for she
is wrong to think that "in the veld you can always find
your way home" (73). Instead of "landmarks blaz[ing]
their permanence" (73), she discovers a landscape altered
by a tumultuous flood "more forceful than anything I'd
ever known as a child" (92). The new landscape bespeaks
horror: the "swirling" flood of black rage that will alter
the South African political landscape beyond recognition.

During the twelve years of Frieda's exile, which conclude in the mid-1980s,[39] that rage has expressed itself.
In the interim, Frieda has felt like "a Martian" in
England, where the view from her window shows not
Hardyesque "bright green meadows" but "lurid yellow of
oil-seed rape sag[ging] like sails under squalls of rain"
(123, 90, 112).[40] Back in a South Africa tense with
black resistance, Frieda is ready both to speak the
unspeakable and to see with a new clarity of vision.

A healing of the wounds of apartheid depends on vision,
and it is with literal, as well as figurative, vision that "A
Fair Exchange" begins and ends. At the beginning, Meid
remembers a girl who was "not blinded but struck

dumb" when she looked defiantly at the midday sun (125). Wicomb hints at, then spares Frieda such a fate: defiance punished not by lack of vision but by lack of words to express the nearly unspeakable pain that she observes. The final section reveals that Frieda has written the illiterate Skitterboud's story, illustrating a type of representation common in societies in which many people are not literate. Frieda gives Skitterboud her glasses, and he gives Frieda his story: it is "a fair exchange." If Frieda can retain Skitterboud's lesson that he knows more than "experts" (140), she will be worthy of writing his "terrible stories" (182).

To prepare Frieda for Skitterboud's story, an ambiguous image of glasses appears in the preceding story, "Behind the Bougainvillea." As she sits outside in the dust—her position disproving the figuratively blind Mr. Shenton's assurance that the newly "civilised" Boers permit coloured patients in the doctor's waiting room (105)—she sees her own face, "bleached by an English autumn," reflected in the "round mirror" of a fellow patient's dark glasses (111). She averts her gaze and buries herself in a novel, finding not escape but "shame" in the English author's racism. Soon after she complicates her own position further by submitting sexually to the "stranger" of the dark glasses, having recognized him as Henry Hendrikse, a friend of her youth turned either revolutionary or government spy. The unresolved contradiction baffles the reader, who does at least know that he is the very same Henry whom her father had reviled years ago as "almost pure kaffir" (116). Perhaps inspired by his African darkness, he has learned to speak Xhosa, which Frieda mistakes for Zulu.

Frieda is too newly returned, too out of touch with

changes, to figure out Henry's relationship to the apartheid government, whether he is its enemy or its tool. The
deliberate lack of clarity is unsettling, and intentionally
so. Ending the story with Mr. Shenton's naïve question
"[W]hat would the government need spies for?" (124),
Wicomb wants her readers to experience the unspoken
answer with the force of the mental "dynamite" of
Frieda's "terrible stories" (182): this is a government built
on spies and murderers. Frieda's cousins, "all UDF people," need no glasses to see the official cruelties to
which Mr. Shenton is blind (170). By the time the
book closes, Frieda is on the verge of her cousins' insight.

Frieda sees many things with new insight, nothing
more so than her own mother. She brings her mother the
same bunch of proteas, the official South African national flower, that her aunt has presented at the airport as a
welcome-home gift, provoking Frieda's "revulsion"
(165). Staring down at the proteas, the mother "has never
seemed more in control," and we remember why Frieda
has had to escape. Now, however, she receives the proteas and "leans them heads down like a broom against
the chair" (169–70).

In "A Trip to the Gifberge," the mother, though still
at times harsh, is different from the rigid, censorious woman
whom Frieda has "killed" in her stories. Whereas in
earlier stories Mrs. Shenton kowtows to the Englishness
in her husband's family, now she burns with long-
remembered anger at the contemptuous epithet "Griqua
meid" (165) bestowed by her father-in-law. Can this be
the mother who disparages little Frieda as a "tame
Griqua" (9)? The mother has Griqua eyes and cheekbones
that contest the "curious high bridge" of her nose that
is her European heritage (164). At the end, mother

and daughter acknowledge with pride their Griqua fore-
bears who inhabited the interior of the Cape when the
Dutch pushed northward in the eighteenth century.

Mrs. Shenton becomes a thematic vehicle for Wicomb's
view of South Africa as she and Frieda travel up into the
mountains, reclaiming both land and ancestry, in a
journey that mockingly emulates the Griqua trek over
the Drakensberg in 1861. When she disputes Frieda's arro-
gant doubt that proteas grow in the mountains, she is
proven right. Her plan to take a bush back for her garden provokes predictable scorn in Frieda: "'If you must,'
I retort. 'And then you can hoist the South African flag
and sing "Die Stem"'" (181).[41] Mrs. Shenton lays claim
to her Griqua heritage, to the land and to the proteas,
with a comprehensive vision that silences Frieda:

> "You who're so clever ought to know that proteas
> belong to the veld. Only fools and cowards would
> hand them over to the Boers. Those who put their stamp
> on things may see in it their own histories and hopes.
> But a bush is a bush; it doesn't become what people think
> they inject in it. We know who lived in these moun-
> tains when the Europeans were still shivering in their
> own country. What they think of the veld and its
> flowers is of no interest to me." (181)

Arguing for the priority and neutrality of nature, and asserting Griqua knowledge of the land, the mother again
surprises us; once an Anglophile, she now finds European
models irrelevant. And Frieda—acknowledging her
"ancestors who roamed these hills" (172), having told her
"terrible stories" (182)—moves toward a closer understanding of her roots.

Returning to South Africa after her father's death, Frieda-the-writer finds herself freed from the eager cringing before European authority and the culpable naïveté that have accompanied his loving indulgence of her.[42] By the end of the book, Frieda feels that there might be a space for her in Cape Town, where—through writing—she would continue "playing with dynamite" (182). When the narrative ends with Frieda's mother's question, " But with something to do here at home perhaps you won't need to make up those terrible stories hey?'"(182), the effect is both rhetorical and ironic. For in bringing forth her brave heroine and in depicting her struggle to find her place as a coloured woman and a writer, Wicomb has paved the way for more stories to be told.

Carol Sicherman
Pleasantville, New York
December 1999

NOTES

This afterword draws, with the kind permission of the publishers, on two of my previously published essays: "Zoë Wicomb's *You Can't Get Lost in Cape Town*: The Narrator's Identity," in *Black/White Writing: Essays on South African Literature*, ed. Pauline Fletcher (Lewisburg: Bucknell University Press; London and Toronto: Associated Universities Press, 1993); and "Zoë Wicomb's *You Can't Get Lost in Cape Town*: A New Clean Voice,'" in *Nwanyibu: Womanbeing in African Literature*, ed. Phanuel Akubueze Egejuru and Ketu H. Katrak (Trenton, NJ: Africa World Press, 1997).

1. For the handling of *coloured*, see the historical introduction to this edition, note 1.

2. In the same mingled vein of serious wit, the narrator remarks that "a tapeworm cannot protect me forever" (40). The allusion is to the adventitious reprieve given to her overdue essay by Verwoerd's assassin, who claimed that a tapeworm had urged him to kill the prime minister (see note 37).

3. The first epigraph comes from Nortje's "Waiting"; the second, from "Immigrant" (in his posthumous volume *Dead Roots: Poems* [London: Heinemann, 1973], 90–91 and 92–94 respectively). Just six years older than Wicomb, Nortje attended the University of the Western Cape, went into exile in England and Canada, and committed suicide at twenty-seven (Hans M. Zell, Carol Bundy, and Virginia Coulon, eds., *A New Reader's Guide to African Literature*, 2d ed. [London: Heinemann, 1983], 437–38). See Nortje's two essays about the University of the Western Cape, "The Staff" and "The Students," in *Arthur Nortje and Other Poets*, 23–31, 8–11 (Athlone, South Africa: Congress of South African Writers, 1988). For an analysis of Wicomb's use in "Ash on My Sleeve" of the final line of Nortje's "Waiting" ("the night bulb that reveals ash on my sleeve"), see Sue Marais, "Getting Lost in Cape Town: Spatial and Temporal Dislocation in the South African Short Fiction Cycle," *English in Africa* 22, no. 2 (1995): 29–43, 38–39. Wicomb seems to allude to Nortje in her story "In the Botanic Gardens," in

which the apparent death by suicide of a humble South African mother's brilliant son, Arthur, brings her to Glasgow ("In the Botanic Garden," in *The End of a Regime? An Anthology: Scottish–South African Writing Against Apartheid*, ed. Brian Filling and Susan Stuart, introduction by Emeka Anyaoku, 126–34 [Aberdeen: Aberdeen University Press, 1991]).

4. Dorothy Driver, "Transformation Through Art: Writing, Representation, and Subjectivity in Recent South African Fiction," *World Literature Today* 70, no. 1 (1996): 45–52, 49.

5. Zoë Wicomb, "Zoë Wicomb Interviewed by Eva Hunter—Cape Town, 5 June 1990," in *Between the Lines II: Interviews with Nadine Gordimer, Menán du Plessis, Zoë Wicomb, Lauretta Ngcobo*, ed. Eva Hunter and Craig MacKenzie, 79–96 (Grahamstown: National English Literary Museum, 1993), 80.

6. Ibid., 92.

7. Ibid., 93. Wicomb has explained her "killing" and then resurrecting Mrs. Shenton as an attempt to counter "the stereotypical way in which black women's writing is viewed" as a autobiographical expression of "our need to air our grievances" (private communication between Wicomb and the author, 15 September 1990; similar comments appear in Wicomb, interview with Hunter, 93). Elsewhere, Wicomb has given a different spin to the mother's death, suggesting that "the reason the mother doesn't have an influence is because she is suppressed, she is silenced by the father. Perhaps her reported death in the early stories can be read as her suppression" (interview with Hunter 94–95). See Marais, "Getting Lost," 38, and André Brink, "Reinventing the Real: English South African Fiction Now," *New Contrast* 21, no. 1 (1993): 44–55, 53.

8. Wicomb, interview with Hunter, 93, 84.

9. Ibid., 81, 89.

10. Ibid., 89.

11. Private communication.

12. Wicomb, as quoted in Thulani Davis and Joe Wood, "To Soweto with Love: Black South Africans Respond to the Release of Nelson Mandela," *Voice Literary Supplement*, 20 February 1990: 25–26, 26.

13. See Wicomb, "An Author's Agenda," *Southern African Review of Books* 2, no. 4 (February/May 1990): 24; interview with Hunter, 88.

14. Wicomb finds some common ground with Bessie Head, the only other well-known coloured South African woman writer (whose fiction, however, is set in her adopted country, Botswana); see Wicomb's essays "Shame and Identity: The Case of the Coloured in South Africa," in *Writing South Africa: Literature, Apartheid, and Democracy, 1970–1995*, ed. Derek Attridge and Rosemary Jolly, 91–107 (Cambridge: Cambridge University Press, 1998), 96–97, and "Reading, Writing, and Visual Production in the New South Africa," *Journal of Commonwealth Literature* 30, no. 2 (1995): 1–15, 10–13.

15. Driver, "Transformation," 52.

16. Annemarié van Niekerk, review of *You Can't Get Lost in Cape Town*, *Staffrider* 9, no. 1 (1990): 94–96, 94.

17. André Brink, "Interrogating Silence: New Possibilities Faced by South African Literature," in *Writing South Africa: Literature, Apartheid, and Democracy, 1970–1995*, ed. Derek Attridge and Rosemary Jolly, 14–28 (Cambridge: Cambridge University Press, 1998), 16.

18. Wicomb, interview with Hunter, 84.

19. Lee Lescaze, "Tales Out of South Africa," *Wall Street Journal* 11 May 1987: 25.

20. Wicomb's international audience includes not only those who have read the original text but those who have read translations into other languages—thus far into French, Swedish, German, Dutch, and Italian.

21. Zoë Wicomb, "Culture Beyond Color?" *Transition* 60 (1993): 27–32, 32.

22. Wicomb, "An Author's Agenda," 24.

23. Njabulo Ndebele, whose essays have propelled South African literary redefinitions, identifies the main characteristic of protest writing as "spectacle" that "documents" and "indicts implicitly; . . . it establishes a vast sense of presence without offering intimate knowledge." Protest literature, he adds, privileges "group survival" at the expense of "dreams for love, hope, compassion, newness and justice" (Njabulo Ndebele, *South African Literature and Culture: Rediscovery of the Ordinary*, introduction by Graham Pechey [Manchester and New York: Manchester University Press, 1994], 49–50).

24. Ibid., 58.

25. Lokangaka Losambe, "History and Tradition in the Reconstitution of Black South African Subjectivity: Njabulo Ndebele's Fiction," in *New Writing from Southern Africa: Authors Who Have Become Prominent Since 1980*, ed. Emmanuel Ngara, 76–90 (London: James Currey, 1996), 76.

26. Ndebele, *South African Literature*, 50.

27. Wicomb, "Shame and Identity," 100.

28. Ibid., 96, 100.

29. Zoë Wicomb, "Comment on Return to South Africa" in *Into the Nineties: Post-Colonial Women's Writing*, ed. Anna Rutherford, Lars Jensen, and Shirley Chew, 575–76 (Armidale, New South Wales; Mundelstrup, Denmark; Hebden Bridge, West Yorkshire: Dangaroo Press, 1994), 575.

30. Judith L. Raiskin, *Snow on the Cane Fields: Women's Writing and Creole Subjectivity* (Minneapolis and London: University of Minnesota Press, 1996), 229.

31. The United Democratic Front, a coalition of previously existing organizations against apartheid, was formed in 1983. As indi-

cated in the historical introduction, the Black Consciousness movement led politically active coloureds to refer to themselves as black. After Wicomb's return to South Africa, Brink grouped her with writers who were neither "outside" nor "inside"—"those who were exiled and have returned, bearing in their writing the scars of both experiences" ("Reinventing," 44).

32. Njabulo Ndebele, *Fools and Other Stories* (1983; reprint: New York and London: Readers International, 1986), 106.

33. Wicomb, "Shame and Identity," 105.

34. Boitumelo Mofokeng et al., "Workshop on Black Women's Writing and Reading," 1990; reprinted in *South African Feminisms: Writing, Theory, and Criticism, 1990–1994*, ed. M. J. Daymond, 107–29 (New York: Garland, 1996), 116.

35. Brink, "Interrogating," 15.

36. Zoë Wicomb, "To Hear the Variety of Discourses," 1990; reprinted in *South African Feminisms: Writing, Theory, and Criticism, 1990–1994*, ed. M. J. Daymond, 45–55 (New York: Garland, 1996), 47.

37. Verwoerd was assassinated on 5 September 1966. The boycott, a mild demonstration in American eyes, must be seen in historical context. In 1960, the student government of the brand-new University of the Western Cape expired virtually at birth when students refused to accede to administration insistence that whites be seated in front during a student-planned event. The head of the university belonged to the Broederbond, the elite Afrikaner secret society that backed apartheid with enthusiasm. See Nortje, "Staff," 25–26.

38. Wicomb, "To Hear," 47–48. Elsewhere, Wicomb says that gender was "*suppressed* by the national liberation struggle" (interview with Hunter, 90). Three of the participants in a "Workshop on Black Women's Writing and Reading" agreed with her, saying: "The women's struggle and the national liberation struggle need to be waged simultaneously"; one, however, argued that the struggle must be private and domestic because "to stand up on a platform . . . would be

like hanging your dirty linen in public" (Mofokeng et al., "Workshop," 121–22).

39. References to the Tricameral Parliament, which was instituted in 1984, indicate that the final stories take place around that time. Moira calculates that "ten, no twelve years" have passed since Frieda's departure (148).

40. Here, it seems, Frieda reflects her creator's experience: "In the latter half of the book the heroine is in Britain, but I refuse to comment on it because my experience there was about being silent. I was certainly not going to give my heroine any voice in Britain" (interview with Hunter, 87).

41. "Die Stem van Suid Afrika" ("The Voice of South Africa") is the Afrikaners' national anthem, celebrating their trek over the Drakensberg; Wicomb discusses the anthem's author, C. J. Langenhoven, in "Five Afrikaner Texts and the Rehabilitation of Whiteness," *Social Identities* 4, no. 3 (1998): 363–83, 369–70.

42. Wicomb herself has commented that "I have to kill off the father, in order for her to speak" (interview with Hunter, 94).